Praise for the novels of RITA Award–finalist
Lynn Erickson

IN THE COLD

"Taut investigative romantic suspense." —*BookBrowser*

ON THE EDGE

"Erickson's suspenseful romance takes readers into the dangerous world of mountain climbing and makes the trip worthwhile." —*Booklist*

"*On the Edge* will excite romantic suspense fans from the first stop on a mountain's side to the final climax. Meredith is an interesting heroine whose pangs of guilt feel genuine . . . Lynn Erickson keeps fans on the edge." —*BookBrowser*

continued . . .

ON THIN ICE

"Erickson creates a masterful suspense with *On Thin Ice* . . . fascinating characters . . . As the tension builds and the pages turn faster and faster, the reader will be swept away in a dangerous world."
        —*Midwest Book Review*

"A highly suspenseful novel. Erickson makes you feel as though you're walking the tightrope with Ellie as she searches for the killer . . . a must-read."   —*Rendezvous*

SEARCHING FOR SARAH

"Erickson builds suspense by expertly weaving romance into multiple thrilling story lines."   —*Publishers Weekly*

"Ms. Erickson teases the reader like a cat is teased with a piece of string. The reader follows the string through all the twists and turns of this well-plotted story all the way to the surprise ending."
        —*Rendezvous*

THE ELEVENTH HOUR

"A fabulous romantic suspense . . . the lead characters are charming . . . Counterpoint to the sizzling romance is a brilliant who-done-it." —*Painted Rock Reviews*

"Layers of depth . . . what a ride!" —*Rendezvous*

NIGHT WHISPERS

"Erickson skillfully navigates the fraught task of portraying the mind of a stalker with multiple personalities . . . The narrative is shadowy and suspenseful, leaving the reader with a creepy, unsettled feeling of expectation." —*Publishers Weekly*

ASPEN

"A deliciously juicy romp through the winter playground of the wealthy and powerful . . . A complex and truly interesting heroine . . . Suspenseful and tumultuous . . . a sharply plotted page-turner." —*Publishers Weekly*

WITHOUT A
TRACE

LYNN ERICKSON

BERKLEY SENSATION, NEW YORK

This is a work of fiction. Names, characters, places, and incidents either
are the product of the author's imagination or are used fictitiously,
and any resemblance to actual persons, living or dead, business
establishments, events, or locales is entirely coincidental.

WITHOUT A TRACE

A Berkley Sensation Book / published by arrangement with
the author

PRINTING HISTORY
Berkley Sensation edition / November 2003

ISBN: 0-425-19325-X

A BERKLEY SENSATION™ BOOK
Berkley Sensation Books are published by The Berkley Publishing Group,
a division of Penguin Group (USA) Inc.,
375 Hudson Street, New York, New York 10014.
BERKLEY SENSATION and the "B" design
are trademarks belonging to Penguin Group (USA) Inc.

PRINTED IN THE UNITED STATES OF AMERICA

10 9 8 7 6 5 4 3 2 1

This book is dedicated to Special Agent Jane of the FBI, whose information was invaluable and whose identity will be kept a cherished secret. Any and all errors in FBI procedure are the fault of the author, and in the name of storytelling, forgiveness is begged.

ONE

Jane Russo was ready. It had taken her seventeen years to reach this pivotal point, and she knew she'd only reached it out of desperation.

She turned off her cell phone and her pager, she put a CD of baroque concertos on her stereo, and she sat in her oversized leather armchair, sketch pad in her lap and three newly sharpened Conte pencils at hand.

This time she would confront her demons: she would remember the face, get it down on paper, and go on with her life.

She could hear the muted sounds of traffic on Denver's Larimer Street below her apartment. The blinds on her window were open, letting in the diffused glow of city lights haloed by snow. She was tempted to get up and look out the window, to watch the people Christmas shopping, going to the trendy brewpubs, or to boutiques open late to grab seasonal customers. But she forced herself to sit there, chewing on her lower lip, her heart beating a heavy cadence in her chest.

She had sketched so many other victims' demons; why couldn't she draw her own?

Blocked. She was blocked. Unable to work, she'd hit bottom in her career, in love, in life itself. And now— tonight—right here in her apartment, she had to face her fears and perhaps begin healing or retreat from the nightmare and wallow in familiar denial. Comfortable but destructive denial.

What did he look like, the man who had raped her when she was only sixteen, who had stolen her innocence?

Young. Had he been young? Somehow she thought so. She also had an impression of dark hair, a vague oval with no clear features. Maybe dark eyebrows, she thought.

Nothing more.

She recalled in acute detail the surroundings—the orange tent, the bright blue down sleeping bag, the green Coleman lantern, her hiking boots stowed neatly in the bottom of her sleeping bag. The weather—cool and dry, the usual Rocky Mountain Indian summer night. Frogs croaked from nearby Reudi Reservoir, and she could still smell the pine and sum- mer dust and smoke from the campfire.

She even remembered the T-shirt she was wearing, which was navy blue with ASPEN VOLUNTEER FIRE DEPARTMENT writ- ten across the front.

But his face remained shrouded in shadows.

She wanted to get up and move around her apartment, the place she'd tried to make into a safe haven. A cozy home. With plants and soft southwestern colors and a few good prints on the walls. A retreat. And she *had* retreated lately, taking no jobs, not traveling at her usual frenetic pace, seeing no one. Another form of denial, she supposed.

She drew in a deep breath, tried to concentrate, took

another breath. His face was in her memory. But memory wasn't a fixed record; it was pliant, subject to stress and fear and distortion. God knows, she'd worked with enough victims to understand that.

Some researchers believed that once a memory was altered, the original was gone forever, but Jane disagreed. To her, memory was like the shaft of one of Colorado's old silver mines—caved in, filled with debris. And her job was to dig out the shaft, go down through the dirt and rock and find the payload.

She picked up a pencil. Maybe the familiar feel of it in her hand would help. When she drew a suspect's face, listening to the victim's description, it felt as if her hand did the drawing. As if her hand was unrelated to her brain. She knew that wasn't possible, but that was the way she *felt* when she sketched.

Why wouldn't it work for her now?

She stared at the window, seeing snowflakes drift across the lights of the building across the street. Snow in Denver wasn't all that common; a white Christmas was the exception, not the rule. She missed the snow. She'd been raised in the Colorado mountains, and the bare dullness of the high prairie in winter was not her thing. Not that she wanted to go back to her hometown. She'd never go back if she could help it.

There you go, running away again. Face it. Face him.

She lay the pencil point on the paper, drew a curving line that was to be his jaw. But her hand wavered, and she knew the shape wasn't right. She rubbed the line out and tried another one.

No. That wasn't right either.

Maybe she should start with the eyes. Dark? Light? Mouth? Nose? Big, straight, pug, hook? She didn't know, couldn't dredge up the deeply buried memory. Couldn't get through the debris.

Okay, try free association. Just let your hand draw. It doesn't matter what you put down on paper.

She shaded in dark eyebrows, a forehead. Strands of dark hair. *Yes, maybe* . . . An ear, an odd sort of flat-topped roll on it. Chin? A few more lines. A cheekbone. A thrill of fear, of excitement, of dread, sparked in her chest.

Her hand poised, ready for the line of the mouth. *His* mouth. She heard in her head his low urgent words, his panting breath. She felt his weight on her, suffocating, his strength. The hard feel of him inside her.

She closed her eyes and pinched the bridge of her nose with her fingers. *Breathe, breathe.* The rape happened seventeen years ago. He couldn't hurt her anymore. Whoever *he* was.

She studied what she'd sketched. Was it familiar? That cheek . . . something about the shape . . . She shadowed the face more with the side of the pencil. It had been dark in the tent that night. A dark late summer's night. A camping trip.

The end of her innocence.

The mouth, a full lower lip. No, thinner but more curved. Almost. Yes. Another line and . . . It was like a word on the tip of your tongue. But she almost had him. She leaned over the sketch pad and rubbed out a line, started to redraw it. Stopped, looked into the middle distance and tried to conjure up the eyes. The eyes were key.

A sound intruded. A persistent sound. She dragged her attention back to the face. A line there, for the nose.

The sound again. What?

She lifted her head, listened. Someone was knocking at her door.

God, no. Not now. *Go away. Leave me alone.* The nose . . . like that . . . or maybe a little flatter there, just . . .

The knock again. Insistent, loud.

Damn it.

Reluctantly she rose, dropped the sketch pad on the chair, and started toward the door. *Maybe it's Alan,* flashed through her mind; maybe he'd changed his mind and come to see her.

But the voice that reached through the door was not Alan's.

"Jane, open up, it's Caroline."

Caroline Deutch. Good Lord, what was she doing here at this hour? She was a special agent at the Denver FBI division office, a friend and mentor, a woman for whom Jane had often worked. She was also the woman who'd told Jane last month to take a sabbatical. Just like Caroline, blunt but right: "You're burnt out, Jane. You need a rest. You're not doing anybody any good when you're burnt out."

Caroline here at eight at night?

Jane opened the door. There she was, flakes resting on her man-short gray hair, her glasses speckled with melted snow, in a shapeless black coat. And she was not alone.

"Caroline?" Jane began.

"I knew you were home," Caroline said. "Figured you'd turned off your phone and pager."

"Uh . . ."

"I told you she'd be home," Caroline said to her companion.

Jane peered into the dimness of the hallway. A man. Tall, a dark overcoat, suit and tie visible at the open collar. The face—she always got an immediate and indelible impression of faces—stern, long, dark slashes of eyebrows, a straight mouth. She recognized the look of him instantly. He was a federal agent, FBI, CIA, Justice Department, something. Oh yes, she knew that look. Her heart sank. This was no social call.

"Sorry for showing up like this," Caroline was saying.

"But it's important." She stood there for a moment, looking up at Jane. "Well, can we come in?"

"Uh, sure." Jane stepped back, closed the door behind them.

Suddenly she recalled the sketch she'd dropped on the chair. She didn't want Caroline to see it. Caroline would ask questions about who it was; she was too perceptive.

But there was no time to turn the picture over, because her friend was studying her as if judging her innermost thoughts.

"What?" Jane asked.

"He did it again," was all Caroline said, but Jane knew exactly whom she meant.

"Oh, God."

"Yup. Guess you didn't see the Amber Alert. But it's the same MO. The girl disappeared after snowboarding. She was with friends. Preliminary reports are sketchy."

"Who . . . ?"

"Her name is Kirstin Lemke. Twelve years old."

"Twelve," Jane whispered.

"We know he likes 'em young, don't we? Younger and younger, it seems."

"You're sure it's him?"

"Same MO. A ski area, she's the same type. Long brown hair, glasses. It's him."

"Oh, Caroline . . ."

"We need you back, Jane," Caroline said, her tone seeped in compassion, at the same time steely with finality.

Jane's specialty lay in being able to crawl into the hidden memories of victims and witnesses, coax to light the faces of suspects when all other law enforcement methods had failed. She'd done sketches for police departments and for the FBI from Miami to Seattle. And her record had been stellar until this case. This rapist, who turned up in ski areas in the West, and who preyed on young girls, was Jane's nemesis.

She had always been able to establish rapport with the people she interviewed. It was her gift, this empathetic ability. She didn't ask questions or push or show the traumatized victims the FBI's *Facial Identification Guide* photographs to choose from. She chatted, she got to know the person, she talked about school or friends or a job or the place the victim lived, and then she eased into the task, interspersing her sketching with conversation.

Her technique worked, particularly with young girls, and she was often called in on a case when previous sketches failed to produce leads.

But this case had stopped her dead. She'd been unable to bring this madman's face to light, and she suspected why. There'd been enormous pressure to find him, because the last girl he kidnapped in Park City, Utah, died as a result of his assault on her. Which meant the stakes were raised from rape to murder. Murder one, in fact.

But worse, this man had hit too close to home, ski resorts like the one she was brought up in, and the girls were too much like Jane herself at that age. Her own trauma was blocking her, and she was no damn good to anyone right now. Caroline knew she needed this break, so why was she here?

"He took a girl here in Colorado this time," Caroline was saying.

"A ski area?"

Caroline nodded. "Snowmass."

Snowmass, one of the four mountains near Aspen. Jane stepped backward and sank into a chair. She'd been born and raised in Aspen; her family still lived there. But she never went home. Never.

She looked up at Caroline. "I can't. I'm not ready."

"Kirstin Lemke," Caroline replied, as if not hearing her words, "twelve years old. Disappeared from the parking

lot at the base of Snowmass. Same as in Mammoth and
Snowbird and Park City. There were two witnesses, her
friends. So far they think they saw a man in a ski hat and
goggles, but they aren't sure of anything. That was two
days ago, and time may be running out for Kirstin. You
know what happened in . . ."

Jane reached up a hand as if to ward off an attack. "I
know. I *know*."

"We need you."

Jane shook her head. She'd already been to Mammoth
and Snowbird and Park City over the past five years. She'd
tried; she'd done her best. She'd been unable to get a
sketch of the rapist's face from anyone. She'd tried, but
nothing came. Not a line, not an impression. Nothing. Just
like her own rapist's face.

"You've been off for a month now," Caroline persisted.
"I know I told you to take enough time off, but this one has
your name on it. Your hometown, for God's sake."

"I won't be able to help. You know that, Caroline.
You're the one who told me to take time off."

"Okay, listen, just do me a favor. Talk to Ray here. He's
just been assigned to our office. He's case agent on this
one. He's got to go up to Aspen tomorrow to join the team
already there. Parker wants you to go with him."

Jane knew Parker. He was the local SAC, the Special
Agent in Charge of the Denver office. And she knew he'd
sent Caroline to twist her arm.

"I can't. I'm sorry, I just can't," Jane said.

Caroline ignored her. "Ray Vanover, Jane Russo. Come
on, Jane, talk to the guy."

She glanced up at the man who stood silently in the
shadows near her front door. He hadn't moved or said a
word all this time. Ray Vanover. His name had a familiar
ring, but she couldn't pursue that will-o'-the-wisp notion

right now. He was tall, his face handsome but distant, devoid of expression. Yet she could feel his skepticism of her ability. She'd dealt with a lot of people like Ray Vanover.

"Look, I'm sorry, Ray," she said, "but you've got me at a bad time. I can't help you."

"I understand," he said, his voice low and a bit gravelly, a strong masculine voice. "Your prerogative."

"I'm not sure you do understand."

He gave an almost imperceptible shrug.

There was something about this man's face. . . . Jane's specialty was faces. Her ability lay in deciphering expression, in reading the set of a mouth or the tilt of a brow. In noting muscle tension and skin tone and facial mannerisms. In uncovering the personality that lay behind—and sometimes hid behind—the collection of features that made up a face.

There was something . . .

He stepped into the light. Dark hair, hollow cheeks, that long face. Startling pale blue eyes under the thick brows. A long thin nose, the slash of a mouth, but now she saw that there was a dip in the center of his upper lip, a slight capitulation to human feelings. And then she noticed the pink scar tissue on his neck above his coat collar. A burn? The disfigurement, she now saw, ran up his neck and along his left jawline. And the injury looked relatively new. She wondered about that for a heartbeat, but there were more important things to think about.

"Will you consider it, Jane? Give it tonight."

"Caroline, really . . ."

"Don't say no right now. Call me tomorrow."

She sighed. "Damn it, Caroline."

The woman smiled. "I can tell you're weakening." Then, to Vanover. "I told you, didn't I?"

"You told me," he agreed, his voice as abrasively caressing as a cat's tongue.

"I'm not promising anything," Jane said.

"Right," Caroline said.

"I'll call you tomorrow."

Caroline faced her, short and square, in a rumpled black coat and old running shoes. "Kirstin Lemke, twelve years old. Don't forget her, Jane."

She felt the small, quick pain, like a paper cut. She put her hand on her forehead. "You're a bulldozer."

"Subtlety is not one of my vices."

"I think Miss Russo would like us to go," Vanover said.

"Yeah, we're going." Caroline stood on tiptoe and gave Jane a hug. "Remember," she said into her ear, "you're the only one who stands a chance at identifying this monster. Kirstin needs you."

"It won't do any good," Jane said sadly. "I can't help you. I can't help Kirstin."

"Tomorrow," Caroline said.

She leaned back against the door when they were gone. They wanted her for a case, another missing girl. Someone's daughter, sister, niece. Someone's beloved child. Missing—what had Caroline said?—two days now. Well, they all knew that a very high percentage of missing children were killed in the first three hours, so it was probably too late already.

Oh, God, she couldn't do it. She wasn't ready. She couldn't face the family's agony, the stress, the rage, the wrenching disappointment. The failure.

No, I can't do it, she thought, wrapping her determination around her like a shroud.

TWO

Taking up her sketch pad again was an impossibility. She walked over and looked down at the attempt she'd made. Ridiculous. A few lines, a generic face. And she'd been worried that Caroline would see it and wonder why she was sketching this particular face. That was funny. No, pathetic.

She ripped the page off the pad, wadded it up, and dropped it in the kitchen trash can.

She paced, her fingers splayed on her temples, thinking. Should she go back? Could she handle the pressure, the awful responsibility? And even if she could handle that, she'd have to start over trying to tweeze the rapist's face from the minds of young girls, and she'd been quite unable to do that the first time around.

She'd call Caroline tomorrow and say no. Firmly.

She got her leather jacket from the closet, pulled on snow boots, and walked swiftly out of her apartment, her mind made up. Damn Caroline and the guilt trip she'd hauled with her and dumped at Jane's door.

She strode the block to Larimer Square through the snow, a tall woman with a determined stride and blunt-cut streaked blond hair that caught the snowflakes as they drifted from the night sky. She wore faded jeans and a man's blue denim work shirt that hung below the hem of her black aviator jacket.

She ordered the usual sandwich from her favorite deli—turkey with cranberry sauce and horseradish—and carried the bag back home. She set the sandwich on a plate on the counter and picked up half of it. Her stomach rebelled. She put the half back down on the plate and stared at it.

Damn Caroline.

Kirstin Lemke, twelve years old. Snowmass Ski Area. The same MO, the same man. The elusive ski-hill UNSUB, FBI jargon for *unknown suspect.* Two days ago. Last year, Jennifer Weissman of Park City had been found dead after ten days. How long did Kirstin have?

Her hand picked up the phone without conscious thought. She pressed the familiar number, one she knew by heart, one she'd called every day, several times a day, up until—how long was it now?—five weeks ago.

"Hello," came his familiar voice, his beloved voice. The same voice that had told her he guessed he wasn't ready for a serious relationship so soon after his divorce. They could be *friends,* couldn't they? he'd asked.

"Alan."

"Jane?"

"Yes, it's me. Alan, Caroline Deutch came by a while ago. He's taken another girl."

"Oh, Christ."

"From Snowmass."

"I see."

"She wants me to go up there tomorrow with the case agent. I can't do it, Alan."

"Did you tell her how you felt?" Calm, masterful, always logical.

"Yes, but she still . . . They have no leads. The girl was reported missing two days ago. My God, Alan, she's twelve."

"Twelve."

"You remember what happened to the last girl?"

"Yes, of course."

"I don't know what to do."

"I'll come over."

"It's late. You don't have to. I mean . . ."

"Jane, I hear that tone in your voice. I'll be there in half an hour."

Alan Gallagher, white knight to the rescue. Funny, he didn't look like a hero. Medium height, smooth features, brown hair. Ordinary looking until you peered into his eyes and saw the triumph over tragedy, the determination, the strength.

His daughter Nicole had been abducted from her own house during a slumber party and had been found two weeks later. Murdered. Sexually assaulted and murdered.

Instead of turning bitter or vindictive, Alan had become a child rights advocate, pushing for stronger laws against child molesters. He was well known on Capitol Hill in Denver and was becoming so in Washington, D.C. Jane had met him when she'd been on the job, sent to sketch the face of the man who'd abducted his daughter.

Alan had lost his daughter in the tragedy, and he'd also lost his wife. As he'd told Jane dispassionately, these kinds of calamities often resulted in family breakups. He still loved his wife Maureen; he always would. But they couldn't live together.

Until a couple months ago, when Maureen had come back into the picture, and he'd started seeing her more often. And then came his speech to Jane on remaining *friends.*

Jane wondered if she was using Caroline's visit as an excuse to see Alan again. Yes, maybe she was. She had no one else to turn to. Alan was always logical, careful, analytical. And Alan was one of the few people on earth who knew about her own childhood trauma.

He lived in the small town of Genesee, on the I-70 corridor west of Denver in the foothills. He made the trip downtown in thirty minutes despite the snowstorm. He'd said half an hour, and when Alan promised something, he never deviated.

She opened the door to his knock and felt a tingle of pleasure inside her. It had been weeks since she'd last seen him, and he looked so good, his duffel coat dotted with melting snow, his brown hair short and neat, his expression somber.

She wanted to fall into his arms, kiss him, feel his skin, his hair, draw him close.

"Jane," he said.

"Hi, Alan."

He moved nearer, but only to let her shut the door. Taking his coat off, he hung it on a wall hook, the same hook he'd always used. Her heart clenched. Everything was the same yet utterly, irrevocably different.

"Now tell me the whole story," he said, sitting on the couch as if he hadn't walked out of her life five weeks before with her incredulous "Friends?"echoing in his ears.

"A glass of wine?" she asked, biding for time, trying to gather her thoughts. Trying not to blurt out the questions she'd asked herself so often: *Why, Alan? What went wrong? How could you leave me just when I needed you the most?*

She poured them both glasses of a white zinfandel she

had open in her refrigerator; she knew he didn't like the sweetness of it, but he'd be too polite to object.

"Come on, Jane. You didn't get me here to serve me a glass of wine."

That was Alan: direct, focussed.

She sat watching the sparkle of light in the pinkish wine. "Caroline came by this evening."

"So you said."

"Another girl is missing. Same MO. They're sure it's the same man."

"And Caroline wants you on the case."

"I'm sure Special Agent in Charge Parker sent her. I just know it."

"That would be like Parker."

"Yes."

"Okay." Reasonable.

"She had another agent with her. A new guy, Ray Vanover, who's the case agent."

"And this is who you'd work with?"

She nodded then wrenched her gaze from the glass of wine to him. "I told Caroline I couldn't."

"But I take it she didn't accept that?"

"No, she didn't."

"Do you feel that you're ready to return to work, Jane?"

She bit her lip, made a fist of one hand. "I don't know."

"If you went back and you couldn't help . . ."

"I know, Alan, I know."

He leaned forward. "I thought you needed time off. I was relieved when you took it, you know, for your sake. You needed to take charge of your life and work on your own well-being. We've discussed this."

He used words like that—*take charge* and *well-being*— as a sort of code to avoid hurting her feelings. What he meant was he thought she'd been completely stressed out, a mess, useless to herself or the victims she was supposed to be helping.

She looked down at her hands, clenched tightly in her lap. "So you think it's too soon. I'd just . . . I'd just screw things up."

He shook his head slowly. "Only you know if you're ready."

She'd thought all along that Alan had backed off from their relationship when he realized how close she was to a breakdown. When he understood how severely her childhood rape had affected her, when he suspected that she was an emotional cripple.

Or was it so much simpler? Was he still in love with Maureen?

"I . . . I don't know. I can't bear to think of what that girl—her name is Kirstin Lemke—is going through. What he's doing to her. It's as if I was there with her, and he's doing it to me."

Alan reached over the coffee table and laid his hand on her knee. "I know," he said gently. "That's what makes you so good with these girls."

"And to sit here, while he's got her, and maybe . . . maybe I could help." She raised her eyes to his. "I don't know if I can say no, Alan."

"There are other people on the case, aren't there?"

"Sure, but . . ."

"And you're not the only portrait artist there is. Caroline will find someone else."

"She wants *me*," she whispered.

"I'm not sure I can help you, Jane."

"God, Alan." She picked up the wineglass to take a sip. The liquid trembled from the shaking of her hand. "She was taken from Snowmass."

"You told me that."

"Do you know how close that is to Aspen?"

"Yes."

"I'd have to go back there. I'd have to deal with the sheriff's office in Aspen. I'd have to . . ."

"See your family," he finished for her.

"Yes."

"Jane." He took a breath. "Maybe you should examine this assignment as a possibility. A blessing in disguise. I've always said you needed to deal with that part of your life."

"Not now."

"Why not?"

"I . . . I can't. I don't want to. I'm not ready."

He smiled sadly. "You can't always choose the timing to suit you."

"I can't *deal* with all of them."

"Or maybe now is the exact time to deal with them."

She stood and stalked around the room, restless. Alan remained seated, relaxed, self-contained, so goddamn calm. Playing devil's advocate.

"The new agent, the case agent, he didn't believe I could help. I could tell. Caroline probably dragged him along with her."

"Was he hostile?" Alan asked.

She stopped and thought. "No, not exactly. He acted as if I was . . . beside the point."

"And that upsets you."

She shrugged. "Not so much anymore."

There'd been a time, earlier in her career, when she'd been terribly sensitive to how she was perceived. When she'd been trying to convince law enforcement officials that her technique worked. She wasn't so sensitive now; her worth had been proven many times. Although there'd always be the skeptical ones. Like Special Agent Ray Vanover.

"But you'd have to work with him."

"Yes."

He picked up his glass of wine, turned it slowly in his fingers. "That's unfortunate. If you knew the case agent and he knew your expertise . . . It's bad timing right now."

"I'd already decided to say no."

He looked up at her. "Then why'd you call me?"

She stopped by the window and stared out onto Larimer Street. "That's the catch, isn't it?"

"Come over here and sit down. Your pacing is driving me nuts."

She sighed and took a seat on the couch. Not too close. She noticed he'd set the glass back down; he hadn't even taken a sip of his wine.

"Okay, so we both agree this is a bad time. And we both know there are plenty of people besides you who can work on the case. Right?" he said.

"Right."

"You wanted six months off, and you've only had— what is it, one month?"

"Uh-huh."

"You feel that you'd be more effective in the future if you took the full six months."

She nodded. God, she wanted to take his hand; she wanted him to put his arm around her and pull her close so that she could bury her face in his neck and draw in his scent.

"And this particular case has caused you . . . uh, well, some trouble."

Some trouble. She'd failed to come up with anything coherent from the victims or the witnesses. Nothing. Not even the color of his eyes or his height. A man, that was all. A man in ski gear, goggles, and a hat. A faint impression.

And that had never happened to her before.

"I let a girl die, Alan. I could have prevented it if . . ."

"The girl's death was not your fault. Come on, Jane."

"Logically I know that, but emotionally . . . I *feel* as if I should have made a difference." She turned to him with a beseeching gaze. "Why can't I get this bastard's face?"

"We've already discussed it. Probably because the situation is so similar to yours, the girls' age and so on."

"Did I try hard enough? Maybe I should have gone back and talked to the victims again. I shouldn't have given up."

"You were ordered to give up. There was no more money in the budget. Remember?"

"Yes, yes . . ." She waved a hand in the air. "But maybe there was something more I could have done."

He cocked his head. "Stop torturing yourself. It's counterproductive."

"I know. I know."

It grew late. Alan was patient, going over the pros and cons of her taking this new case, putting her concerns in perspective. And yet, his full wineglass sat like an unspoken barrier between them.

By eleven o'clock, she'd decided she was definitely not going to take the case. There were too many reasons not to. Kirstin Lemke would have to do without her.

"Okay," Alan said, "do you feel better now? It's all straight in your mind?"

"Yes, I think so."

"You better know so. Caroline can be persuasive. Are you prepared to stand firm?"

"Yes."

"Remember, you'll be able to help more victims in the future if you take time off now."

"Absolutely." She smiled at him. "Thanks. Thanks so much for coming over. It really helped."

"I'm your friend, Jane. That's what friends do for each other."

There it was again. *Friends.* The word was like the red cape that bullfighters flared to taunt the bull.

She turned her face away and wondered if he'd noticed her reaction. Probably. Alan was an astute judge of people. Was that why he'd retreated from her?

He rose and unhooked his coat, shrugged it on. She went with him to the door, her arms folded across her chest. Defensively.

"Call me tomorrow and let me know how it comes out," he said.

"Okay."

He put his arms around her. "Be strong," he murmured into her ear. He kissed her. On the cheek. A chaste, brotherly kiss.

And then he was gone, and she was alone in her apartment, the glass of pale pink wine still sitting untouched on the coffee table.

THREE

It had snowed all night in Aspen, making the old mining town picture-perfect for the Christmas visitors. The airport, Sardy Field, had been shut down by the storm the previous day, causing vacationers to be stranded, their choice either waiting for the weather to clear or driving two-hundred miles over the high mountain passes between Denver and Aspen.

At five-thirty in the morning it was still pitch black. A stark-white contoured blanket of snow lay on every roof and bush and fence rail and bare tree limb. Quiet, peaceful, even the late-night revelers gone to their dreams.

Headlights pierced the darkness, spearing the last few gently floating snowflakes: a pickup truck, its tires cutting distinct furrows in the snow as it drove. A single lonely truck with a rusted iron plow attached to its front bumper made its way through the predawn stillness to its first job clearing a driveway.

The driver of the truck liked to work alone, and he liked

winter. He pushed his glasses up on his nose and peered through the windshield whose center was marked by a spider web crack caused months ago by a rock spit from under a Range Rover's tire.

The weather didn't bother him; it insulated him. He'd plow driveways, one after the other, until midmorning. Then the rest of the day was all his.

The phone awakened Jane, startling her. She rolled over in bed and groaned, reaching for the receiver on her night table. "Hello?" she mumbled, her voice sleep-drenched.

"Jane, it's me. Did I wake you?"

Alan.

"Um, yes," she managed, squinting at her alarm clock. It said 9:04. My God. How on earth had she slept so late?

"Sorry, but it's important."

"Um . . . what?" She sat up against the headboard, her heart bounding. Hope blossomed in her chest, warm, almost bringing a sob. He was going to tell her they should get back together. Maybe after last night he'd realized how he'd missed her.

"Caroline Deutch called me this morning."

"Caroline?" Her mind whirled. Sure, Caroline knew Alan, but what in hell did she have to do with . . .

"She wanted me to talk to you." A pause. "About the case, the one in Aspen."

Oh. So that's why he was calling. What an idiot she was, assuming he still loved her, assuming . . .

"Jane, damn, I knew you'd be pissed. I told Caroline so, but you know her."

"I'm not pissed."

"Okay, sure."

She pulled her knees up, hair hanging in front of her

face, huddled under the duvet. "Well, what did she want you to say?"

"Look, I know what we decided last night. What *you* decided. I told Caroline it was too soon for you to go back, that I agreed with you about that."

"And?"

"I told her Aspen was the last place on earth for you to start working again."

"Did she ask why?"

"Well, she was a little curious about that."

"You didn't . . ."

"No, no. I just said you don't get along with your family."

"An understatement," she said under her breath.

"What?"

"Nothing."

"Jane, honestly, you know I wouldn't call you if I didn't think . . . if it wasn't important."

Of course not, she thought.

"Jane?"

"Go on, get it out, Alan."

"Caroline told me the portrait artist who tried to draw the suspect came up empty. There are two witnesses in Aspen, two girls, and he couldn't get a face from either of them. She still wants you to try."

"Was it Ed Staley?"

"Who? What?"

"The portrait artist who couldn't . . ."

"Oh. I don't know who it was."

"Just curious."

"Caroline wants you to talk to the girls. She thinks you'll get something. It's another opportunity to put a face to this guy."

"But, Alan, damn it . . . What was all that about last night then?"

"I know what I said. I think I was wrong. Okay? I changed my mind."

"Caroline's a goddamn tank. She runs over people, she . . ."

"She made sense, Jane. I'm sorry, but I have to admit I agree with her. What if someone like you could have saved Nicole? What if there's even the slightest hope that another parent won't have to go through what Maureen and I went through?"

Oh Jesus. He'd pounded her with a left and a right, then he'd dealt the knockout blow. Below the belt.

Her heart squeezed, and her fingers dug into the receiver.

Special Agent Ray Vanover picked Jane up at noon. She was waiting in front of her building on Larimer Street, overnight bag and artist case in hand, the strap of a black leather bag over her shoulder. He almost didn't recognize her because she was dressed in a long tweed wool coat, tall black boots, and a violet turtleneck sweater over a calf length black skirt. Her hair was pulled back severely into a bun. Nothing like the casual woman with her honey-blond hair down, jeans, a loose denim shirt and socks patterned with red and green chili peppers on her feet.

"Pull over there," Ray said to Phil, the agent driving them to the airport.

"That her? Not bad," Phil said.

She was a good-looking female, more like handsome, with a straight nose, wide mouth and high, chiseled cheekbones. Blue eyes and arched brows a shade darker than her hair. She was flat chested, Ray had noticed, and very tall, probably five ten. Easily six feet in those high-heeled boots, very close to standing eye to eye with him. He didn't like to admit that her height disconcerted him.

The woman with the *gift*.

He'd assumed she was unavailable after yesterday's futile visit. She'd made that quite clear. Why had she changed her mind when she called Caroline this morning?

He really hadn't wanted to work with her anyway. She wasn't FBI; she was a freelancer. She worked for whoever paid her. And Ray distrusted the civilians the FBI contracted with. Better to keep the job in-house, where everyone understood the rules.

Then, out of the blue, some guy named Alan Gallagher had apparently persuaded Jane Russo to take on this case, Gallagher being a vocal and respected child rights advocate since the murder of his own teenage daughter five years ago.

Yeah, and what else was Gallagher to Miss Jane Russo? Why did he wield so much influence over her?

Phil pulled up to the curb, and Ray got out.

"Hi," she said, a half smile frozen on her face. Nervous, a bit awkward.

"Get in. Phil's dropping us at the airport."

She ducked and got into the backseat, her long legs folding gracefully. He probably should have let her sit in front.

"Phil McEachen, Jane Russo."

"Nice to met you, Jane." Phil turned and flashed her a smile. Ray felt a spurt of irritation.

Nobody talked much on the drive to Denver International Airport. If Jane was getting bad vibes from him, it was tough. She was useless baggage as far as he was concerned.

How had Gallagher changed her mind? Or had it been

.

someone else who had actually persuaded her? In any case, *someone* had influenced her to revisit this case. One she'd unsuccessfully tackled three times in the past. At the Mammoth ski area in California, at Snowbird, and Park City in Utah. Some *gift*.

Phil dropped them at the terminal, the distinctive one with the enormous white multipeaked roof that duplicated the ranks of snow-capped mountains to the west.

They went through security, showing their IDs. He filled out the requisite papers for his weapon and noticed that Jane pointedly looked away as he did so.

Doesn't like the rough stuff, he thought. *Just wants to draw pictures.*

The short flight to Aspen on United Express was bumpy, due to the remnants of yesterday's storm. Below them the mountains rose, jagged and glistening in the sun, with the line of the interstate highway meandering along the valley floor, taking the path of least resistance. Cloud shadows skimmed the ground below. They crossed the Continental Divide, and the plane began to descend, passing through a layer of fluffy white clouds, homing in on a runway that was a speck in the midst of the Rocky Mountains.

Jane sat next to him. She'd tried to make conversation, attempting to create a relationship with him, the way he supposed she did with the subjects she interviewed. He was barely polite, being an asshole. Maybe because she was so damn attractive, with her long legs and strong-boned face and blue eyes that looked right at you, no evasions.

"I'm a little nervous," she offered.

"About flying?"

"No, no." She smiled. "Not that. I fly all over the country. It's just that I haven't been home . . . I mean back to Aspen in . . . well, years."

"You still have family there?"

"Yes." She bit her lower lip, a habit he'd noticed.

She probably wanted him to ask why she was nervous, get him involved in a conversation, but he wasn't in the mood.

When she gave up and buried her head in the *Aspen Times* newspaper, he found his fingers reaching up to trace his scars, scars that ran down his neck and along his arm. Pink shiny scar tissue that puckered and felt tight and had made it hard to bend his elbow for months of painful physical therapy.

The doctors had said last year that the scars would fade in time. Or he could have more skin grafts. More surgery.

No, thanks.

He figured the scars didn't matter that much; hell, he was thirty-seven. Got over youthful vanity a long time ago. He should consider himself lucky to have survived the incident with only a few scars. But today he was self-conscious, glad it was winter and a sleeve covered his arm. She'd noticed. Sure she had. He'd seen that quick glance, the abruptly veiled gaze that switched away too fast. The silent questions. Well, it was none of her damn business.

"Does it hurt?" he heard her ask.

He dropped his hand too quickly. "Hurt?"

"Your injury."

"No, it doesn't hurt," he replied then turned his head to look out the window, not uttering another word until they landed in Aspen.

A Pitkin County sheriff's deputy met them in front of the terminal, a courtesy not always accorded to federal agents. They were often on their own where transportation was concerned. The deputy introduced himself to Ray as Bernie, then grinned and hugged Jane.

"I volunteered for the airport run when I heard you were coming. Welcome back. It's been a long time."

"It sure has," she replied.

Obviously they knew each other. But then, why not? She'd been raised here. Still, he resented the fact that it was Jane who'd gotten them the service.

Enough of this old-home-week crap. "Has Sid Reynolds contacted you?"

"The agent from Glenwood Springs?" Bernie asked.

"Yes."

"He's already in town."

"Good." Ray had called Sid yesterday from Denver, asking permission to work in the area covered by the Glenwood Springs resident agency, forty miles from Aspen. Protocol and a formality, but one that could not be overlooked. Everything by the book.

"Do you have any new leads?" Jane asked as they settled themselves in the department's big SUV, Ray in back, Jane next to the deputy.

"Not a one."

"The witnesses?"

"Pretty shaky."

"That's what it sounded like."

"We'd sure like to catch this guy," Bernie said, shaking his head, steering out of the airport.

"So would a lot of people," Jane replied.

Ray had never been to Aspen; he'd only moved to Denver a few weeks ago. Moved out of the center of things to a dull backwater. Federal agents in Denver were lucky to pick up a bank robbery or an interstate truck hijacking now and then. Mostly they did boring surveillance, gathered evidence on a petty drug dealer or a fraud artist. Naturally, since 9/11, everyone was on high alert, even in Denver, Colorado. But it sure as hell wasn't what he'd been used to in Seattle, on the coast and so near the porous Canadian border. Then, of course, Seattle had its good points and its bad points. Some very bad points.

"Where are you staying, Jane?" Bernie asked.

"Oh, I guess at my sister's."

Ray wondered at that—hadn't she called anyone to tell them she was arriving? He knew the Denver agency's budget didn't include hotel expenses for her. And it was a week before Christmas. Aspen must be full up.

"You want me to swing by Gwen's then, so you can drop your bag?"

"Uh, sure, I guess so. They won't be home." She sounded relieved.

At a traffic roundabout Bernie turned up a road that ran between mountains, ski runs on the right, houses built on a hillside to the left. Another ski area lay ahead—he saw the sign for Aspen Highlands, but they turned left before reaching it.

Bernie pulled up in front of a two-story wood and stone house, nice, solid-looking, not one of the pretentious starter castles he heard abounded in Aspen.

"I'll just be a sec," Jane said.

Don't people lock their doors here? Ray wondered. He guessed not, because Jane walked right in the front door. She was back in less than five minutes. "I left them a note," she said to Bernie a little breathlessly. "Told them I might be late."

"Yeah, you might be." Then, a mile or so on he said, "Have you seen the new high school?"

"No, I heard about it, though," she said.

"There it is. All those good times in old Aspen High. It's hard to believe the town grew so much."

"Um, it's a nice building," she said, looking out her window.

"Don't you miss it?"

Silence. Ray could swear her shoulders tensed. "Not so much," she finally said.

The drive to the sheriff's department only took a few minutes. Idly Ray studied the old mining town turned ski resort. Gracious Victorian houses lined Main Street, which was bordered by tall cottonwood trees, bare-branched now in December. Old-fashioned lampposts with evergreen and lights twined around them stood at intervals. A few old ski lodges: the Christmas Inn, the Molly Gibson—all very cozy-looking, with a sixties atmosphere.

To his right above the snow-covered rooftops he could see Aspen Mountain's ski runs, bright white in the mid-afternoon sun, skiers tracing turns down to the gondola at the base of the mountain.

The sheriff's department was housed in the basement of the imposing redbrick Pitkin County Courthouse on Main Street. The Aspen Police Department shared the quarters. The place was crowded, the focus point of the search for Kirstin Lemke. Coordination between the police, the sheriff, and the federal agents was mandatory in a case like this. None of the macho "this is my turf" stuff you saw in movies.

Local law enforcement knew the people and the territory. The feds had the technical know-how and the clout. Where Jane Russo stood in this hierarchy, Ray didn't know. Nor did he give a damn.

Extra phone lines snaked across the floors. The basement offices echoed with ringing phones and voices. The electronic hum of computers filled the air. There was a large chalkboard set up in the hallway, scribbled with names and dates and times and phone numbers. Off-duty Aspen police and sheriff's deputies milled about, and a secretary sat at a desk on the phone, her brows drawn, busily writing something.

A lot of sound and fury, Ray thought, *probably signifying nothing.* They had no leads.

Special Agent Sid Reynolds out of the Glenwood agency was waiting in the sheriff's office, a heavy man with a craggy face and thick black eyebrows. Ray hadn't met Reynolds before, had only spoken to him by phone.

He introduced Jane to the man, who nodded and said, "I've heard of your work."

"Good or bad?" Jane asked, smiling.

"Good."

Had everyone but him heard of Jane Russo? he wondered.

"Hey, Vanover, see you finally made it," came a voice from the doorway. Bruce Dallenbach from the Denver office.

"Hey, Bruce. How's it going?"

But Bruce's attention had switched away from him. "Well, well, if it isn't Jane Russo," he said, grinning. "I heard you were on your way."

"Hi, Bruce," she said, and when he held his arms out, she stepped close and embraced him.

So she knew Bruce, too.

Sheriff Kent Schilling of Pitkin County was also among her acquaintances, as were two of the deputies in addition to Bernie and one police officer. Ray was beginning to find the situation ridiculous.

"So you've brought Jane home," Schilling said to Ray. "About time." He was a bear of a man, with grizzled curly hair and a wide mouth with a space between his front teeth. He'd put his arm around Jane, but she'd extricated herself. Politely but deliberately.

"I'm working, Kent," she said, her smile fixed.

"Does your mom know you're here?"

"Not yet."

"She'll be glad to see you."

"Um."

"And your dad?"

"You mean my stepfather." There was a distinct edge to her voice.

"Well, sure, but it's been so long I forget. How's Roland been?"

"I don't . . . um . . . really keep in touch. I'm so busy, well, you know, it's hard."

"Oh, big city girl," Schilling teased, oblivious to the discomfort Ray saw so clearly. What was going on here? Was Schilling why Jane hadn't wanted to come to Aspen? Or was it the stepfather?

"Well, now, you give Roland my best. And your mom, too. We should get together. Especially now that you're home."

"I'd like to get down to business, if you don't mind," Ray said, trying to keep the impatience out of his voice.

"Sure, sure."

"Can we sit down and go over everything you have? And I'd like copies of all reports and forensics."

"Not much in the way of forensics," Schilling said. "Nothing, in fact."

"The witnesses?"

"Got all their stuff for you. Two young girls. Can't get much out of them." He shot a gap-toothed grin at Jane. "But I bet Janey here can."

They sat around a table in a room that barely contained them: Schilling and his deputy Frank Keane, Sid Reynolds, Bruce Dallenbach, Ray, and Jane. If Jane was ill at ease at being the only female, Ray, saw no sign of it. But she *wasn't* comfortable around the sheriff, even though the big man seemed glad to see her. More than glad.

"Okay, Kirstin Lemke," Schilling began, passing out

copies of the missing persons report along with a photograph of Kirstin. Long brown hair and bangs, glasses, a broad smile. "Twelve years old. DOB February three, nineteen hundred ninety-two. Five feet six inches, one hundred eighteen pounds, brown hair, brown eyes. Address two hundred twenty-four Medicine Bow Road, Brush Creek Village. Last seen three days ago when she and two friends got down from snowboarding and were waiting in the Fanny Hill parking lot for the shuttle bus to where Kirstin's mother Suzanne was to pick them up. All they could say was Kirstin was there one minute then gone the next. A man driving by in a truck asked her directions, and she walked over to point out something, and that's the last they saw of her. They thought the man was dressed like a skier, could have been any one of thousands of skiers at Snowmass that day. Hat, parka, goggles pushed up on his ski hat. Glasses. One of them *thinks*." He shrugged. "Not much to go on."

"It's day three," Ray said. "Now, we know Jennifer Weissman was kept alive for a little over a week, and the two other girls,"—he looked down at the report in his hands—"one from Mammoth, California, and one from Snowbird, Utah, were let go." Ray met the eyes of each man at the table. "We may have up to a week left to find Kirstin. We may not."

"Listen," Schilling said, "If that son of a bitch is in this county, we'll find him. The valley isn't that big. If we had any kind of description on the guy, we could get it out right away, get the whole damn population of Pitkin County on the lookout for him."

"Okay, that's all fine, but we need evidence, we need a lead, a vehicle, a face, something. A man acting strange. A new guy in town," Bruce Dallenbach said. "Have you checked out all the children's programs around, where a pedophile might volunteer?" Dallenbach knew, as all of them did, that child molesters very often worked with children, as if they needed to be near them, to get friendly, and then perversely try to hurt them.

"That was easy," Schilling said. "Only new volunteers are women."

"Schoolteachers? Coaches?"

"It's being done," Deputy Keane said.

"Anything like parental kidnapping? An estranged husband?"

"Nope. Solid family. Mother and father live together."

"Was she a problem kid?" Ray asked. "You know, a runaway, hiding out for attention?"

"A good girl according to her parents," Schilling said.

"Boyfriend? They have them so damn young nowadays," Sid Reynolds asked.

"No one special. She was more interested in volleyball and her horse than boys."

"All right, we had to ask," Dallenbach said. "What's left is a kidnapping."

"By the same UNSUB as the three previous ones," Ray put in. "A man dressed as a skier, snatches a girl at the end of the day, in a parking lot where a getaway is easy. Uses a knife to control them. Never lets them see his face well. We know he likes winter resorts. We know he likes young girls. He likes them tall, with long brown hair and glasses." Ray rubbed the back of his neck. "What we've got here is the sadistic type of child molester, the kind who abducts and murders his victims. We know that when the victim is a child, rather than an infant, statistically the UNSUB is probably not a family member, is probably male and is probably motivated by sexual needs. There isn't enough data yet for a geographical profile, and we can assume he gets around in a vehicle, so he can strike anywhere."

"Damn little to go on," Schilling said.

"Our profiler suggested the UNSUB may wear glasses himself," Sid Reynolds said, then he held up a hand. "I know, it's thin."

"So we have a pedophile skier who probably drives and may wear glasses," Dallenbach said. "Whoopee."

"The witnesses?" Ray said.

"Melanie Steadman and Crystal Brenner," Schilling replied. "Both thirteen. Hysterical." He shrugged again. "We interviewed them. And your artist guy Staley did, too."

"Can we get them down here?" Ray asked. "Talk to them again, get Jane here to try her hand?"

"Sure can. I can call . . ." Schilling began.

"No, please, it's better if I go to their homes," Jane said, the first words she'd spoken.

"Why?" Ray raised a brow.

"I want them to feel secure, in familiar surroundings." She shook her head. "Not here. They'd be scared to death."

He looked at her. *What the hell?*

"They need to be interviewed at home," she insisted, obviously noticing his reaction. "Otherwise it's a waste of time."

"Whatever," he said, once again irritated by her, by her supposed talent, by her hometown coziness with men who were strangers to him. "I'll take you to see them."

"Not with that attitude, you won't," she said coolly.

FOUR

"I know the bureau is tight-fisted these days," Sheriff Schilling said. "So I figured you guys could use one of our vehicles."

She was surprised at the alacrity with which Ray accepted the offer: "Thanks, Sheriff, that'd be a big help."

"Kent, I go by Kent," the sheriff replied.

"Kent it is. Have you got something inconspicuous?"

"Pretty close. White Ford Explorer parked out front. No light bar, but there's a department logo on both sides."

"That will do fine. Thanks."

She listened to the exchange and waited while Kent fetched the keys and a vehicle sign-out sheet. She said nothing, instead tried to keep her focus on the upcoming task. But concentration was difficult for a number of reasons, not least of which was being home in Aspen, the sights and sounds and the smell of streets and sidewalks wet with melting snow as the sun finally pushed its way through the clouds left hugging the mountainsides. A brilliant sun even in December. But shortly it would dip below the shoulder of Aspen Mountain—Ajax to the locals—and by five this time of year you'd need to turn your headlights on.

Familiar territory. Yet so transformed since her youth. Her feelings were jumbled. Faces from the past surrounded her, some conjuring up fond memories, like seeing Bernie again. Others were muddling her thoughts. Like the sheriff's familiar countenance. Kent Schilling had been on the Reudi camping trip seventeen years ago. He'd been her stepfather's friend. He'd also been her friend, hadn't he?

Kent was pointing out the window to where the vehicle awaited, and she stared fixedly at him, trying to gauge whether . . .

"Coming?" Ray asked.

"Ah, yes, sure." She shook off the unsettling memories. "Let me get my stuff."

She probably should have changed clothes earlier. Worn jeans and a casual sweater. But she'd just thrown her bag inside her sister's house, hastily scratched a note—Gwen was going to be stunned by the unannounced visit—and made a quick getaway.

"You know where Melanie Steadman lives?" Ray asked when they were outside.

Melanie. Kirstin Lemke's friend, witness to her abduction. *Right. Focus, Jane.*

"Sheriff said fourteen-oh-three Cemetery Lane?" Ray prompted.

"Uh-huh, yes, I know where it is. Head back out Main Street the way we came."

"Is it far?"

"Ah, no, couple miles at the most."

He opened her door and waited while she settled in the passenger seat, her purse and artist's case by her feet. How polite, she mused, holding the car door for the lady, but knowing, *feeling,* the truth. Ray thought her talent was pure crap.

He drove up the gentle incline of Main Street and got stuck in stop-and-go traffic leaving town. In ski season the traffic was always murder this time of the afternoon. Lots of workers driving home downvalley, hordes of tourists heading to lodges or God knows where, probably sightseeing. Construction trucks. She couldn't remember a year without the lines of pickups and dump trucks crowding the roads. The building and tearing down in this valley was ceaseless. One of the less attractive aspects of so much disposable income.

"Schilling's called the Steadmans to let them know we're on our way," Ray said, the fingers on both hands impatiently tapping the steering wheel. "Is the traffic always like this?"

"In the afternoon. In the morning it comes upvalley."

Cars were barely moving, a county snowplow with its blue light flashing making a last slow sweep ahead of them. "Turn here," she said, remembering you could sneak under the bridge and take the steep narrow road up the other side of Castle Creek, bypassing the standstill traffic. "But you might need four-wheel drive. After all this snow, the road might be . . ."

"I think I'll figure it out," he said.

"Fine," she muttered. *Focus.* She couldn't afford to let him get under her skin. She needed to put her mind on Melanie and the necessity of being at ease, of putting *Melanie* at ease.

Still, she glanced at Ray in the waning light. Handsome as hell. Today he was wearing a scuffed brown leather jacket, a turtleneck sweater and cords. And yet the casual attire did not invite intimacy. He was nasty. Had he always been mean? Or had the disfiguring scars burned down into his soul?

Not her problem. "Turn right here," she said, pointing. "This is Cemetery Lane."

"Pretty neighborhood. Doesn't fit the name."

"No, it doesn't. But there's a cemetery behind that row of cottonwoods. Everybody in town has friends and relatives there." *Including my real father,* she thought.

"That should be the house, there on the right. Or maybe the one next to it. I can't quite make the numbers out."

"That's the one," Ray said, craning his neck. "Fourteen-oh-three." He pulled up in front. "You going to be able to get out in that snowbank? I could back up."

"I'll manage. This is fine." What wasn't fine was his attitude. She could feel the intense vibes of his total reluctance to be here with her. This was never going to work.

He began to open his door. "Ray," she said, "hold up a minute."

He shot her a look.

"We need to talk."

"We *need* to interview the witness," he stated flatly.

But she shook her head. "You're totally uptight, and I can't do my job with you scowling and hovering over my shoulder. I don't know what your problem is, but I need to go in there relaxed. I'm about to crawl into a young girl's mind, perhaps a very wounded mind right now. Melanie's friend is missing. These girls are in their teens. They watch reality TV and go to violent movies, and they aren't dumb. She knows what's at stake here, and I've got to put her at ease. She has to feel safe."

"Safe."

"Absolutely. She'll block me out otherwise. She's already blocked the FBI artist you sent here."

"*Parker* sent Ed Staley."

"Okay. Whatever. Your boss sent him. And you're new to the case, new to Colorado. I'm aware of all that. And maybe you don't want to be here. But for the victim's sake, for Kirstin Lemke's sake, please don't hinder me."

The air seemed to grown heavy in the car, his silence weighing on them both.

"Look," she said with intentional softness, "Ed Staley may have already muddied Melanie's memory trying to get a sketch. I don't know. I only know this interview is going to take time. Maybe hours."

"Swell."

"That's exactly what I'm getting at. Your attitude." She drew in a breath. "Ray, I do things a little differently. Police artists normally do a composite. They combine features taken from a book. It's really two dimensional and frankly, barely resembles a human being."

"In your opinion."

"Yes. In my opinion. They use the standard book of facial features and try to blend them into a real face. But they're never even close."

"Come on."

"Have you seen my work?"

"No."

"Well, there you are."

"Where am I, Jane?"

"Doubting. Skeptical."

"Maybe."

"You most certainly are."

"Are we arguing?"

"Yes."

"I thought you needed to relax."

She'd let him get to her. *Damn it.* The silence between them stretched and twanged with tension.

She shut her eyes and let out another long breath. "I really am good at what I do. It doesn't matter what you think. Just try to believe this man's face, this *murderer's* face, or some other detail, might be imprinted on Melanie's brain. The memories are retrievable if I can establish a rapport. And I'm going to go in that house and try to do precisely that." She opened her door. "I only pray Staley hasn't messed everything up."

"It could be," Ray said, opening his own door, "that Melanie didn't really see the man."

Jane stopped in the snowbank, which was over the top of her boots. *Great.* "I'll bet she saw *something*," she said over the hood. "They always do whether or not they know it."

They were nearly at the front entrance when he put a hand on her arm. "You've tried before to get this man's face from witnesses, right?"

Oh God, she thought.

"And you've come up empty," he pressed on. "Before we go inside, is there something I need to know about you and this case?"

Her throat constricted. She couldn't tell him the truth. How could she possibly tell this officious stranger that for nearly two decades the face of her own tormenter had been hiding in the blackest corner of her brain, and that she couldn't rid herself of her own demon?

How in God's name had she let herself get talked into this? But her sudden onslaught of doubt was interrupted when the front door of the Steadman house opened and a man appeared, nodding at them, a frown on his brow.

Ray produced the requisite ID and introduced them to Barry Steadman, who was quick to express his opinion of a second police artist.

"Melanie was very upset after that man . . . Staley left here. She tossed and turned all night and cried over Kirstin most of the day. She's had about all she can take. Plus, I don't see the point in another attempt. She didn't see a damn thing."

"She feels guilty," Jane said gently.

Steadman stared at her a moment then shook his head. "Damn right she does. She feels as if she's letting Kirstin down, and, my God, if her friend is . . . harmed. . . ."

"All the more reason why I've been sent here, Mr. Steadman. Barry. Young adults are my specialty. You need to know that. I freelance. Here in Colorado and all over the country. And if I don't get a sketch, then I do my best to help the witnesses understand they aren't to blame."

"I'm not sure."

Again, Jane carefully phrased her words. "Barry, Melanie probably did see something, something that she doesn't even know she saw. It could be insignificant to her, but it could be a huge break to the FBI. Melanie deserves the chance to let me help her recall any forgotten details. What if, years later, she remembers something and has to live with that? Let's give her a second chance."

He gave in, finally, and the door swung open. Behind her she heard Ray say, "Very persuasive, Miss Russo," but she didn't react, merely followed Barry Steadman into his cozy living room.

They waited while Steadman went to get his daughter. The mother appeared, unsmiling, nodded her head to them, holding a dish towel, then disappeared without an introduction. Jane could hear an oven door open and close, and the aroma of baking Christmas cookies wafted through the air: butter, almond, vanilla, and browning cinnamon. The house was decorated for the holidays, a tree in the corner of the living room, a fire in the stone fireplace, holly and a handmade evergreen bough draped artfully across the stones, stockings already in place, bowls of spicy dried fruit on tables, dishes of foil-wrapped candies, Christmas cards sitting open on every available space.

Idly Jane wondered if her mother still decorated the

Aspen house. Probably. She'd do it for herself if not for Jane's stepfather and her stepbrother Scott, who was a couple years older than Jane and still hanging out at home, sponging off his father. Not to mention the grandchildren, Gwen's boys. Her mother's house appeared in her mind's eye, a sudden vision of warmth and comfort. Christmastime as a child. She shut the thought down.

Melanie appeared and again introductions were made. Barry led them into a small but comfortably appointed den, with two couches facing each other and a television set and computer desk, even another fireplace, which was also burning.

A pleasant, inviting setting. Now if Jane could only concentrate. And where was Ray going to wait? This was bound to take a while.

He didn't leave then, though. He insisted on sitting off to the side and observing. Short of upsetting the already ill-at-ease young girl, Jane didn't dare risk an argument. She only hoped he kept his mouth shut.

Melanie sat opposite Jane. She scrunched close to the arm of the couch, held two throw pillows against her chest. All the young people Jane interviewed reacted much the same way. Nervous, defensive, wishing they were anywhere but here, wishing, of course, they were with their friends, and nothing in the world would ever harm them.

Melanie was a very pretty thirteen-year-old . . . going on twenty. Jane was quick to realize. She was savvy and more outgoing than a lot of girls her age. Probably quite the leader of her peer group in normal circumstances. She was also well developed for an eighth grader. With her long curling blond hair and dimpled cheeks, she was going to knock boys dead in high school next year.

Jane explained about her job and how she liked to get to know the witness and for the witness to get to know her.

Melanie picked right up on Jane's intent. "I don't know if I can remember anything, Miss Russo."

"Jane."

"Jane." She ducked her head for a moment. "I didn't remember a thing for that other guy, Mr. Staley."

"That's okay. In fact," Jane stretched the truth, "it's better you didn't. This way we start fresh and we get it right. Okay?"

"Okay." Dutifully.

"So tell me about yourself, Melanie. I'll bet you ski."

"Um, well . . ."

"Oh, I always forget, it's snowboarding—nowadays, shredding."

Melanie nodded.

"Do you play school sports? Volleyball, basketball?"

"Uh-huh. I'm captain of the middle school volleyball team."

"Good for you."

They talked about school and boys and drugs, the kids that hung out on the downtown malls and drank and skipped classes. "Not like in the city or anything," the young teen was quick to explain, "but that stuff is here, too, you know?"

And that was Jane's opening to tell Melanie that she herself had been born and raised in Aspen and graduated from Aspen High School. She chatted with Melanie about the mundane, and Ray was almost forgotten. Almost. Melanie seemed oblivious to his presence in the room, but Jane was only too aware of him.

"There are these real geeks who try to hang with us," Melanie was saying, the pillows having fallen to her side, her legs not so tightly curled beneath her.

"With us?" Jane asked. "You mean you and your girl-friends? Like with you and Kirstin?" The first time she'd spoke Kirstin Lemke's name.

The reaction was to be expected. Melanie seemed to have forgotten Kirstin, but now she remembered, and tears sprang to her eyes. "Oh God," she said, her hands going to her cheeks, "poor Kirstin. Why can't the police find her? I don't understand."

"They're trying their best," Jane said. "That's why I'm here and the FBI has sent their agents. We're all trying really hard, Melanie."

"Why didn't he take me or Crystal? We were both there, too."

Guilt. Survivor's guilt. Again, to be expected.

Jane knew that her next words were going to alarm Ray, but this was the way she worked. Too bad if he didn't like it.

She leaned forward and held the teenager's gaze. "This will all come out soon, but I'm going to ask you to keep this to yourself and maybe your mom and dad for a while. Okay?"

"Okay." The girl sniffed.

"We don't think Kirstin's abduction was an accident. We believe Kirstin was carefully selected. This man, if he's the one we think he is, has taken girls before. And they always look similar—on the tall side, long brown hair, glasses, a certain shyness."

"Oh my God," Kirstin whispered, and while she digested the news Jane turned just enough to catch Ray's scowl. She met his glare and shook her head imperceptibly. He had to see why she was confiding this to Melanie, and he must know it was going to come out in the end anyway.

He kept his counsel, thank heavens, but Jane could feel the disapproval emanating from his corner of the room.

Then Melanie asked the inevitable question. "If he's done this before, I mean, are the girls . . . okay?" Her eyes were so wide they dominated her features.

"I can tell you that Lisa and Allie, those are the girls, are perfectly fine," Jane said, not mentioning Jennifer Weissman, found dead in Park City last year. "So, Melanie, this man would not have taken you or your other friend Crystal even if you'd offered to exchange yourselves for your friend. You understand that, don't you?"

"I guess so."

Jane reached into the case then and produced her favorite tool, a hunk of neutral-colored Play-Doh and handed it to Melanie.

"What's that for?"

"I just want you to form it into shapes while we talk. Okay?"

"You mean . . . you think I can like make his face or something?"

Jane smiled. "Goodness, no, but sometimes it helps you to remember the littlest things while you fool with it."

"I . . . I didn't *see* him."

"I know. But we can talk about that day with Crystal and Kirstin, can't we?"

"I guess."

Melanie was dubious but willing. A whole different person from the uptight teenager who'd sat down an hour ago.

"So," Jane began, "you were skiing—*boarding*—at Snowmass?"

"Uh-huh."

"Because Kirstin lives near Snowmass, or is it the best boarding?"

"We just like it there. The Big Burn. You know." A shrug.

"Oh, yes, I remember. Was it a cold day?"

"Real cold. But then a storm began to move in, and it started getting windy and a little warmer."

Jane nodded. It always did before a good dump of snow. "What runs did you ski?"

They talked about the trails and the lifts they rode and friends from school they ran into then ditched after having lunch with everyone on top of the mountain. All the time Melanie half-consciously played with the hunk of pliable plastic, rolling it in her hands, forming vague shapes: a pretzel, something resembling a ski, a hot dog. The other witness Crystal had had a hot dog and fries at lunch.

Melanie talked about riding the ski lift after lunch and then her face grew very still. "There was a lift line," she said, recalling, her brown creasing. "And I rode up with Crystal. Kirstin was pissed, you know? She had to ride with some dude. We were laughing at her."

"There's something about this man, this dude, isn't there, Melanie?" Jane kept her tone even, but she *felt* something was there.

"Um, I don't know, just some guy."

Jane was losing her. "And this guy, he didn't ride up with you or Crystal, did he? He rode with Kirstin on purpose?"

"No, I mean . . . Well, maybe I was in line sort of more with Crystal. And Kirstin was kind of stuck behind us next to him . . . Yeah, maybe."

Without realizing it, Melanie had made a ball with the clay.

"Was he wearing a hat?"

The girl thought. "Yes. It was dark colored. Black or maybe dark green or something. I remember thinking it was a dorky hat. And a neck gaiter. That was dorky, too."

"Do you remember what color the neck gaiter was?"

"Um, dark. Oh, and goggles. I remember because he was wearing glasses under them. Weird, you know?"

"I sure do. Geeky."

"Kind of."

Melanie's hands were working the Play-Doh into the shape of a head. Round at first, then a long oval. Jane took up her sketch pad and Conte pencil. She kept her body language unobtrusive. "Do you remember what kind of glasses he wore?"

Melanie wrinkled her nose. "It was hard to see with the goggles, but I think, um, I think they may have been wire-rimmed ones." She paused. "Like my mom's driving ones."

"Do you recall the shape of the glasses?"

"Like my mom's, I think. Oval, I mean, I *think* they were. I didn't see the guy very well. Honest."

Oh, but you did, Jane thought. A part of Melanie's mind had registered more than she knew.

"So," she said, sketching now with her pencil while keeping her focus on Melanie, "what kind of ski clothes was he wearing?"

Melanie frowned. "It was a parka. I think. Maybe black."

"A dark color, anyway?"

Melanie nodded. "Black. And maybe it had red bands around the sleeves?"

"More than one band?"

"Um, I can't remember."

"That's okay. But he was on skis, not on a board?"

"Ah . . . skis. Skis for sure. I remember he was leaning on his poles before he got on the lift with Kirstin."

"Um. You don't recall what kind of skis?"

"No way. I'm pretty into boards."

Jane strayed from the subject for a few minutes, giving the girl a break. She talked about snowboards and the different weight shifts you made to carve turns, about the distinctive baggy clothing shredders wore and how the local ski corporation had prohibited snowboarders from Aspen Mountain, its premier mountain, for years until giving in to the new wave.

"Dad said they gave in because of the bottom line," Melanie told her. "Lots of families come to Aspen and kids snowboard now, you know? So Aspen Mountain was losing business to the other resorts because the families like to ski together."

"I see. And I take it snowboards can screw up a slope for regular skiers?"

"People say that." Melanie again shrugged. She was still working with the Play-Doh. "They say boards mess up the moguls."

"And snowboarders are a little wild, too, I bet."

"I'm not."

"I'm sure you're not. So, this man who rode up with Kirstin . . . did he have a beard under the neck gaiter, or maybe a mustache?"

"Ah . . . I don't know."

"Maybe you saw his cheeks? Were they red from the cold?"

"Um. I don't know. He had whiskers, I think."

"Interesting." Jane shaded with the side of her pencil, adding shadows to the featureless, long oval face behind the goggles and glasses and cap and neck gaiter. "Not a beard. But maybe he hadn't shaved."

"Maybe. I don't know."

"So I guess he was an older guy, seeing as he was on skis."

"Uh-huh. Older."

Age was tough for teens to decipher. After all, twenty was old to them. And parents were downright ancient.

Jane took a workable path. "I suppose this guy was your dad's age then."

"Not *that* old."

"Oh. Then maybe the age of a teacher at school? Or a coach?"

Melanie thought a minute. "Maybe Mr. Crawford's age. He's my homeroom teacher."

"How old is Mr. Crawford?"

"He's, like, thirty-something. You know, from the TV show? He jokes about it, but he's not very funny."

Jane smiled. "Okay. Thirty-something it is. Was he as tall as Mr. Crawford?"

"Mr. Crawford is short. *I'm* taller than he is."

"Oh, I see. So this guy was tallish then? Or was he your height?"

"Tall. I think."

"Taller than you?"

"Uh-huh. More like Dad. He's six feet."

"Was he trim like your dad? It's hard to tell under a parka, but maybe you got an impression?"

"I guess like my dad."

Jane would have put Barry Steadman at around one-seventy. Lean for a six-foot man. She was sketching when Melanie said, "The dude had Mr. Crawford's nose. I *think* he did." She tried to form a nose on the Play-Doh with little success. Unfortunately, Melanie was no artist.

"And what's up with Mr. Crawford's nose?"

"He broke it last year. He helps with the JV baseball team and Cory Grossman . . . he's the pitcher . . . anyway, he threw a wild pitch and caught Mr. Crawford on the nose. There was, like, a ton of blood."

Jane sketched. "Wow. Did you see the accident?"

"Um, no, but the guys were all laughing about it the next day. I think it's really gross."

"Crooked nose . . . with a bump, too?"

"Huh?"

"From the break?"

"Oh." She shook her head. "I don't remember."

They talked about when the girls got off the lift at the top. Evidently, the man had skied off immediately. Melanie wasn't sure if Kirstin had said anything about him, but she thought her friend had been pissed that Crystal had jumped on the lift with Melanie and left Kirstin to ride with the stranger.

"So did you see him again that afternoon?" Jane asked.

"Ah . . . no. I don't think so."

And then, as Jane had known he eventually would, Ray inserted a question. "Melanie," he said, leaning forward on the computer chair, "did you happen to see this same man in the parking lot after skiing?"

Melanie pivoted. The lump of clay fell, forgotten, to her side.

Goddamn it, Ray.

"I . . . I . . . I don't know," Melanie said, suddenly alarmed, as if she should have seen him.

Jane tried to repair the damage. "That's okay, honey, if he's the man who took Kirstin, he would have done everything he could not to be seen."

But the thread was broken. Still, Jane tried. "How did you and Crystal get separated from Kirstin near the bus stop?"

"We, ah, that is Crystal and I were rushing to catch the skier's shuttle bus . . . Kirstin's mom was supposed to meet us at the parking lot where the shuttle lets you off. I think it was four-thirty. And, anyway, we got in line . . ."

"You and Crystal?"

"Uh-huh. We got in line, and I turned around to tell Kirstin we weren't going to fit on this bus, it was so packed, and I was thinking Mrs. Lemke was going to be pissed, but Kirstin wasn't there."

"Um, okay," Jane said. What Melanie had told them just now agreed with what she'd told the police. The man, the rapist had driven a pickup truck in Mammoth and Snowbird. The witnesses and victims had known that much. But, evidently, Melanie had been oblivious to any vehicle, just concerned about getting into the bus line.

How *had* he gotten Kirstin to go with him? Surely, he hadn't wielded a knife in public. The victim from Snowbird had been duped into giving the man directions to a gas station and then, when they were away from her friends, he'd shown the young girl his knife and forced her to wear a stocking cap pulled over her eyes, forced her into a windowless room somewhere and kept her tied in the dark for days. In this case, ten days, Jane thought she recalled. And then he made her wear the same hat pulled over her eyes when he dropped her on a remote road, in the dark of night. Her body abused, her mind ravished . . .

"I don't remember anything else," Melanie was saying, her glance going furtively to Ray now, her demeanor growing more and more tense.

They left the Steadman home a few minutes later.

Ray started the cold engine. "Well, that was . . ."

"I can't believe you did that," Jane cut in.

"What?"

"Broke her concentration like that."

"Huh," he said, then, "It doesn't matter. It was a waste of time."

"Oh, really? We got . . . I got a few details at least. Height, weight, maybe hair color, the glasses, no beard or mustache . . ."

"What the hell makes you think it's even our man? Some stranger rides a lift with a kid. Hardly a federal case." He pulled away from the snowbank and drove too quickly down Cemetery Lane. "I'll drop you at your sister's," he said curtly.

"Fine. Whatever."

"It's too late to interview the other witness, what's her name?"

"Crystal."

"It's too late tonight. I'll arrange for it tomorrow. Right

now I've got to get back to the sheriff's and meet up with the team."

"You'll go to the Lemke's then?"

"Yes."

"That will be rough. The poor parents . . ."

"It's always rough."

"You've handled kidnapping cases before?"

"Not really."

"So what was your field before you transferred to Denver?"

"Antiterrorism, domestic militant groups."

"Um." And again, something itched in her brain. Ray Vanover, militants, terrorism . . . But she still couldn't get a handle on the annoyingly vague notion that she knew something about this man. "Turn right at the light," she said, "then you go around the traffic circle to . . ."

"I remember the way."

"Fine."

But he didn't remember the turn to her sister's house, and Jane had to direct him. All he muttered was, "They should have goddamn streetlights."

"That's the place," she said, pointing.

He pulled into the drive. "I'll make the arrangements to get you with the other kid . . . Crystal."

"Good." She opened her door, her purse and case held to her breast. Fleetingly she thought about the time—it was past seven in the evening—and wondered where Alan was, who he was with. She spent most of her evenings thinking about Alan and what went wrong. Thinking and regretting and aching for companionship. Then she came back to reality with a jolt. *God.* She was in Aspen. At her sister's. And the man dropping her off was not Alan.

"I'll call you early," Ray was saying.

"I'll be waiting." She knew her next move was childishly

calculating, spitefully so, but she reveled in the moment anyway. She half closed the car door, then said, "Oh, by the way, about the crooked nose on the UNSUB?"

"Yeah? What about it?"

"If you check my case file notes, I think you'll find that the Snowbird victim from three years ago described her abductor as having a crooked nose." With that she shut the door and started up the walk, her entire focus abruptly shifting to her family and the confrontation that was sure to come.

FIVE

On his third pass along Main Street in the space of a few hours, Ray's impression of Aspen solidified. Walt Disney could have created this winter wonderland nestled between towering peaks in the middle of the Colorado Rockies. The town bore little resemblance to the outside world, with its turn-of-the-century lampposts, the bare-branched cottonwoods standing in stately ranks along snow-packed Main Street, its quaint pastel-painted Victorians with gingerbread trim and funky ski lodges. Heavy snow blanketed the pine boughs in a quiet park, and the gazebo at its center was adorned with twinkling white lights.

Yeah, a fairyland. And all he'd seen was Main Street. And the courthouse, of course, with the sheriff's department in its basement.

His thoughts turned back to the Kirstin Lemke case. Turned to Jane. He'd give her points for her well-timed dig about the Snowbird witness's description of the UNSUB. The crooked nose. He didn't believe in coincidence. The

odds of two witnesses, hundreds of miles apart and years
between their interviews, coming up with the crooked nose
were astronomical. Had to be the same man. He had studied
the case histories in detail, and mentally he ran through the
other victims and their locales: Mammoth, California;
Snowbird and Park City, Utah. Now Aspen. All ski resorts.
That was the connection. Which told him nothing new.

He parked the Explorer in the official space across from
the courthouse and thought harder about the connection,
the ski angle. All abductions had occurred in the winter. So
was the UNSUB tied into the ski industry? A patrolman,
ski instructor, lift operator, snowcat driver? A lot of possibilities the team was working on. Too damn many.

The crooked nose, most likely broken. Was it worth
checking hospital records in Mammoth and Snowbird? What
were the chances the guy had broken his nose within the time
frame of this case? Unacceptably low. The man could have
fallen off a bicycle when he was a kid. To order an investigation of hospital and clinic records was a waste of bureau
resources. They needed to nail the UNSUB right here in
Aspen. For Kirstin's sake, they had better do it quickly, too,
because last winter the kidnapper had only kept his Park City
victim a little over a week. Jennifer Weissman. Raped repeat-
edly and left to die in a rundown shack of an abandoned
motel. Jennifer. She'd never seen her fourteenth birthday.
Special Agents Bruce Dallenbach and Sid Reynolds had
gone to the Lemke's Snowmass home right after Ray had left
with Jane for Melanie's house. The FBI electronics specialist,
Special Agent Howard Canning, was already at the Lemke's,
having flown in yesterday afternoon to set up the requisite
phone taps, though no one believed for a minute the UNSUB
was going to call the Lemkes. He hadn't taken their child for
ransom. He'd taken her to fulfill his sick urges.

Sheriff Kent Schilling was still in his office along with

deputies Bernie and Frank, who were waiting to escort Ray to the Lemke house.

"I take it there hasn't been any news?" Ray asked when he rapped on the open door and strode in.

"Not a thing," Schilling replied.

Ray nodded at the deputies.

Schilling rose from behind his oak desk and stared out the garden level window. He hitched up his pants and said, "Jane have any luck with the Steadman kid?"

"Not much. The guy might be tall and lean, maybe. And he might be fair-skinned and blondish, maybe. And he might wear oval, wire-rimmed glasses, maybe. And he might have a crooked nose, *maybe*."

Schilling pivoted. "Well, that's a damn sight more than we had earlier, I'd say."

"If any of it's factual." Ray shrugged.

"If that's what the kid told Jane, then my money's on it."

"Um," Ray said.

"Jane's good. She's had a knack since she was a kid. She's got genuine talent, that girl."

Ray stared at him. "You've known Jane for a long time?"

"God, yes. Since she was, oh, maybe eight or nine. Her dad, that's her *stepdad*, really, is a good friend. Roland Zucker. Hell, he was sheriff here in town when I was new to the department. When he decided not to run for office again, Roland backed me all the way. And as for Jane, heck, my wife Lottie had her in art class at school here for years. Lottie always said Jane had a gift. And she does."

"Um." Ray was noncommittal. He turned to the deputies. "I'll follow you out to the Lemke's now, if that's okay? I'd like to keep the Explorer."

Ray spoke to Schilling again. "Sheriff, would you also do me a favor and set up a time tomorrow to get with the other witness . . . Crystal? As soon as possible."

"Crystal Brenner. Sure, I'll ring her mother and make the arrangements."

"I'd appreciate it."

"I'm here to serve."

"Uh-huh," Ray said, his thoughts already shifting to the upcoming task, talking to Kirstin's mother and father. *Christ.*

The Lemkes lived six miles from Aspen in an area called Brush Creek. The houses in the development dotted a snow-covered mountainside at the turnoff to Snowmass Village, the resort where Kirstin had been boarding with her friends on the afternoon of her disappearance.

He followed the two deputies up a precipitous, curving road called Medicine Bow to a house perched on the hillside with a steep driveway running down to the garage. The house was gray clapboard, quite modern in style, with a great view of the valley below.

There were several vehicles parked in the neatly plowed driveway, several more up on the road. Ray knew Special Agents Dallenbach, Reynolds, and Canning were there with a car, and presumably a couple of the vehicles belonged to the Lemkes. The others could belong to friends or even relatives. Ray was going to have to cut the number of nonofficial visitors down for the time being. His job was to extract information from the distraught parents, not to baby-sit their anxious friends. Somehow the UNSUB had spotted Kirstin; somewhere he had seen the girl and made his selection. Her abduction had not been random. It had been well planned and thought out for days, if not weeks or months in advance. He had even known the time of day Kirstin usually quit the slopes with her skiing buddies, known that the light was dim near the winter solstice. It was no coincidence that all the victims had been taken near the shortest day of the year.

Merry Christmas, Ray thought, following the deputies to the door.

There were indeed a lot of bodies crowded in the Lemke home. The three FBI agents were there, manning phones, making calls themselves, and a sheriff's deputy named Teresa Morales was on duty. There was a minister and several friends of the Lemkes. He had no idea which ones were Kirstin's mother and father.

People gathered in sober clusters, in the living room and the kitchen and what appeared to be the library. Ray's presence along with two more deputies went unnoticed.

Until he stood on the broad shallow step of the bi-level living room, cleared his throat and got everyone's attention. "Excuse me, folks, I'm Special Agent Ray Vanover, and I have a request. I know you want to be with your friends in their time of need, but right now I have to ask that all nonessential persons give us some working space here with the Lemke family. You can certainly call anytime you like and speak to Deputy Morales or Special Agent Reynolds. They'll give you a dedicated phone number for that purpose. Okay, folks?"

All heads swiveled towards him. There was an angry buzz from the gathered people.

"Look," Ray said, "I know you all want to help, but the best thing you can do right now is to let us work. You want Kirstin back safe, right? You're going to have to let us do our jobs."

There was a slow, reluctant movement to find hats and coats and gloves, but they were leaving. Thank God. No confrontational ones to deal with.

"Thanks, everybody, we appreciate your cooperation," he said as they filed out, ushered by the other agents and the deputy on duty. Like a funeral procession.

Ray wasn't used to dealing with shattered families; his

expertise had been in a different area—shattered buildings and bodies and vehicles. He guessed he'd done all right, though.

A man appeared from the master bedroom and strode over to him. Kirstin's father. He looked terrible. He'd probably once been a nice-looking, fit man in his mid-forties. Medium height, with light brown hair, thinning at the crown, close set blue eyes, a cleft in his chin. Now Josh Lemke's eyes were red and puffy, his skin ashen, his lips quivering.

He went for Ray like an attack dog. "So you're the goddam case agent?"

"That's right."

"And it takes you fucking three days to get here from Denver? Our child, our *baby* is out there somewhere with . . . a maniac, and you sit on your ass in Denver! No goddamn wonder the FBI takes so much shit!"

"Just hold on right there," Ray said in a barely audible voice. "Mr. Lemke, you're going to have to control yourself. This kind of behavior is counterproductive."

"Counterproductive," Lemke spat.

"We're here to get your daughter back." Ray said.

Lemke stopped and his shoulders sagged. He put his hands to his face and stammered something unintelligible.

"Listen," Ray said, "I understand what you're going through, but getting angry at me isn't going to help."

"You have no goddam idea what I'm going through," Lemke said hopelessly, dropping his hands. And then his jaw went slack and his lips began trembling. His eyes filled. "Our baby," he moaned, "our *baby.*"

Ray could sympathize with the man, because he recognized his rage on a very personal level. Hell, for the past eighteen months he'd suffered the same uncontrollable emotion, ever since those bastards had murdered Kathleen, scarred him for life, and gotten away scot-free.

But he couldn't let Lemke give in to that emotion. He needed him. "Mr. Lemke . . . Josh," he said, "I need to sit down with you and your wife, and I need you to be clear-headed. Can you do that?"

Lemke wiped angrily at his eyes. He sucked in a breath and nodded. "Yes, sure. But Suzanne, she's taken some mediation her doctor prescribed, and . . . Well, I don't know if she can think too straight."

Wildly erratic behavior on the father's part, Ray thought, *and a sedated mother. This is getting better and better.* "Let's find someplace to talk," he suggested, catching Bruce's gaze, while Bruce rolled his eyes. The other agents went about their business. Very quietly.

Ray walked down the hall to the master bedroom, where Suzanne Lemke lay under a blanket, several pillows behind her head. She was awake, her eyes glazed over, her expression blank.

Bruce Dallenbach followed them in with a notepad and settled on a window seat. Josh Lemke sat on the side of the king-size bed and took his wife's hand, while Ray moved to a chair by a dresser. He pushed aside the ottoman, sat with his knees splayed, hands on the armrests, trying to appear relaxed. This was a first for him. A helluva first. And again he thought for a split second about Jane. How well she'd handled Barry Steadman and Melanie, reassuring them, setting them at ease, making them feel necessary to the investigation.

"Safe," Jane had said. The witness—or victim—had to feel safe. Maybe he shouldn't have dropped Jane off, maybe he should have asked her to tag along.

"Okay," he began, and he introduced himself to Suzanne, who blinked and squeezed her husband's hand.

She was an ordinary-looking women, around forty, medium weight. She wore her brown hair blunt cut to her shoulders, and she had bangs. Ray observed a pair of glasses on the night table. Clearly, Kirstin resembled her mother. There was even a shyness he recognized through the drugs. Yeah, if Suzanne Lemke were twenty-five years younger, she'd be just the rapist's cup of tea.

Ray took a breath. "Okay," he repeated, "I'd like to start by telling you exactly what the FBI knows so far, and level with you about what we don't know. I won't whitewash the facts, either, because I believe the faster we come to terms with what we're dealing with here, the better our chances of apprehending our man."

"Why . . . why hasn't he called?" Suzanne stammered. "We have money. . . . My parents could even help. We'll get whatever he asks, anything, *anything*."

Bruce, who was at the window seat, caught Ray's attention by clearing his throat. He shook his head, as if to let Ray know that the parents had not been informed about the UNSUB.

Shit, Ray thought. He had just made his first blunder, on his first kidnapping case. He'd assumed that someone had told the parents, had told them the facts or at least the possibilities. Obviously no one had. That was the job of the case agent. *His* job. He should have known that. FBI Procedure 101. Textbook crap.

"What the hell?" Josh Lemke was saying. "Do you *know* who has Kirstin? I don't understand what the hell is going on here. If you know . . ."

Ray put up a hand and Lemke subsided. "Here's where the case stands. Everything about this abduction is pointing to a serial kidnapper of young girls."

Suzanne gasped, moaned.

Ray went on. They deserved the truth. "We think the UNSUB, sorry, that's jargon for unknown subject, we think this man has abducted at least three other girls over a five-year period."

"Oh God," Lemke whispered.

"The first that we know of was a thirteen-year-old girl in Mammoth, California. The next was three years ago, out in Snowbird, Utah. And last year a girl was taken from Park City. All of the girls were the same age, on the tall side, same complexions, same hair coloring and styles, right down to the bangs. And they all wore glasses. Even their personalities were similar."

"And the girls . . . are they . . . ?" Suzanne asked.

"Two of them are fine, Mrs. Lemke," Ray said gently. He knew what the next question was going to be.

Lemke. "And the third girl?"

Ray shook his head.

Suzanne clung to her husband and wept, while Josh held Ray's stare, obviously steeling himself. And again he took on the look of a man ready to burst with fury.

"Her death," Ray said with care, "may have been an accident. You need to know that. We believe she was all right when her kidnapper left her." *All right. Sure.* Raped and abused for days on end. Left tied to a broken bed—Ray had seen the crime scene photos—in the boarded-up motel ten miles outside of Park City, no heat or food or water, the middle of December. *Yeah, she was perfectly fine.*

"What . . . what does this man, this horrible man want with these girls?" Suzanne began, but then she realized through the haze of sedation, and she began to sob again.

"Look." Ray hardened himself. "You need to put your heads together and try to think about any out-of-the-ordinary situations or incidents Kirstin may have experienced these past weeks. Someone approaching her on the street, at the grocery store, the movies, at school, or a volleyball game, on the ski slopes. Right here in Brush Creek. Anything. Anybody. Agents Reynolds and Canning and the sheriff's department are making calls as we speak to Kirstin's friends and teachers, and we're canvassing neighbors and everyone we can conceive of, but as her parents you'd know more than anyone. Try to recall if Kirstin was upset about something. Even if she didn't talk about it to you, she might have confided in someone, a girlfriend, a . . ."

"You've *talked* to her girlfriends, haven't you?" Josh said tightly. "They were right there with Kirstin, for chris-sakes. How could they *not* have seen him?"

"We've talked to Melanie Steadman. We'll see Crystal Brenner tomorrow. But you have to understand that our man is a very careful planner. He pulls off his abductions in mid- to late December when the light is so dim it's hard to see. He waits till after a day of skiing, as late as possible, at the bottom of the slopes crowded with the last of the skiers, the parking lots full of people. He wears nonde-script dark clothes, hides his hair color and face behind a neck gaiter and goggles. Of course, we've interviewed the witnesses and the victims themselves, but either due to trauma or shock or his cleverness, we've gotten no con-crete description of him. One fact we have is that he drives a pickup truck. Dark in color. *Maybe.*"

"But surely the other victims, the two girls," Suzanne said in a moment of clarity, "surely they saw the man. They must have if he . . . he . . ."

Ray shook his head. "The man kept his face hidden, as I explained, during the actual abductions, and he pulled a stocking hat down over the girls' eyes when he drove away. He took them to an unknown location and kept them in the dark, literally. He released them the same way, blindfolded. All they ever saw of him was his hat, a neck gaiter pulled up over his mouth, goggles. We do believe, according to two witnesses now, that he might have had his nose broken at one time. We have approximate height and weight and skin coloring, maybe even hair coloring." *Too many maybes.* "The point is, no one has been able to give us enough detail for a composite sketch."

Or give Jane a damn thing, either, he thought. She'd interviewed both living victims, all the witnesses to their kidnappings, and other than the possible eyeglasses, the crooked nose, clothing, and pickup truck, she'd utterly failed. Great *gift* she had. Yet she'd had amazing success with other cases, or so SAC Parker had assured him. Successes all over the country, her talent sought after by state and federal law enforcement agencies. So why was she stumped on this case? Why the sabbatical right now, with Special Agent Caroline Deutch having to talk her into taking on this particular case? And Aspen. What was with her curious relationship with her family here or, more to the point, her *non-relationship* with them?

"How long?" Lemke was asking.

"Excuse me?" Ray said.

"How long did this . . . this bastard keep those girls?"

"Up to ten days," Ray replied, and Suzanne moaned like a wounded animal.

There was plenty more Ray could have told them, but he chose not to. There was the UNSUB's weapon of choice to subdue his victims, a curved, approximately eight-inch-long knife. And he certainly wasn't going to get into statistics, tell these poor people that with each crime, rapists and serial murderers grew more needy; not only did the time between crimes diminish, but the level of brutality increased exponentially. No doubt that was why he had left Jennifer to die when he'd previously released his victims.

How could he tell them that Kirstin's prospects were not very good at all?

He sat with the Lemkes for some time, asking a lot of questions about their daughter's habits, her routine, her friends. He kept in mind what Jane had said, that the people she interviewed had to feel safe. He asked about any odd circumstances, a man hanging around, a stranger talking to Kirstin. He got nothing from them, nothing but tears and threats and the sight of a mother and father pushed to unbearable dread.

Finally he nodded at Bruce. Time to go and give the parents a little privacy. They had to be going through living hell. Not that he had any children, so what did he really know?

Bruce closed the bedroom door behind them and followed Ray to the FBI's makeshift workstation, where Howard Canning sat with headphones on, waiting to record a call that was never going to come. Sid Reynolds was on a cell phone, finishing up a call to one of Kirstin's teachers. The agents and deputies had made dozens of calls and would make dozens more, hoping, praying for a break, no matter how insignificant. Maybe a janitor at school, or an assistant coach or another parent or a school bus driver had noticed someone loitering where he shouldn't have been, someone in a pickup parked too long somewhere.

Then there were the Snowmass ski area employees, lift operators, ticket sellers, patrolmen, ski instructors—a seemingly endless list of people to interview. And very little, pathetically little, in the way of a description of the UNSUB to give them. The bureau was always shorthanded these days, with so many agents pulled off street crimes to work on terrorist activities, and cases like this one suffered from the lack of manpower. He looked around at the men on the phone, doing their best to find Kirstin Lemke, and shook his head. He could have used more men.

Deputy Morales was at her post at the door. Mostly, she

headed off well-meaning visitors, turning them away, and accepted dishes of food from gracious friends and neighbors who felt completely helpless. He was again reminded of a wake, where everyone automatically brought food. It was all they could do.

He decided to leave Canning and Reynolds at the Lemkes to take the night shift, and he and Dallenbach would head into town to try to catch a few hours sleep at the suite that had been rented yesterday at the Mountain House, reportedly a nice but inexpensive guest house. Dallenbach had told Ray they'd been damn lucky to find an open suite at Christmas. And then only through the offices of Sheriff Schilling, who happened to know the owner of the place. Aspen was a small town.

"See you early in the morning," Ray told Canning and Reynolds.

"Oh, say," Reynolds snapped his fingers. "Kent Schilling phoned to let you know that Crystal Brenner—the other kid who was with Kirstin—well, you can interview her tomorrow, but not until the afternoon."

Ray frowned. "What's up with that? We need to see that kid as soon as possible."

"Don't know," Reynolds said. "Something about the mother. I guess she keeps late hours. It's her call."

"Great." Ray put on his leather jacket, which he'd left draped over a couch. "Okay. You've got my cell number and the Mountain House number. We'll probably stop on the way for a bite. You okay here?"

"We're fine," Canning said.

Ray drove. On the ride into Aspen they talked about the Lemkes, in particular, Josh Lemke's mood swings.

Ray said, "This is my first kidnapping case, and I feel I should be able to handle the man better than I have."

"I think you handled him just fine," Bruce said.

"I don't know. The truth is, if Lemke found out who this asshole is, and if he went after him, I'd be tempted to turn my back."

"Who wouldn't?"

"Rhetorical question?"

"Absolutely."

The difference was, Ray knew, a professional at his level—case agent—shouldn't even consider the idea. Yet he did. It was his own bottled-up rage. He didn't even have to look in the mirror to feel the anger and frustration. He wondered when Bruce was going to ask him about the burns. Eventually everyone did. At dinner, probably.

He was right. They stopped at a rustic log cabin restaurant at the edge of Aspen. Place called the Hickory House. Schilling had suggested it to the agents as an eatery for locals to get a good, fast, down-home meal.

Over barbecued ribs and chicken, Bruce said, "You . . . ah . . . have a lot of skin grafting done on those burns, Ray?"

"Some." God, he hated the subject. Hated the time squandered in surgery and doctors' waiting rooms, the memories of that afternoon eighteen months ago. He hated remembering Kathleen, dead, her family, the waste of her life. And for what? Now here he was in Colorado, a backwater posting as far as he was concerned. Seattle had been a happening place, near Canada, a gateway to Asia. There had never been dull moment. But from what SAC Parker had told him, Denver was going to give Ray a break.

Well, Ray hadn't wanted a break. But orders were orders.

"Not that they . . . ah . . . the burns show that much," Bruce hastened to add, then he got busy with his french fries.

"It didn't seem important," Ray said. "In view of what happened to the other agent in the car."

"Yeah, we all heard. A woman, right?"

"Right."

"Um," Bruce said. "And we haven't caught the perps yet. That sucks."

"Uh-huh."

He steered the conversation to a more comfortable topic, the present assignment. "I'd like to spend some more time on the old case files from California and Utah. I've been over them, but I need to look again. Case got thrown in my lap only the day before yesterday."

"We'll both review them," Bruce said. "Everything's back at our suite, and I don't think I could sleep much, anyway."

"Okay," Ray said, pushing aside his plate, signaling the waitress for the check.

The Mountain House was situated on the east side of town. Everything was within walking distance, even the gondola up the face of Aspen Mountain. But because it was on the perimeter of town, and an older set of buildings, offering only the essentials, the rates were fairly reasonable.

The suite assigned to the FBI team sat around the corner from the small lobby. It consisted of two rooms separated by a wooden blind that could be pulled across between them. The bathroom could be accessed from both rooms. In the living area there was a small fridge, microwave, and coffeemaker, a green plaid couch that pulled out into a queen-sized bed, two workable chairs, a dark wood coffee table, an end table, and lamp. Everything was clean and neat but dated, and the lighting was not the best.

Bruce had brought along all the material the bureau had on the kidnappings and the Park City murder case. The notes and files and tapes took up two boxes, and yet not one piece of paper or tape contained a single solid lead on the UNSUB.

By midnight, Bruce was in sweatpants and Ray in cords, their shoes kicked aside. Papers littered every useable surface in both rooms. They were keeping separate notes. Ray finished up with the last file while Bruce washed his face. Ray sat back in his chair, scrubbed his hands over his stubbled cheeks and stretched.

When Bruce reappeared, it was time to compare notes. Ray began. "Okay, we've got four abductions that we know of, including the present one. We've got all victims from ski areas moving west to east over a five-year period. We've got Allison Sanchez from Mammoth. Christmas five years ago. We've got Lisa Turchelli from Snowbird, three years ago, and murder victim Jennifer Weissman from Park City last Christmas. Agreed?"

"That's the sum of it." Bruce yawned.

"The time period tells us the UNSUB is a settle-in type. Okay, Snowbird and Park City are only a few miles apart, so it's safe to assume our man spent at least two years in the same area of Utah. When he moved to Colorado is an unknown. I think it's also safe to assume that he at least finishes out a winter season in the resorts."

"Okay," Bruce allowed.

"Here's my reasoning. Given the difficulty of finding a place to rent during the season—I don't think he's a property owner—I'd have to believe he makes his moves during the off-season. The Weissman girl died last Christmas. Let's say he moved to this valley in the last seven months since the ski area in Utah closed. So, what's the feasibility of checking every recent newcomer to this valley who owns a pickup?"

"Impossible."

"Not impossible," Ray corrected, "but damn impractical given the time we have, and I'm figuring a week or less now. And that's only if his MO hasn't changed. So we go a different route. What we know is that he's most likely a skier. Especially because other witnesses than Melanie Steadman have reported the possible sightings of our man on skis prior to the abductions."

"So he skis. I agree."

"All right, then. And he's somewhat mobile. Most likely unmarried."

"That agrees with the profiler's report," Bruce put in. "Single, white, age twenty-five to thirty-five, blue collar worker, above average intelligence."

"Uh-huh," Ray said. "And a calculator. Our boy takes very little risk. He picks Christmas, close to the shortest day of the year. He's a careful dresser. About the only things visible on him are his cheeks and nose, which we now think may have been broken. And he may wear glasses."

Bruce took up the thread. "He also never takes risks when he makes the actual abductions, does it in crowded parking lots, tons of vehicles to shield him. He invariably waits till his victim is a few feet away from her friends and then, according to the Mammoth victim, he asks for directions—in her case it was to a lower parking area—gets her to take a few more steps away from her friends by asking her to point him the way, then he shows her the knife, and she's history. Once she's in his vehicle—the pickup . . ."

"Maybe dark in color," Ray added.

"Yeah, the maybe-dark truck, he forces her to wear a stocking cap over her eyes."

Ray stood and went to the window, drew aside the blind. A pine tree blocked his view, and he could see a light snow drifting from the black sky. He dropped the blind. "I wonder what our boy would do if he couldn't get his target alone for a second? Would he put off the snatch till the next evening or the next? Is he that controlled, or has he just been lucky?"

"Lucky four times?" Bruce shook his head. "No way. My money is on him stalking them for as long as it takes for the perfect opportunity to arise. Shit, he can't chance letting anyone see his license plate or get a good description of his vehicle."

"I agree. Way I see it, the holiday abductions work for him first because of the poor light, and second because the girls are all on school break and reportedly ski or board almost every day. He has several opportunities for the snatch."

"You know," Bruce said, "that angle doesn't work well if our guy is a ski area employee. I mean, how's he going to get several days off in a row in the middle of the busiest time of year?"

"Maybe he's a night worker. Snowmaking? Trail grooming?"

"Could be."

"Then again, all the victims were abused at night. Every night for up to ten days."

"Right. Damn," Bruce said.

"We can assume that they were taken to his own place. The girls were fairly certain they were held in places with at least one bedroom and a kitchen and living room, because they could hear kitchen noises and, on occasion, a radio from another room. And he has to keep them isolated. Can't risk having a neighbor see or hear anything."

"So no condo or apartment."

Ray blew out a breath. "Probably not. Probably a free-standing place. Isolated. Maybe a cabin? I can't see this man affording a house."

"Unless he doesn't work at all. Unless he's a trust-funder and just dressed in nondescript ski clothes and drives a pickup as part of his cover."

"Remember the profile?"

"Yeah, okay. Probably not a trust-funder."

They discussed the possible employment opportunities in the ski area, everything from maintenance man to dishwasher to ski patrolman to snowcat driver. And they compared the similarities between victims. Ray ticked them off. "Twelve to fourteen years in age, relatively tall, brown hair worn straight, bangs, eyeglasses, shy in nature."

"Easily handled by our man," Bruce said. "Pliable."

"A goddamn monster," Ray said under his breath. Then, to Bruce, "You know, when I was a kid my parents told me monsters weren't real. But they are."

"Oh yeah." Bruce nodded.

They were ready to try to catch a few hours sleep, picking up files, making some order out of the disorder they'd created, when Ray came across Jane Russo's file, which he'd put aside earlier.

"You know Russo very well?" He held up her file.

"Not real well. I know she's worked with her friend, a guy named Alan Gallagher."

More than a friend? Ray wondered.

"Gallagher's kid was abducted and murdered, oh, say, five or six years ago. He's quite the child rights advocate now. Been to Washington, all over creation. Good man."

"Huh. So he brought Jane in on things, recommended her?"

"He didn't have to. She's made her reputation with law enforcement agencies across the country on her own. Gives police sketch artist a whole new meaning."

"You ever work directly with her?"

"Oh, sure. Once, anyway. Case in Durango. That's a smallish town in southwest Colorado in the Four Corners area. There was this young girl, think her name was Samantha. Anyway, she witnessed her mother's murder, but was too traumatized to give the police a thing. I went

down with Jane and damned if she didn't get a sketch out
of the kid that I swear was a photographic likeness to a
local deliveryman. I never saw anything like it. Yeah,
Jane's good. Hell, she's great."

Ray looked askance at Bruce. He couldn't help playing
devil's advocate then. "I wonder what's up with her so-
called gift on this case? I mean, she's pretty much failed,
I'd say. She's interviewed a half dozen witnesses and two
victims over the past five years and come up empty."

Bruce lifted his shoulders and dropped them. "Beats me."

"You know she's from Aspen?"

"I guess I did."

"Any clue about her relationship with her family?"

"Nope."

"Um."

He would have asked Bruce if he knew the exact nature
of Jane's involvement with child rights advocate Gallagher, but he figured that info had no bearing on this case,
so he let the subject drop. Still, he wondered.

They had both finally dozed off, Bruce on top of the
bedspread in the bedroom, Ray stretched out on the couch,
when his cell phone rang.

He was instantly up and alert.

"Sorry, Ray, to call you at this hour," came a man's
voice—a familiar voice.

"Stan? Stan Shoemaker?" Ray said. *What the hell?*

"I know, it's got to be, what, two in the morning there?
Anyway, I knew you'd want to hear this right away."

Stan was a former coworker from Seattle. If he was calling at this hour, it was important.

"The Seattle office just arrested two men in Washington
State," Stan said. "For security we're moving them out of
this district. We'll be bringing them down to L.A. at the
end of the week."

Ray felt his blood begin to boil. Stan didn't even have to tell him who the men were. Ray knew.

"I figured this was one plane you'd want to meet," Stan went on. "Friday. Friday at eight AM."

"Got it," Ray said, "and thanks."

"No problem."

He clicked off the phone and set it on the end table. The plane would land in L.A. on Friday. And Ray was going to be there waiting for it.

SIX

It was five o'clock in the morning. Only a single dim light shone out of the front window at the Lemke house. Two inches of fresh snow lay on the shake roof and on the hoods of the cars parked in the driveway.

Too many cars.

Ordinarily, he would have made a sweep down the drive and charged the clients the regular fee for the plow job, but he guessed with all the vehicles, he'd have to skip the normal routine. Oh well.

He sat on the road for a moment, truck idling, contemplating the single lamplight in the living room window. Cops. Had to be. His own window was rolled down, and he peered through the darkness, his breath pluming in the brutally cold air. He was wondering how the occupants of the house were feeling, what nightmare thoughts ran through their minds in the predawn.

He rolled his window up halfway, put the truck in gear, and drove off to the next job.

*   *   *

Somewhere a door slammed, and a minute later another one.

Voices echoed in the hall. "Come on, Kyle, get out of the bathroom. *Mom*. Kyle's being an idiot. *Mom!*"

Jane turned over in the guest room bed, opened her eyes, looked at the digital clock: 5:30 AM.

"Go screw yourself, Nicky," came Kyle's voice as he apparently exited the bathroom, slamming the door again.

Then Gwen's voice. "Cut it out, you two. Don't you know your Aunt Jane is trying to sleep?"

"Oops," one of the boys said, followed by a giggle.

The day began early at the Grinell house. Gwen and George operated a restaurant on the top of Buttermilk Mountain, the base of which was only a couple miles from their home. Breakfast was served by nine at the restaurant, and that meant the family was up and running by five. Usually Gwen left a box of cereal and milk on the table for the boys, as they wouldn't leave for school till eight, but school was out for the holidays. Both fourteen-year-old Nicky and Kyle, who was twelve, worked at the mountain restaurant, too.

Jane sat up, rose, padded to the guest bath. Good God, the tiles were cold. She shivered.

She didn't bother dressing, instead tugged a sweater over her striped pajamas, ran a brush through her hair, and appeared in the kitchen, groggy, stifling a yawn.

Another door slammed in the bath. "Damnit, Kyle," George called out, "you slam one more door and you'll wash dishes all day. I'm dead serious."

Fully dressed, Gwen appeared in the kitchen right behind Jane. "Sorry, I know it's impossible to sleep in the mornings around here," she said, pouring them both a cup of freshly brewed coffee. "This place is a zoo all winter. But you'd know that, Janey, if you ever bothered to come for a visit."

"I'm here now, aren't I?" Jane settled on a stool at the kitchen counter while her sister tore open packets of sugar—portion-controlled packets obviously brought down from the restaurant—dumped two packets in each mug, then stirred in skim milk.

"Here," Gwen said, handing Jane a cup. "Oh, how do you take yours?" An afterthought.

"This is fine," Jane said.

That was Gwen. Several years older than Jane, she took after their mother, a control freak. She'd always been direct to a fault, bossy, and manipulative. Age, Jane decided, had done nothing to temper her sister.

The boys appeared in their ski clothes and parkas, hats jammed on heads, ready to go, pushing and shoving each other as they made hot chocolate, spilling it on the stove. Gwen gave them a reproachful glare, and they subsided.

"Kyle spilled his, I'm not cleaning it up," Nicky announced.

"Did not," Kyle countered, giving his brother the finger behind Gwen's back.

"I'll clean up after you guys leave," Jane said.

"I'll get it after work," Gwen said automatically. She'd never liked anyone in her kitchen. After all, no one could cook and tidy up better than Gwen.

"Aunt Jane, you coming up skiing today?" Kyle asked.

"Well, I . . ."

"Of course she is," Gwen cut in.

Then Jane's brother-in-law appeared, car keys in hand. "*Are* you coming up today?" he asked. "I thought last night you said you were on the Lemke girl's case here, so I assumed . . ."

Gwen waved him off as she picked up her thick gloves. "Go warm the car, George."

Dutifully, George went to the garage, the boys tripping and shoving each other behind him, wired at 5:45 in the morning on the sugar in the hot chocolate.

"Now, Jane," Gwen continued, as if nothing had been said, tucking her auburn hair up into her ski hat, "I'll call down to the ticket office. The office moved from when you were here before, but you'll just have to find it. So there'll be a ticket waiting for you. Just take the quad lift to the top. You know where we are. Oh, and there's skis and poles and boots galore in the garage. Parkas, hats, gloves in the hall closet. "You still wear a size nine shoe?"

"Gwen." Jane sighed. "There's no way I have time to ski. There's a girl missing, and we have to find her. I appreciate the offer, but . . ."

Gwen turned on her. "You're telling me you don't bother to visit or even call in years, and you can't give me one lousy hour?"

"Gwen, look, I really . . ."

"You just be at the restaurant by eleven. We can ski or sit on the deck and talk. But by noon, I'm maxed out at the cash register."

Jane took a sip of coffee. What was the point in arguing? You couldn't win with Gwen.

By now George was standing in the door, awaiting his wife. He rolled his eyes at Jane.

Gwen walked past him, then called back through the open door. "Don't forget George and I are catering a Christmas party tonight for some people on Red Mountain, so it's a perfect time for you to have dinner at Mom's. Roland will be there, of course, but make sure Mom calls Scott and tells him to come, too." Scott was their stepfather Roland's son from a previous marriage. Not only did Jane dislike her stepfather, but she didn't much like his son, either.

"I'll see you at eleven," Gwen finished, and she hurried to her car.

Phew. It wasn't even six, and her nerves were scratching at her skin.

Then George took an extra second to stride over to her and give her a peck on the cheek. "I'll tell Gwen you couldn't make it to the restaurant when the time comes. Don't worry. You know how bossy she is. But, hey, Jane, it is great to have you here, really it is. Got to run."

She waited till he was gone, the door securely closed behind him, the house suddenly drenched in blessed silence. And then she felt disgust ripple in her stomach, and she wiped his kiss away. He'd been there, too, on the Reudi camping trip seventeen years ago. Gwen's hot new love, restaurant school graduate George Grinell.

It *could* have been him. It could be his face that was so buried that she couldn't even begin to sketch the first detail.

Or maybe it had been her stepfather. Pitkin County Sheriff Roland Zucker at the time.

Kent Schilling had also been there with his wife Lottie and their very young twin girls. Kent, her mentor. Her most fervent hope was that it wasn't him.

But Scott . . . Her stepbrother had been a senior in high school, Jane a sophomore. Scott the athlete. The ladies' man. The *asshole.*

Jane automatically began to clean up the kitchen. To hell with Gwen's "I'll get it after work" routine.

What am I doing here? she thought, sponge in hand. She must have gone mad. At least Gwen and George were busy tonight. The catering job. And Lord only knows what Kyle and Nicky had planned. Not that she minded them. In fact, she wished she'd gotten to know her nephews better. A true regret.

By six-thirty, with another cup of coffee on the vanity, she was in the shower, her mind reverting to the Lemke case and the upcoming interview of the second witness, Kirstin's friend Crystal Brenner. Maybe she'd have a breakthrough today with Crystal.

Shampoo in her hair, she paused, growing still beneath the hot stream of water. Where was Kirstin at this precise moment? Terrified somewhere in the dark? Alone and dreading the sound of approaching footfalls? Or maybe she was asleep, asleep and mercifully numb.

She couldn't, she just *wouldn't* consider the other possibility, that Kirstin was no longer suffering, that she was . . .

No, no, no. It had only been a few days. The girl was alive, in terrible danger but alive. She could survive this; she could heal, given enough time. But only if they found her. The clock was ticking.

Ray picked her up shortly after nine. He'd dressed in jeans, boots, green turtleneck, tan sweater, and his leather jacket. She wore casual clothes as well, black jeans and boots, a coral turtleneck sweater, one of Gwen's parkas, a silvery blue.

The morning had dawned clear and bitter cold, and her boots crunched on the packed snow beneath the fresh dusting on the walk. Ray still had the Explorer, and the heat was on high.

"Morning," he said from the driver's seat, and she noticed again the unique timbre of his voice, that low rough purr that made every word he uttered as intimate as a kiss.

"Morning. Brrr, it's cold out there."

"Heat's as high as it goes."

"Did you get hold of the Brenners last night?" She was

ready for the interview, mentally prepared to go for that breakthrough.

"Schilling talked to the kid's mother, and we can't see Crystal till this afternoon." He backed out of the driveway.

"What?"

"Nothing I could do about it."

"Damn," she muttered.

"So, we've got some time to kill. Hurry up and wait."

Kirstin *is the one waiting,* she thought. *Every second like an hour. Every day like . . .*

"I thought we'd grab a bite. Have you eaten?" he asked.

"Ah, not really. Plenty of coffee, though."

"Okay, then, we'll get something quick and then we'll head out to the Lemke's."

"I take it you saw them last night."

"Yeah, sure did."

"And? Oh, turn right toward town, we can go to the bakery. If it's still there, that is. This town's changed so much since I was here last. So how was it . . . the Lemke's?"

"Rough."

"I bet. I assume there's been no news?"

"Nothing."

She pursed her lips and blew out a breath. "Ah, take a right on Galena Street. There." She pointed. "Paradise Bakery is three blocks up."

"So *this* is Aspen," Ray said, searching for a parking spot.

"Uh-huh. Heart of downtown."

"Not bad. Everything looks turn-of-the-century."

"Well, it was a silver mining boomtown, after all. And the hysterical society . . ."

"The what?"

"A joke for the *historical* society. Anyway, they make sure everything, every building and entry and window and lamp and awning stays in original form. You can't even put a planter in a window without their okay."

They found a spot in front of the Independence Building across from the Paradise Bakery. The aroma of freshly baked muffins and cookies and rich, blended coffees filled the air. Locals and tourists crammed the tiny place, more sat outside on a brick patio with several comfortable benches and a perfect view of the gondola on Aspen Mountain.

At Jane's height she'd always been able to eat pretty much what she wanted and keep her weight under control. Alan often joked that she ate as much as a man. She stood on the patio next to Ray in the morning sun munching on a cinnamon bun and thought about Alan, wishing she didn't think about him so darn much.

She glanced at Ray. He was eating a banana nut muffin and sipping steaming hot Colombian coffee. Her eyes strayed to his scars, which showed in the bright light of day, his collar not high enough to hide them. Or maybe he didn't care about hiding them. He was nevertheless a very good-looking man, the patch of shiny, pink skin lending him a kind of mystique.

She shifted her attention to the gondola crawling up the face of the mountain. All the happy, excited skiers on holiday, shivering on their first ride up the mountain, but ready to tackle the powder snow, oblivious to the ordeal of Kirstin and the FBI presence in the picture-perfect resort.

Ray tossed the white muffin bag and napkin in a tidy wooden trash can. "Maybe you want to stay in town," he said. "No need for you to tag along to the Lemke's. You could shop or whatever, and I can pick you up later or meet you at the sheriff's."

"Trying to ditch me?" She felt a spurt of irritation. She was just an annoyance to him.

"Hey, take it easy."

"Come off it. Ray. You don't want me here. Fine. But your superior does. And did you think I could *shop* while that poor girl is being held prisoner and the clock's running? My God. Are you sure we can't get to see Crystal before this afternoon? Maybe if I went alone?"

"Apparently the mother sleeps late, and she won't let anyone in till afternoon."

"I can't believe anyone would do that."

"I guess Mrs. Brenner cares more about her beauty sleep than a kid's life."

On the ride to Brush Creek he was painfully withdrawn. *It's me,* she thought. She did her best to convince herself she didn't give a damn about his opinion of her, but that was a lie. She cared. She always cared what her coworkers felt about her abilities. Then again, she remembered, she hadn't given Ray a reason to appreciate her. Maybe this afternoon she'd finally have success on this case. It had been too many years. Why couldn't she drag this monster's face into the light of day?

Bruce was back on duty at the Lemke's, and Howard Canning was still manning the phones, nonstop for almost two days. The only rest he'd gotten was a few hours sleep here and there on the Lemke's couch. Sid Reynolds had gone to the Mountain House earlier to catch some shut-eye rather than making the forty-mile drive down the valley to Glenwood Springs where he lived. Jane was familiar with the all-out dedication of the agents; she'd seen it often. Too often.

Her old friend Bernie from the sheriff's department was on duty. He told them, in whispers, that Josh Lemke was still on the verge of losing it, and the mother Suzanne was no help with her husband—she languished under the haze of too much medication.

"Maybe you could calm Lemke down," Bernie said to Ray. "We sure as hell aren't getting anywhere."

Surprising Jane, Ray didn't appear in the least concerned. He only said, "Yeah, I'll talk to him." He seemed preoccupied. Just as he had been on the ride out here. *Maybe he's deciding what direction to go from here,* she thought. The sheriff's department and the FBI were running out of options, people to interview, calls to make. They'd gotten absolutely nowhere. Glancing around the Lemke house, *feeling* Kirstin's presence, she was nearly overcome by the need to make progress in the investigation.

Ray finally talked to Josh Lemke, who was wandering from room to room, mumbling to himself, bursting into short spells of sobbing anguish every time he passed Kirstin's bedroom door. He must be tortured by possibilities they could barely imagine.

Ray steered the man into the kitchen and asked him to sit. There was some argument from Josh before he sagged onto a stool, head between his hands.

"I'll kill the bastard when I get my hands on him," Lemke kept saying.

Surprisingly, Ray seemed to empathize with the man. He said, "Look, Josh, if Kirstin were my child, I'd feel exactly the same way. And you'll get your chance. But for now I think you need to sleep. You can't do a damn thing in your condition. If not for yourself, get some rest for your daughter's sake. Something's bound to break soon, and we need you sharp, okay?" His voice was soothing, the velvety rasp low and confidential.

She was touched. He could have pulled rank and threatened the poor man, but he hadn't. He'd actually shown some compassion, more than she would have given him credit for.

Josh listened, rubbed his face with a hand, and disappeared

into the master bedroom. The agents seemed to heave a collective sigh of relief. But she suspected the calm wouldn't
last.

It wasn't ten minutes later that the bedroom door
opened again, and Josh Lemke came out, yelling, "Goddamn it, why can't you find her? What goddamn good is
all this . . . this shit . . ." He stabbed an accusing finger
toward Howard and the electronic equipment. "It's useless! Useless!"

"Okay, Josh," Ray said, "you feel better now? You got it
off your chest? Yeah, this stuff hasn't helped yet, but it
might. Hey, it might. Isn't it worth trying? We're doing
everything we know to get your daughter back."

Lemke's shoulders slumped, and he turned away and
stumbled blindly down the hall without saying another
word.

Jane looked in on Suzanne, sitting on the bedside and
introducing herself, explaining her role. No matter how
false, she felt as if she had to give these people a shred of
hope. Without hope, they were lost. When Suzanne took
both of Jane's hands and squeezed them, her eyes pleading,
saying, "My baby's all right, isn't she? She's got to be all
right," Jane felt as if someone had drilled a hole in her
heart.

Just before noon, Sid Reynolds arrived back and the
agents found a quiet room to put their heads together. She
could see them through a half-open door going over lists,
assigning tasks. She knew the routine. They'd talk to everyone in the valley who'd had contact with Kirstin, interview
them over and over until something gave. Or didn't. And
Bruce was still working with the ski area employee angle.
He left for Snowmass Village, where Kirstin had disappeared, immediately after the strategy session adjourned.

Jane wandered into Kirstin's bedroom. She felt curiously

guilty as she stood looking at photographs and school mementos on shelves and walls, a blown-up photo of a horse, a poster of Britney Spears. She felt as if she were letting the child down, the weight of the entire case on her shoulders alone. And here she was, waiting to talk to Kirstin's friend, held up by Crystal's mother. Marking time.

Carefully, she picked up photos and ran a finger lightly over Kirstin's face in one of them. Her heart was beginning to sink. She knew, she *knew* firsthand what it was like to have a man steal your innocence. Your body healed in time. But your mind never would. Not entirely. Not until you had justice. And Jane had never found that justice. Was it possible her own personal ordeal, her own weakness and, yes, her *cowardliness* would cause another child to lose her life?

Eyes swimming with tears, she stared helplessly at the pink-and-yellow-striped duvet on the bed, the lacy pile of pillows, the tattered teddy bear lying on its side near the foot of the bed. *Oh, God.*

She wiped her eyes hastily when Ray stuck his head in the door. "I've got to go into town," he said, "check in with Schilling before we see the Brenner girl."

"Ah, yes, sure." Damn Caroline Deutch and damn Alan for talking her into this. And she couldn't voice her fears and doubts to Ray. She couldn't run or hide. She was in too deep.

There was still too much time before the appointment with Crystal Brenner. Ray parked at the courthouse on Main Street, and they talked to Kent Schilling, updating him. Not that there was anything to update him on. He had half the department on the case, too, making their own calls, pounding the sidewalks. They must have given out a hundred photocopies of Kirstin's picture. No one believed for an instant that she was anywhere but locked up in her abductor's hideaway. But they had to follow protocol.

"Well, you'll get some info out of the Brenner girl," Schilling told Jane. "You always do."

She smiled weakly. She wasn't about to admit her helplessness to the very man who'd launched her career, dubbed her ability a gift. But she felt the heft of Ray's doubt. The room swelled with the weight of his skepticism.

Thank heavens Schilling dropped the subject. He snapped his fingers and said, "Good Lord, I almost forgot to tell you I just ran into your mother over at the shop, and she acted as if she didn't even know you were here, Janey. Didn't you even call her?"

"I . . . uh . . . I took the case so quickly, Kent, and then last night at Gwen's we all hit the sack right after dinner. I . . . um . . . assumed Gwen had called Mom. Oh, gosh," she finished lamely, "I guess . . ."

"Well, I told Hannah that soon as I saw you I'd send you over."

"Oh, well, you know, we've got to get to the Brenner's. I'll call Mom as soon as . . ."

"We have an hour," Ray put in, and she shot him a look.

"There, you see?" Kent said. "Hannah's only three blocks away."

"Oh," she said, "I thought it was much later." *No way out.*

"I'll walk with you," Ray offered. There was no way out of that, either.

She suspected he was curious now, even more than he'd been yesterday. Part of his curiosity was pure cop. The other part, she figured, was a sense he could understand her better if he ferreted out her relationship with her family. Or was she so unnerved that she was making something of nothing? *Maybe,* probably. He didn't give a damn about her or her family. He was walking her to the shop to kill time.

They crossed Main Street and went past the rectory of

the old Catholic church, St. Mary's. She had been to confirmations there, weddings and funerals and the annual holiday performance of Handel's *Messiah*. She'd cast her first vote in a presidential election in the basement of the stately church.

Past city hall, a barn-shaped brick building with a glaring tin roof. Then across Hopkins Street, past the Gap. Her mother managed an interior design and gift shop on the corner of Galena and Hyman Streets in the 1880s-era Elks Building. The core of the downtown high rent district.

She and Ray entered the store; Ray was obviously taken aback. "Jesus," he said, "I've never seen so much stuff in one place."

At first glance the shop was overwhelming. The owner had crammed merchandise from all over the globe into a maze of aisles that towered twenty feet high. The goods were pricey. Right now it was full of Christmas wares, from the live, eight foot tall, decorated trees to life-sized stuffed reindeer and sleighs laden with gifts. There were stacks of holiday paper goods, ornaments, fine china, crystal glasses, and brightly painted pottery. There were menorahs from the Holy Land. Glass balls, ceramic wreaths from South America, exotic potpourri. Even holiday toilet seats.

"Now there's a unique item," Ray said, raising a brow at the holly- and berry-painted seat.

How could he be so calm when they needed to be looking for Kirstin? Was the girl just another case to him? Impatience clawed at her, but was it due to the need to find Kirstin or the fact that she was going to have to deal with her mother?

Jane didn't spot Hannah till they were in the second room of the wall-to-wall, floor-to-ceiling goods. It was hard to spot anyone in the jumble of elegance, shoppers wandering up and down the aisles. When she saw her mother, she stopped short. It had been years. And Hannah had aged. Jane knew it was silly to be surprised; everyone got older. She should have expected it.

When Hannah saw her, she put her hands on her hips and frowned. "So *here* you are. And Kent had to be the one to tell me you were in town. Let me look at you."

Her mother held Jane's arms and studied her, cocking her head from side to side. "You look wonderful," she announced. "I like your hair longer like this." She hugged Jane. "I phoned Gwen at work and gave her hell for not calling last night. You girls. I thought I raised you better. And how come you didn't call me? You could have stayed with us. Your sister's got enough of a household to deal with." And then, without taking a breath, she said, "Weren't you supposed to meet Gwen for lunch on the mountain?"

She'd quite deliberately forgotten. "Oh, I guess I should have called the restaurant. I'm too busy to go skiing, Mom."

"Because of this case? The Lemke girl?"

Jane nodded soberly. Then she remembered Ray. "Mom, this is Ray Vanover. He's with the FBI. Ray, my mother, Hannah Zucker." They shook hands, eyeing each other.

She couldn't help wondering what their first impressions were. Hannah was still an attractive woman at sixty-one, five foot eight, large-boned but not heavy, her light-brown hair showing more gray, swept off her face and held at the back with a silver clasp. Her blue eyes were sharp, her complexion smooth, her makeup discreet. She was wearing a white blouse under a cherry-red cardigan and a calf-length black skirt that flattered her wide hips. Silver earrings and silver bracelets jingled on her wrists. *Yes,* Jane thought, *Hannah looks a little older but just fine.*

And, on quick assessment, her mother wasn't skipping a beat, still the workaholic. Jane couldn't recall a quiet day or night from her childhood. There never seemed to be downtime or, for that matter, an abundance of family time.

Jane had never known a true bonding with her mother or even Gwen. Certainly never with her stepfather or Scott. At Hannah's insistence, everyone in the family was kept busy from dawn till dusk, and when Jane had declared she was going to the art institute rather than college, Hannah had been appalled.

"That's your goal in life," her mother had said, "to withdraw into a shell and sit on your butt all day?"

Hannah was sizing Ray up, not even making a pretense of it. She gave him a full inspection even while she asked, "Those poor people, the Lemkes. What they must be going through. Have you gotten anywhere with the case?"

How did Hannah see him? As Jane did, handsome, with his long narrow face and shrewd blue eyes, the dark curly hair and ever-so-slight whisker shadow on his cheeks? She knew her mother hadn't noticed his scars yet. But she would. As soon as Ray turned, Hannah would notice.

And she did. Without missing a breath, Hannah was, as always, direct to the point of rudeness for to some, refreshing for others. "My goodness, what on earth happened to you?"

Jane felt heat prickle on her cheeks. *Oh, God.*

"You mean this razor burn?" Ray reached up to touch the scars, his expression devoid of emotion.

Hannah opened her mouth to say something, then she closed it and shook her head, wagging a finger at him. "You're putting me on, young man."

"That's right," he said, "I'm putting you on."

Jane cringed. She should have known her mother would have something blunt to say. If she didn't get Ray out of there things would only deteriorate.

She found her voice. "Uh, Mom, we have to run," she said. "Got an appointment. Really."

"That's fine," Hannah said, "the store is busy as hell, and I've got customers. But I'm organizing dinner tonight.

In your honor. Gwen said she already suggested it. We'll catch up then."

"Mom, I don't know if I can make it. This case . . ."

"I insist. Come up to the house as soon as you're off for the evening and Ray, you're coming, too. No arguments."

"I'll stop by if I can, Mom, but if something comes up with this case . . ."

But Ray broke in. "Thank you, Mrs. Zucker, I'd love to. Can I bring anything?"

"Just yourself. See you after work." She gave Jane another hug and kissed her on the cheek. "It's so good to have you here, honey."

The cold air was a relief from the warm, crowded shop, and Jane sucked in a breath. "God," she said. Then she looked up at Ray. "That's so typical of my mother. She just blurts things out without thinking."

"No big deal," he said. "I was burned in an explosion. The scars show. People wonder. I just get tired of telling the story." He shrugged.

An explosion. Something again nagged at her, and she nearly had it, but the wisp of memory dissipated before she could grasp it.

She let it go. "Look, Ray," she said, "no way do you have to do the dinner thing. I didn't argue in there because there's no point making a scene, but Mom will have to understand."

They began to walk back toward the courthouse. "Dinner sounds fine," he said. "Assuming we have the time. I could use a home-cooked meal."

She paused, her brow knitted, but he took her elbow and guided her across the street. On the far side, passing city hall again, he kept his hand on her. She couldn't recall the last time a man had done that. *Alan.* Most likely Alan used to touch her like that.

She needed to call him. If for no other reason, she knew he was wondering how the case was progressing. Tonight. She'd phone after dinner. She might even have good news after the interview with the Brenner girl. She prayed she would. They'd talk about the case, and his optimism for Kirstin's well-being would be infectious.

She was tempted to pull out her cell phone and bring up his preprogrammed number. It would be so easy, and she was suddenly dying to talk to him.

Ray finally let go of her elbow when they approached the courthouse. Idly she wondered if he'd been aware he'd been touching her at all or if his gesture had been an automatic response.

An explosion, he'd said. He was tired of telling the story. She gave him a surreptitious glance, noted the perpetual crease of his brow. Well, maybe he *was* tired of the story—whatever it really was—but the pain was still written all over his face.

SEVEN

Crystal Brenner lived only minutes from downtown in a mobile home at the foot of Smuggler Mountain. A relic of the old mining days, the mountain stood sentinel on the opposite side of town from Aspen Mountain. Once Smuggler had been a beehive of activity. The long-gone Rio Grande Railroad depot had been located at its base, along with huge silver smelteries, and the mountain itself was still perforated with slope mines. Now the monolith loomed quietly over the city, welcoming hikers, bicyclers, hunters, and campers to its forested slopes.

It's about time, Ray was thinking as he followed Jane's directions through town and up the road that led to Smuggler Trailer Park. They'd been waiting all goddamn morning for this interview, and he wasn't the least bit predisposed to like Crystal Brenner's mother for causing the delay. Didn't she know what was going down here?

"Now this is a surprise for Aspen," he couldn't help commenting when they arrived at Crystal's mobile home, one of many in a decidedly middle-class neighborhood.

"Rent-controlled housing," Jane explained. "The park was here long before Aspen became so trendy. I grew up with lots of kids who lived right here. This is the real Aspen."

"Is it?"

"Trust me."

Parking was tight in the narrow streets, but he squeezed the big Explorer between the Brenner trailer and a NO PARKING ON STREET sign. Who'd tow a vehicle with PITKIN COUNTY SHERIFF'S DEPARTMENT stenciled on the doors?

"I don't suppose you'd wait out here or come back for me later?" She looked hopeful. "I could ring you on your cell phone?"

Ray shook his head.

"Didn't think so."

He opened a creaking gate and was met by an old black lab with a wagging tail, graying muzzle, and thirty extra pounds on him. "Good guard dog," Ray said.

"You don't need guard dogs here." She bent to stroke the lab's floppy ears.

"Tell that to Kirstin Lemke."

Abby Brenner, Crystal's mother, opened the door to greet them, and the dog waddled through, nudging everyone out of his way. Even before they were inside, Ray was instantly assailed by the distinctively pungent odor of pot.

"Whoa," he couldn't help saying, and Jane, who must have detected the smell, too, shot him a warning look. As for Abby Brenner, she made no apologies, merely invited them to sit in the living room, saying, "I'll get Crystal."

They found seats in the clutter. The lab ambled over and settled half on the soiled shag carpet, half on Ray's feet. A corner of Jane's mouth lifted in a smile.

Ray pivoted to see a man open and close a bedroom

door down the narrow hall, then pad into a bathroom.
Shirtless, his jeans undone, he was skinny as a toothpick
and had a graying ponytail that straggled halfway down his
back. Crystal's father? But, no, the sheriff had told them
Abby Brenner was long since divorced.

As for Abby, she was a leftover sixties hippie. She wore
her salt and pepper hair parted in the middle and hanging,
several ear studs and hoop earrings, a lavender-flowered
shirt over a dark blue shapeless dress, socks and Birken-
stock sandals. Her neck and wrists were adorned with
beads. And she had a silver nose stud.

Lovely, he thought while they waited, his glance straying
to an ashtray the size of a hubcap in the center of the coffee
table, cigarette butts and well-smoked roaches stubbed out
in it along with melted down candles and burnt sticks of
incense. Everything in the crowded room was dusty and
faded. The couch Jane sat on, the India print shawl draped
over its back, the throw pillows, the easy chair he'd taken, the
shag carpet, the thin wood-paneled walls. A string of bells
hung from the corner of the divider between the kitchen and
living room, where unwashed wineglasses sat.

He took the place in as the Brenner woman called down
the hallway to her daughter. "Those people are here. Turn
off the CD and come out here. Jeff and I will be in my
room."

Jeff. But he wasn't Ray's concern, nor was their lifestyle.
He met Jane's eyes as the music stopped, and a door opened
down the hall. Jane shrugged and lifted a brow. He knew
she was as impatient at the delay in talking to Crystal as he
was, but she hid it better.

Crystal Brenner was a petite girl wearing a rust-colored
sweatshirt with the face of a female rock star on its front,
black sweatpants with a white stripe up the side, and fur
animal slippers. Tigers. Her reddish-brown curly hair was

cut short, and the style framed her heart-shaped face. Her eyes were green and big and fringed with long lashes. She wasn't going to be a knockout like her friend Melanie, but she exuded an aura of sweetness and intelligence.

He and Jane stood to shake her hand and introduce themselves, then settled back into their places. He was sure dust rose from his chair cushion. The dog stretched back across his feet and let out a groan of contentment.

"If Sherman bothers you," Crystal said, "I'll put him out."

"He's fine." Ray returned the girl's smile. She seemed a nice enough kid.

She seated herself on the far end of the couch from Jane, hugging a pillow to her chest exactly as Melanie had done. *Predictable,* Ray thought. Defensive, anxious. Would Jane handle this girl the same way, or did she size up each person individually?

"You haven't found Kirstin," the girl began, her attention on Jane. "If you had, you wouldn't be here."

"No, we haven't."

Crystal drew in a lungful of air, and tears shimmered in her eyes. "I was hoping you'd call and cancel and then I'd know she was okay. Do you think she's okay, Miss Russo?"

"It's Jane. And to answer you as best I can, I'm very optimistic we'll find her soon."

"Oh, that's good news. Mom, she said . . . But Mom doesn't know."

Jane nodded indulgently.

"I hope I can help. I really *want* to help. Melanie called and said you were much better to talk to than the other one, Mr. Staley."

"That was sweet of Melanie."

"All he did was show me this book, you know, with different face shapes and noses and mouths and hair? I wanted to help, but it was very hard."

"I imagine it was," Jane agreed. "I don't work like that. I don't have any book of features. I try to get the features from you without any help. I've found that works better for me."

Crystal seemed far more savvy than Melanie, eager to proceed, her anxiety more from impatience than fear of failing her friend Kirstin.

She also took to Jane quickly. He could read the admiration in the girl's eyes, the way the kid looked Jane over, even subconsciously emulated the way Jane cocked her head and the way she bit her lower lip when concentrating.

He could see why a young girl teetering between childhood and womanhood would look up to Jane Russo. Not only was she nonjudgmental and sincerely compassionate, but she was really quite striking, the kind of woman who made the simplest clothing look great, with her endlessly long legs, a terrific figure, a good face, wide-set blue eyes, dark blond hair that swung with each movement of her head and made you want to feel it against your fingers. Her smile was infectious. He was growing used to her body language, too. The feminine pitch of her head, her long legs crossed, her slim fingered hands gesturing or poised in patient anticipation over her sketch pad. Her voice a soft but firm contralto, like rich flowing honey. She had a voice people listened to. He was even getting used to the different inflections of her speech, the hidden meanings.

He caught himself musing, his gaze riveted to her, and he had to rouse himself mentally. There was a kid out there, alone and terrified, hurt, praying for them to find her. And there was another fly in the ointment, a big one; this Friday Stan Shoemaker was escorting to L.A. the murderers Ray had waited eighteen months to get his hands on. And Ray was determined to meet that plane. Damn right he was.

He hadn't realized he was staring into middle distance,

the back of his fingers massaging the scars. He focused, and he found Crystal's attention on him. He dropped his hand.

Jane took her time befriending the girl, as if they had nothing more to do than fritter the afternoon away. They talked about figure skating and hockey at the funky old rink on the west side of town, and the new recreation complex that would replace it. They spoke of the new high school and, of course, in Crystal's case, boarding and the terrain park at Snowmass. *Hell,* Ray thought, growing impatient, they covered summer hikes and campgrounds and hidden hot springs in the mountains. He began to wonder if Jane had a clue as to why they were there. After all her fretting at having to wait so long to talk to Crystal. *What crap. She has a gift, all right, the gift of gab.*

It was finally Crystal who ducked her head and said, "Melanie told me she remembered this guy who rode the ski lift with Kirstin. I don't think Melanie and I should have talked about it, because you might think she gave me the idea."

"It's okay if you talked," Jane said, but Ray was sure she would have preferred that they hadn't. Then again, she had not given Melanie any instructions before they'd left the Steadman's. In her defense, she had been pissed at him for speaking up, asking his own question. Maybe so angry she'd forgotten to inform Melanie of the rules.

Jane finally produced the hunk of Play-Doh, which Crystal took to rapidly, no questions asked, no explanations given.

She was a straightforward, eager-to-please girl. She immediately shaped an oval face with the wad of plastic, and she said, "I'm pretty sure that guy on the lift followed us a lot that day."

"Oh?" Jane cocked her head, and again he found himself staring at her, the way the heavy curtain of hair swung against her cheek. Then he caught himself. The UNSUB had followed the three girls . . .

"Uh-huh," Crystal was telling Jane. "And I'm not just saying so because Melanie remembered him. I saw him over on the Big Burn and even the Elk Camp runs."

"Why did you notice him, Crystal?"

"He was alone. Ski patrol guys ski alone and sometimes locals, who have an hour off work for lunch or something, but mostly people ski with friends."

"That's true," Jane said. "So did Melanie tell you anything else she remembered about him?"

Crystal shook her head in earnest. "We decided we'd compare what we remembered when you leave here. We figured you wouldn't mind."

"I don't mind at all. And I think it was awfully smart of you girls to know better than to talk too much. So, what can you tell me about this man? What pops into your head?"

Crystal looked at the Play-Doh she was molding. She sighed. "Um, he was pretty much covered up, you know? Like he wanted to be. I mean, I didn't think that at the time, when he rode the lift with Kirstin, but now I'm sure that's why he looked so creepy, all covered up like he was."

"Covered up?" Jane prompted.

"Oh, you know, he had on goggles, Bolle goggles."

"Uh, Bolle, for sure?"

"Uh-huh. Real old with scratched lenses, uh, what are they called? Amber? Or maybe polarized? But they were so geeky with the glasses under them."

"Glasses?"

"Yeah, the oval kind with metal, or I guess they were wire frames. Kirstin wears ones like that, it makes her eyes look big, kind of weird. But not all the time," she hastened to add.

Jane began to sketch, and Crystal played with the lump of plastic. She talked easily and with assurance about the man's ski clothing, describing the hat and neck gaiter and parka much the same as Melanie had done. She even thought she recalled the make of skis he used, K2s. An older model, not the newer-shaped skis. Jane kept steering the girl back to the man's face, and eventually Crystal talked about his ugly nose, how crooked it was.

"That's good," Jane said, sketching.

"Did Melanie remember his nose?"

Jane hesitated, then she said, "Yes, she did."

Crystal looked pleased.

Ray listened, wishing the kid would give them something new, but he was as pessimistic as ever. He studied her at length, watched her mold the Play-Doh. She had a certain knack, an artistic talent that Melanie had lacked. At least the plastic looked a little like a human head.

He compared the three girls. Could see them on the mountain, baseball caps on backwards, carving down the slopes together, laughing, falling, dusting snow from their clothes. Melanie, the rich kid, with the latest, coolest gear, outgoing, the leader of the pack. And Crystal, the poor relation, all grown up before her time because of a mother left back in the sixties. Crystal in her shabby ski clothes, probably secondhand stuff, but the anchor of the group. And Kirstin. He'd only seen photos of the girl. But he knew her to be pretty, even in her wire-rimmed glasses; she'd be a follower of the popular Melanie and the more serious-minded Crystal. She'd be easily manipulated. Molesters were excellent at preying on the pliable ones, just as lions unerringly zeroed in on weak prey animals.

He noticed that Crystal had picked up a paper clip from the littered table and had straightened it. She began to poke holes in the Play-Doh.

"Um. What are those?" Jane asked.

"Whiskers." Crystal was concentrating intensely. "I'm not doing this very good, and they should be blond."

"Blond."

"Uh-huh."

Jane drew.

"And I can't do the hair very good, either." She dragged the end of the paper clip through the clay on the cheeks. "Um, he had like curling hair here and here. It stuck out some."

"On the side of his head?"

"Uh, the sideburns. Sort of long."

"Good, Crystal, that's good."

"Oh, and the earring."

"The earring?"

"On his right ear. No. That would be his left ear, 'cause he was facing me."

"What sort of earring?"

"A gold stud. Round. You know."

Jane sketched, and Ray could see the true shape of a face with a few details, the earring, the longish curling sideburns, whisker stubble, crooked nose, eyeglasses beneath Bolle goggles—Jane had drawn the word Bolle on the elastic band over his ear. Still, there was too much missing, the neck gaiter covering his mouth, the nondescript hat pulled low, obscuring the forehead, eye shape and color unknown. *Hell,* Ray thought, *the guy could be totally bald or partially balding or have the thickest, curliest hair in the world under that hat.*

And Crystal's memory of his height and weight disagreed with Melanie's. This girl thought he was of very average height, five eight or so, and much leaner than Melanie had believed.

They still had practically nothing but another wasted

afternoon to show for their efforts. The sketch was not complete enough to distribute.

At one point, trying not to disturb Crystal or Jane, he quietly went outside, dog following him, and called the FBI team at the Lemke's, speaking with Bruce. There was nothing new to report on Ray's end except the earring and curling blond sideburns, but Bruce was following an anonymous tip. Apparently a ski lift mechanic at Snowmass had a prior conviction and had done jail time for involvement in a California kiddie porn ring. The guy had lied on his employment application. Right now Sid Reynolds was talking to the man at his home in Basalt, a bedroom community twenty miles down the Roaring Fork Valley. The trouble was, the guy had moved from California and worked for the ski company for the past three seasons. Of course, they were also checking sick time and days off, any leaves he may have taken during the holiday season, but so far he wasn't looking too promising.

"And he's overweight and short, five foot five. Also dark-complected and no glasses," Bruce said. Plus, Ray knew, in terms of criminal profiles, kiddie porn was a world apart from kidnapping and molestation.

"Well, keep after it," Ray said, clicking off.

He and Sherman went back inside. Ray quietly sat in the same chair, the dog at his feet. Jane only gave him a cursory glance, then continued talking to Crystal. Ray studied the dust motes dancing in a spear of light from the front window.

"So, you girls were rushing to catch the shuttle bus to the parking lot after skiing," Jane said, obviously trying to cue Crystal's memory.

"Oh, right." Crystal tilted her head and worried her lower lip. A miniature Jane. The kid really did need a role model. "Kirstin's mom was supposed to pick us up and

Melanie, I *think* it was Melanie, was making us hurry. Still, there wasn't room on that bus anyway."

"Was Kirstin worried her mother would be mad?"

"Um, I don't think so. Mrs. Lemke is pretty cool about that stuff. But Melanie, well, she can be dramatic sometimes, you know? Not that we *mind*."

Jane waited.

"Anyway, Melanie was ahead of me and Kirstin was behind. I think. It was pretty crowded in the parking lot and you had to stop for people and move aside and stuff. I think Kirstin was behind. I'm kind of fuzzy on that. But I do remember when we got to the end of the line, the bus line, that is, Melanie was saying we'd never make this one, and I was going to ask Kirstin if we should call her mom or something before she left the house to meet us, but Kirstin wasn't there."

"Go on," Jane said softly.

"Anyway, I sort of looked around for her, but I'm pretty short, and it's hard to see. It was getting dark out, too. Not *real* dark, but . . . What's the word?"

"Dusk."

"Yeah, dusk. And that's when I saw the truck. It was pulling out of the parking lot. I saw it from behind, sort of, and I thought this girl in the passenger seat kind of looked like Kirstin. Melanie and I didn't think much about it for a long time, because we were pissed at Kirstin. I feel so bad about it now."

"Don't," Jane said. "Anyone would have felt the same. You didn't do this to your friend, Crystal. You know that, don't you?"

"Uh-huh."

"Okay. Good. So it was actually you who saw the truck?"

Another uh-huh.

"Okay." Jane waited, and Ray felt his muscles tense. How much had the kid seen? If she had noticed the truck from behind—*if* it was the pickup belonging to the kidnapper—was the plate number or even a partial stored in her memory?

"So," Jane said. But Crystal was looking fixedly at the Play-Doh, not shaping it, just holding it. The girl's brow furrowed. Jane repeated herself, "So?"

"Oh," Crystal said, her eyes snapping up. "It was . . . the *truck* was burgundy, like the wine, you know? Faded, I think, and sort of metallic, that silvery sort of paint you see."

"Go on," Jane said smoothly.

Ray was ready to spring out of his seat.

"Oh, *right*," Crystal said abruptly, "it was a Ranger. A Ford, you know?"

He couldn't stay silent now. He leaned forward. "Ah, Crystal," he began, holding up a hand to ward Jane off, "why a Ranger? What makes you so sure?"

Crystal looked at him as if he were dumb as hell. "Because my dad has one. Same color. Well, he *used* to have one. The bank took it away."

"Your father had the same truck? A Ford Ranger pickup?"

"Uh-huh."

"You don't happen to know the year?"

"Ray," Jane said.

But Crystal said it was okay. "I think it was a ninety-two or three. Pretty old. Dad bought it used."

"Okay," Ray said. Then, even though she'd told him the bank had repossessed it, he had to ask, "Where is your dad now, Crystal?"

"New Zealand. He's a Kiwi. I'm half-Kiwi, you know?"

"No, I didn't," Ray said.

"Um, he split, like, three years ago. I got a Christmas card the first year."

The information she'd given them, if accurate, might prove invaluable. There were, of course, hundreds of pickup trucks on the road. In the heart of the Rockies, in remote rural areas like so much of the Roaring Fork Valley, the number could be in the thousands. *Still.*

Then, despite the glare from Jane, he had to ask, "I don't suppose you saw a license plate?"

She shook her head.

"Did you get the state?"

Another head shake. Her eyes were fixed on him. "I'm sorry," she whispered, still staring.

Damn. "That's okay." Mentally he was estimating the time it would take to run a check on every Ford pickup in the valley, on every truck, for that matter.

"Mr. Vanover?"

Ray had to focus. "Yes, Crystal?"

"Can I ask you something?"

"Sure."

"How did you hurt yourself?" She touched her own jaw. "Were you, like, in the war or something?"

He was trapped. Out of the mouths of babes . . . He couldn't be angry at the kid; the question was innocent. And what was the point of giving her his usual sarcastic reply? Might as well tell the truth. "I wasn't in the war, not the kind you mean," he said. "Two of us were investigating a militant group in Seattle and some members of the militia put explosives in our car. I only survived because I'd gone back to the office to get a file I'd left behind, and when I got back to the car it was on fire. I tried to pull the other agent out, but . . ."

"He was killed?" she breathed.

"*She.* The other agent was a woman." He felt the oppressive weight of Jane's stare. *Screw it,* he thought. To Crystal he said, "Hey, I'm the lucky one."

He didn't feel lucky, though. He felt only survivor's guilt and a familiar surge of red-hot rage. But this coming Friday, in Los Angeles, he was going to get a shot at payback. He didn't know exactly how or when, but now that the bombers were under arrest, he was going to avenge Kathleen. He had a fleeting thought then—what about his career, his life? But the notion fled as quickly as it had come. Nothing mattered, the fucking murderers were going to pay.

EIGHT

His profile was grim as he drove. He'd been in a strange mood all day, up and down, and she wondered what was bothering him. And now, in a few minutes, he was going to meet her whole absurdly dysfunctional family. *Great*.

How had she let herself get into this spot? She shouldn't have gone to see her mother today. Damn it, she should have known better. She should have ended this farce before it went this far. Why hadn't she told Hannah she had an interview this evening? In the midst of a gut-wrenching search for a kidnapped girl, with a life on the line, she shouldn't have to deal with her family. It was just too much. Why hadn't she made an excuse?

"Sorry, Mom, but I have to see one of the witnesses. Work, you know." That's all she'd have had to say.

But Ray—damn him—with his uncharacteristically bland, "Thank you, Mrs. Zucker, I'd love to."

Oh, the evening was going to be ugly. They'd all ask her why she hadn't been to visit in five years; they'd dwell on her absence and ask and ask and ask. And she'd have to be nice to Roland, whom she truly disliked. And his self-centered son Scott.

She clenched her hands into fists in her lap, realized what she was doing, and made herself relax. And she knew she was biting her lip nervously, removing all the lipstick she'd carefully applied.

Did Ray notice her unease?

"Where's the turn?" he asked.

"Oh, the next one. Left, up the hill."

So familiar, the twists and turns of the highway, bordered on the right by the Roaring Fork River and on the left by rising mountainsides studded with houses set among aspen groves and scrub oak. The stone walls announcing the subdivision of Mountain Valley, the turn, bumping over the drainage channel and recessed sewer cover.

"How far is it?" he asked.

"Oh, a ways. Top of the hill. Keep going."

Up the hill, every house as well-known as a friend's face, their bright windows and outdoor lights and Christmas decorations transporting her back decades. How many times had she driven this road?

"Bear left," she said at the intersection halfway up.

"Good thing we've got four-wheel drive," he said.

"Um."

"Did I tell you we've put out an APB on the truck?"

Her mind fought to return to the present. "No, you didn't tell me."

"It's a long shot. Dark red or burgundy Ford Ranger, maybe faded. Year and license plate unknown."

"Not much to go on. There's probably thousands of old pickups in the valley."

His shoulders hitched under his leather jacket. "It's all we've got."

"I know."

"We also put out a description of the UNSUB. Medium height, slim build. Maybe blond, *maybe* wears glasses. Maybe a broken nose. Maybe a gold stud earring."

"Well, that's more than we had yesterday."

"The truck may help us. Sounds like the same truck a witness described in Mammoth."

"He could have bought a new one," she said in a low voice.

"Yeah, and this one could be a different UNSUB."

She shook her head. "No, this is the same man. I know it is."

"The likelihood is high, I agree."

"Maybe we'll get lucky. Crystal was a good witness."

"Her mother was an ass."

"Her mother doesn't matter anymore. Crystal has an eye."

He was steering around the last narrow switchback to Hannah's house, the town laid out below them in a grid of sparkling light. Across the valley, Aspen Mountain rose like a frozen wave forever ready to break.

"Nice view," he said.

"Uh-huh." She turned toward him. "You know, today, when you told Crystal what happened to you, I remembered the news stories. I knew your name sounded familiar. I should have put it together. I'm so sorry about your partner."

He grew silent, his profile carved from stone, the light from an oncoming car gilding his features, then sweeping on. She was acutely uncomfortable. She was as bad as her mother, never knowing when to keep her mouth shut.

"That . . . uh, it must have been terrible for you," she went on, compounding her discomfort. *Shut up.*

He shrugged again. "Shit happens." The words dripped with bitterness.

She was abruptly struck by an overwhelming feeling of sympathy for this man. Sympathy and an urge to help him, to understand and aid the healing process. She caught herself. He didn't need her help; he didn't need *her*. He thought she was a charlatan. And didn't she have enough man trouble?

"There's the driveway," she said, pointing. "Just go on down and park there."

Two vehicles were already parked on the road, the sheriff's SUV and another car. Scott's? The outdoor floods were on, and there were tiny white lights twined among the bare scrub oak branches bordering the stairs down to the house, a red bow and sleigh bells hung on the front door.

The tang of wood smoke filled the air when they got out of the car. The Zuckers had a fire going. Cozy.

Jane took a deep breath. They had a couple hours before Ray had to be back at the Lemke's. Two hours. She could stand two hours in her mother's house.

She'd barely set foot in the place in years, not since she'd gone away to art school. She'd been raised in that house, a warm happy childhood until Roland Zucker had entered the scene and stolen Hannah away from Jane's father.

And until that awful camping trip, the worst night of her life.

The man who'd raped her could very possibly be in there, just down those snow-covered steps, waiting to greet her and kiss her and wish her Merry Christmas.

She put her hand on the wrought-iron railing and took a step down. "I never should have agreed to come," she said. "Bad idea."

"Care to elaborate?" Ray said from behind.

"My mother and I . . . we never really got along that well." She stopped, holding onto the railing as if it were a life preserver. She shivered from the cold.

"She sure seemed happy to see you this afternoon."

"It's been a while."

He moved past her down the steps, put a hand on her arm to urge her on. She shivered again. "I think . . ."

The door opened, a rectangle of light and warmth, the murmur of conversation. Christmas carols and the scent of ham cooking and something sweet in the oven.

"I thought I heard a car," came a familiar voice. Her stepbrother. Tall and blond and handsome. More mature looking, his face thickening in that way men have when they've reached their prime. Like the muscled neck of a stallion. Scott Zucker.

"Come on in. God, it's freezing out," he said. "Jane, you look wonderful, just terrific. You haven't changed a bit. And . . . ?"

"Ray Vanover." Ray held out his hand, and the two men shook, toe to toe, eye to eye, one blond, one dark. A kind of unspoken message passing between them. A male thing.

They were inside then, Scott taking their coats, the fragrant warmth hitting them like a soft blow.

"Mom," Scott said, "look who's here."

Mom, Jane thought.

Hannah was wearing an apron. She'd been checking something in the oven, and she straightened, her face flushed. "Oh, Jane, I'm so glad you could make dinner. And Ray . . . It's Ray, isn't it? Welcome and Merry Christmas. Roland, get them both drinks, will you?"

"Jane, Jane, Jane. Boy, are we glad to see you. How long's it been? And this is . . . ?" her stepfather said.

"Roland Zucker, Ray Vanover. He's . . . ah, we're working on the Lemke case together."

Roland, tall and broad across the chest and shoulders, his blond hair thinning and buzz cut, his features rough-hewn but exceedingly masculine. He thrust out his hand.

"Heard of you. Kent told me. Awful thing about the Lemke girl. You got any leads?"

Of course Roland would ask. He'd been the sheriff of Pitkin County for years before he retired, and his protégé Kent Schilling had gotten the job.

He was in his mid-sixties and still in great shape. He ran a martial arts studio now, Jane knew, and she could easily picture Roland in white pants and coat and belt, crouched, throwing students to the mat.

Kent was there with his wife Lottie, a pretty lady with prematurely gray hair worn in a shoulder-length pageboy. Her face lit up when she saw Jane, and she came over and hugged her, then held her at arm's length. "Jane, you haven't changed. How long has it been? It's so wonderful to see you."

"Hi, Lottie, how's school?"

"Good, very good. We have a new high school. Did you . . . ?"

"I saw it. Looks great."

"You should see the art room. I'm in heaven." Lottie was the high school art teacher; she'd taught Jane, recognized and nurtured her talent.

"How're the twins?"

"Just fine. Home from college for Christmas break now. They're baby-sitting tonight. Can you believe that?" Lottie said. "Remember when *you* used to baby-sit for *them*?"

"I sure do." Jane smiled. She really liked Lottie Schilling, and she owed her so much. Jane had done her first police sketch for Kent while she'd been on spring break from art school. Lottie had suggested that he ask Jane to try to draw a suspect's face from a witness to an attempted murder. She'd done the interview and sketch, and the likeness had been extraordinary. Kent had arrested the man, a well-known local developer, the DA had tried and convicted him, and Jane's career had been unwittingly launched.

There was only one person in the gathering she didn't know. A pretty redhead in tight jeans and a cream-colored sweater that showed her perfect breasts. *Scott's date,* she thought. Typical. He shuffled one lady *du jour* for another, always had, even back in high school. How old was Scott now? Thirty-five? He was a ski instructor, a top dog in the ski school, booked all winter with private lessons. Wanted by the rich and famous for his expertise, his charm, his looks.

Scott brought Jane a glass of wine, pulling his lady friend over. "Jane, this is Cherie, from Houston. Jane, my little sister."

"Hi," Jane said, taking the wine. "How is Aspen treating you?" *Little sister.*

"I just *love* this town," Cherie gushed. "I am having *so* much fun. And Scott's *such* a good instructor. And so nice to invite me for dinner."

"Fantastic." Jane put on her party smile.

Kent and Roland were monopolizing Ray, talking about the Lemke case. Cop stuff. Lottie was chatting with Hannah in the kitchen. Scott nuzzled Cherie's neck, eliciting a giggle.

Jane looked around the house. It was the same, the golden-colored pine floor, the earth-toned oriental rug, the off-white sectional. Re-covered, she saw, with a new fabric. The same prints on the walls, the thirty-foot span of sliding glass doors that opened onto a deck overlooking the valley, concealed now by drapes to keep in the warmth on a winter's night. The huge stone fireplace in the center of the room, complete with a crackling fire. The dining table set with crystal and linen. She remembered her mother ordering that table from Denver, so thrilled when the truck arrived, and the deliverymen carried the table into the house. How many meals had she eaten at that table?

Without a bridging thought, a scene appeared in her mind's eye. The time was late summer, the drapes were open, morning sun splashing across this very table. Jane and Hannah were arguing. She'd been going into her last year of art school and was getting ready to leave for the fall term. Maybe that's what had given her the courage to blurt the truth out, to throw in her mother's face the secret she'd borne alone for years.

She couldn't even remember what they'd been arguing about—probably something to do with Scott or Roland. But she'd been angry at Hannah and feeling put upon.

She recalled her exact words: "You think Roland is so great, the love of your life! Well, think again, *mother.* I was raped that fall we went camping in Reudi. I was raped, and it could have been that macho jerk you married."

Hannah had been coldly furious. "You are a sick person," she'd said.

"Well, if I am, it's *your* fault! Letting Dad die like that. My *father.* And marrying Roland and worshipping the ground Scott walks on. You love him ten times better than me. You don't even *like* me."

"That's not true!"

"Oh, yes it is." She'd drawn a quavering breath, tears stinging her eyes. "Just think about that, your beloved Roland. Raping me."

"You're a goddamn liar."

"Okay, right. I'm making it up. Ask him! Ask him!"

"Are you out of your mind?"

Jane had stormed out of the house that day, left for school shortly after and hardly spoken to Hannah since. The fight had been hideous. It still lay between them like a lit fuse.

She looked around and remembered and ran her fingers

along the tablecloth and stared down at her grandmother's flowered china. So familiar.

She couldn't believe she was here, in the very situation she'd avoided for years, surrounded by inescapable memories of that awful night, surrounded by people who had been along on the camping trip. Probably in the same room with the man who'd raped her, the others who couldn't save her, her mother who hadn't believed her.

Ironically brought full circle by another young girl's plight.

You can't escape, Jane told herself bitterly. *No matter how hard you try.* The man who'd hurt her so could have been one of these men drinking, talking, at home in the house where she'd grown up. It could have been one of these men—Kent, Roland, Scott—whose face she knew so well yet could not dredge from memory to put on paper.

"Isn't it wonderful to get together like this?" she heard a voice say. Lottie.

"Oh, yes, it sure is."

"We've missed you. Your mother has missed you."

Jane felt her mouth twist. Too late. Lottie saw the grimace and cocked her head. "I know mothers and daughters sometimes have problems. But honestly . . ."

"It's okay, Lottie. Let's not get into all that. I'm here."

"And with a handsome man, too."

"We're working together."

"I know, but still . . ."

Jane smiled. "I'm too old for you to be playing matchmaker."

"You're never too old, my dear."

There were eight for dinner, all of them longtime acquaintances except for Ray and Cherie. At the center was Roland, big and overbearing. Pompous. The man who'd swept Hannah off her feet while she was still married to

Doug Russo. The man who'd destroyed Jane's family. Doug Russo had moved to Telluride after the divorce, leaving his daughters in the care of Sheriff Roland Zucker. He'd been found alone in a cabin several years later—dead of liver failure from heavy drinking.

Funny, Gwen had never disliked Roland so much. But Gwen was older, and she hadn't been forced to live with him all those years as Jane had.

Roland sliced the ham. There were bowls of garlic mashed potatoes, yam casserole, hot rolls, salad, and green beans and water chestnuts. A feast. Prepared by Hannah, who'd been at work the entire day.

Wine was poured all around. A lovely cabernet from the Grape and Grain, Roland pointed out. Cherie had already had several glasses and was giggling at everything, her blue eyes glazed.

Alcohol and eight thousand feet of altitude, Jane thought. *They don't mix.*

The conversation was the usual Aspen banter: what celebrities were in town; who'd returned from a trek in Nepal; how crowded the town was with Christmas vacationers; where the best snow was to be found on which mountain. Gossip about friends, questions about children, kids the older adults had seen born and grow and leave to go to school and return married with kids of their own.

"Do you remember Asia Schultz?" Lottie asked Jane. "She was, oh gosh, I think a year behind you at school?"

"Sure, how is she?"

"She got married last year and is expecting. Her mother—Pam, remember her?—is so excited."

Asia Schultz a mother. Jane felt a pang of envy. *Someday . . .*

"I saw Erica Frankel the other day," Hannah added. "Did you know her son Evan is an associate professor at Stanford?"

"Evan Frankel?" Jane said. "He got in trouble burning the track coach's running shoes. He's a professor at Stanford?"

"People change," her mother said meaningfully.

Jane was aware of Ray, not talking much, listening intently. Was he curious about her screwed-up family?

What did he see at this festive table? A bunch of pleasant people getting together to celebrate the holiday? Did he recognize the undercurrents of tension and resentment? He couldn't have the faintest idea that she shifted her gaze from Roland to Scott to Kent, asking herself: *Was it him? Or him? Or was it Kent?* No, not Kent. It couldn't have been him, with his wife Lottie and their kids.

There was a man missing in this circle of friends. George Grinell, her brother-in-law. He and Gwen had only just met seventeen years ago. *Could* it have been George? Lord knows, all the men had been drinking, and George had always been a flirt. But so was Scott.

Had one of them violated her? It had been dark in the tent. Maybe she couldn't pull his face from her subconscious because she never really saw him. Maybe it was as simple as that.

Hannah finally set her sights on Ray between coffee and dessert.

"So," she said, smiling graciously, "you're working with Jane for the first time?"

"Yes, that's right," he said.

"She's really good at what she does. Isn't she, Kent?"

"Absolutely," the sheriff replied.

"Have you been to Aspen before, Ray?"

"No. Actually, I only moved to Denver a few weeks ago."

"Oh? And where did you move from?"

Jane thought, *She's got her talons into him now.*

"Seattle."

"Nice city." Roland put in. "But the *rain*. Well, you know, we're used to the sun here."

"Yeah, it does rain there," Ray said pleasantly.

"Are you from Seattle originally?" Hannah asked. No deviation, straight on target.

"No, I'm from the Boston area. I was born in Connecticut, raised in Lexington."

"Lexington and Concord and the Minutemen and all that?" Lottie asked.

"Yes, all that. But it's been years since I've been back."

"Do you have family in the East?" Hannah asked.

Mother, for God's sake, Jane thought.

"Some cousins."

"Any family in Seattle?" Hannah pressed.

Ray smiled and answered her in that rough-velvet voice of his. "If you're asking if I'm married, the answer is no."

"Well, I *was* sort of curious," Hannah said, unabashed.

"Mom, I think you've asked enough questions," Jane began.

"No, it's all right," Ray said. "I don't have anything to hide. I'm not married, never was. I was almost engaged once, but . . ." He gave a quirky smile of regret. "I guess you could say it didn't work out."

Hannah was like a dog with a bone. "Oh? And what happened to her?"

Ray locked his pale gaze on Hannah. "She died."

An awkward hush fell over the company. Finally Hannah said sincerely, genuinely, "I'm so sorry."

"Yes, ma'am, so am I. But it was a while ago."

"Have another glass of wine," Roland said, his usual loud voice softened. As if he really cared. Jane looked at him, surprised.

She cringed inwardly at her mother's grilling, but she

realized she'd learned more about Ray in the last five minutes than she had in two long days. A woman he'd been almost engaged to. A woman who'd died. The car bombing in Seattle. *Of course!* She'd known the agent killed in that bombing had been a woman, but . . . Ray's lover? His almost fiancée? My God. And on the drive up here she'd told him she was sorry his *partner* had been killed.

"Is that why you moved to Denver?" Hannah was asking.

"Not really. I was reassigned."

"Maybe it was good to get away from the memories," Lottie put in. "A new start."

"Maybe it was."

Hannah got up to pour more coffee, and Jane took the opportunity to lean across the table. "Look, Ray, I apologize for my mother. She's so darn nosy."

"Doesn't bother me. It's nice having someone that interested in me."

"We could go now. They're expecting you at the Lemke's."

He glanced at his watch. "Bruce is there. We've got a few minutes."

Hannah returned to her seat. "So, what exactly did you do in Seattle, Ray? I know you're an FBI agent, but I'll be damned if I know what you guys do."

Roland laughed. "I can tell you what they do. So can Kent. We've worked with the bureau lots of times."

"Now, Roland, I want to hear it from Ray."

Ray leaned back in his chair. "I was in the domestic counter-terrorism unit."

"Wow," Hannah said. "In Seattle?"

"My home office was there, but I got posted all over, especially after nine-eleven. New York, Miami, Djakarta, Manila."

"Interesting. Did you like the travel?"

He lifted his shoulders and let them drop. "Mostly I was in offices working."

Hannah was leaning on her hand, elbow on the table, eyes fixed on Ray. "It must have been wonderful, though."

"It was work."

"Oh, you're just being modest."

"No, Mrs. Zucker, I'm not being modest."

"But all those exotic places. The intrigue. The danger."

"I was never in any danger. Mostly I dealt with government bureaucrats and reports."

Hannah flapped her hand. "I don't believe that for a minute. Were you undercover?"

"Hannah," Roland put in, "listen to what the man said. Boring government stuff."

"*Shush*, Roland." She turned to Ray again. "No close calls? No dangerous situations? Come on, Ray."

He fixed his pale blue eyes on her, thick brows drawn together. "The only time I was ever in danger was in Seattle. When I got this." He put his fingers up to his neck.

Roland frowned. "Sure, I remember that. Those militia crazies, the ones who liked to leave car bombs. You ever catch them?"

"As a matter of fact," Ray said, "they've been apprehended in Washington State just recently."

"Well, you know the saying," Roland's voice was filled with oily joviality, "you always get your man, right?"

"We try."

Jane realized, with a spurt of surprise, that Roland was impressed with Ray because he was a federal agent. She studied her stepfather, his face flushed from wine, and she thought, *So he has some chinks in his armor.*

The women began to clear the dishes, uncovering the tablecloth spotted with crumbs and splotches of wine and drips of gravy.

"Oh, leave it all," Hannah said. "I'll do it in the morning."

"You will not," Lottie replied. "You have to go to work. And I'm on vacation from school. Let's get this done."

The men sprawled on the sectional sofa in front of the fire. Ray stepped aside and took his cell phone out, probably checking in with Bruce. Cherie joined the men. She'd been very quiet, pale, sipping water, sitting close to Scott.

"That girl drank too much," Hannah said, running water into the sink.

"The altitude gets them every time," Lottie observed.

"Scott should know better."

"Scott likes them like that," Jane said. "Softens them up."

"*Jane.*"

"It's true." She scraped scraps off dishes into the trash.

Lottie deliberately changed the subject. "And how's your young man, Jane?"

"Alan?"

"Yes, Alan."

"Well, we haven't been, uh, seeing a lot of each other lately."

"You haven't?" Hannah asked sharply. "I thought you were a couple. On the phone last summer you told me . . ."

"We were, Mom. But lately, I don't know . . ." She piled the scraped dishes on the counter and began to stack coffee cups.

"Is there someone else?" her mother asked.

"You mean for him or for me?"

"Either one."

Jane lied. Straight out lied. It was none of her mother's business. "No, no one else."

"So what's the problem?"

"Who said there was a problem?" God, her mother could get her back up.

"You just said you haven't seen much of each other. That means there's some kind of problem." Hannah rinsed dishes and put them in the dishwasher.

"*Mom,* stop interrogating me."

"You're my daughter. Can't I even ask about your boyfriend?"

Jane turned to gather some more dishes from the island and found herself face to face with Ray, who was setting empty wineglasses down.

Had he heard the conversation? Had he heard her mother questioning her about her *problem* with Alan? She felt herself burn with embarrassment. *Damn it all.*

"So, you and Alan are no longer an item" Hannah was saying, her back turned as she scrubbed a pot. "He sounded so perfect. You should have . . ."

"Mom, please." Low, taut.

Hannah glanced over her shoulder, caught sight of Ray and said, "Oh, sorry. Family stuff."

Jane felt her face grow hotter. Damn her mother, damn her whole family.

"Mrs. Zucker, I want to thank you for the great meal," Ray said, not missing a beat. "I enjoyed it a lot. I don't get much home cooking. But Jane and I have to go now."

"So soon?"

"Yeah, well, duty calls."

"Ray, you're welcome anytime," Hannah said. "You'll be here for a while?"

"No, ma'am, not really. I'm leaving tomorrow."

Jane swiveled her head toward him. *Leaving tomorrow?* That was news to her.

"Well, you come back soon. You and Jane."

Jane felt as if she'd been released from jail. She walked up the steps to the car, got in without giving Ray a chance to open the door for her, slammed it, and hunkered down in the passenger seat. Now she remembered why she didn't visit her family.

"Bad idea," she muttered.

Ray was sliding in behind the wheel. "What?"

"I said it was a bad idea to come here."

He started the car and drove up the steep driveway, the defroster going full blast, melting a semicircle of frost on the windshield. She hugged herself, looking out the side window, her breath condensing on the cold glass.

Finally he spoke. "Look, it's pretty damn obvious you have a problem with Aspen and with your family. Now, I know you think it's none of my business, but when your problem impacts my case, it becomes my business."

Her temper flared. "You're right, it's none of your business."

"I'm waiting to see some results from this *gift* of yours I keep hearing about. I'm waiting, but I'm not seeing any. You got some kind of hang-up about the Lemke case?"

"I got results from Crystal, and you know it. You're just predisposed to think I'm a waste of your precious time."

"I'll admit to some of that. Hey, I was willing to give you the benefit of the doubt. But time's running out for Kirstin. And I have to fly to Los Angeles tomorrow. So I figured you'd want to go home. You've interviewed the witnesses. Your job's done."

"Why are you going to L.A.? The Lemke case is *here*. Kirstin is *here* somewhere."

His features hardened. "I have some personal business."

"In the middle of a case?"

"In the middle of a case, yeah."

Home. She could go home to Denver and call Alan. She needed to see him, to tell him she still loved him before it was too late. And he'd want to know how the case was going, so she had the perfect excuse to call him.

After all, he was the one who'd convinced her to take on the kidnapping.

Why did she feel the need for an excuse to call him?

An urgency gripped her. *Forget about Alan.* Kirstin needed her more right now.

"I want a little more time. I know I can draw something. I can come up with something. But not if I'm in Denver." She knew she sounded lame. And desperate. She had so little to go on. A vague sketch she'd done at Crystal's. A generic male with a crooked nose wearing a hat and goggles. An earring. Next to nothing. Maybe Ray was right, and she should go home. See Alan . . .

No. Kirstin was out there somewhere. Kirstin needed her. There were no leads, and time was short.

"I'm going to L.A. with you," she stated.

"The hell you are."

"Yes, I am. I'll pay my way if I have to."

"What in God's name do you think you can do in L.A.?"

She shook her head. "No, I mean I'm not staying in L.A. I'll go on to Mammoth. I need to interview Allie again, and the witnesses to her abduction. Now that I have more information. . . . And Utah. I should see the victim and witnesses there, too. I have to."

"You already talked to them. I saw the reports. You got nothing. It'll be a waste of your time."

"No, no. I can get more now. I know I can. I have to talk to them again."

"Oh, for chrissakes."

"I'm going."

"You're obsessed."

"Maybe I am. So what? If it gets results my obsession is okay. It's good, in fact." She drew in a breath. "Okay, I admit it, I have a problem with my family. I don't like Roland or his son, and my mother and I don't see eye to eye about a lot of things. There's some history there—I won't go into details—and there's some . . . *stuff* that may be interfering with my ability to draw the UNSUB's face. But I can overcome that. I can. And I need to go to California with or without you."

She readied herself for an argument. Scorn, skepticism. Those dark brows drawing together in a scowl. Instead, he gave her a sidelong glance as he drove down the hill, a long, searching glance, then said, "Okay, come along. Knock yourself out. And after I finish my business, I'll go to Mammoth with you."

She waited a beat, then another, the car heater blowing warmth onto her face, banishing the cold night. "Thanks," she finally said in a small voice.

He drove her through town and out to her sister's house.

"You remember how to get to the Lemke's?" she asked as he pulled into the Grinell's driveway.

"I do."

He seemed impatient now, distracted, as if he wanted to get rid of her. Maybe he was regretting his momentary lapse, letting her get her way. Maybe he didn't give a damn whether or not she went to Los Angeles with him. He'd never believed in her anyway. Or perhaps he was still mourning the death of his lover and wasn't interested in other women's company. Was that why she got such negative reactions from him? He was being true to a dead woman, and Jane was an affront to him.

"What was her name?" she couldn't stop herself from asking.

"What?"

"Her name, your . . . partner."

His eyes bored into hers, and for a moment she was afraid, as if she'd blundered into the cave of a dangerous predator.

"I'm sorry . . . you don't have to . . ."

"Kathleen. Kathleen Bachman."

"Oh."

"She was only twenty-nine years old," he said in a voice of vast sadness.

"I'm so sorry."

"Yes, I know."

She wanted to put her hand on his, to comfort him, but she knew that was impossible, and then he seemed to straighten and shake off his pain. He cleared his throat. "I've got some things to finish up in the morning, so I'll try to get us on an afternoon flight to Denver," he said as she got out of the car. "I'll pick you up at, say, three."

"Okay, that's fine."

"Don't make me wait."

In the house, the two boys were watching television and eating chocolate chip cookies out of a bag.

"Hi, Aunt Jane," Kyle said. "Mom and Dad are still working that party. They're gonna have fits it's lasting so long."

"Don't you boys have to be in bed?" she asked.

Nicky rolled his eyes. "Guess you don't remember how old we are."

"Oh, sorry."

"You ever see this movie?" Kyle asked, pointing at the TV.

She glanced at it: a man with a machine for half his body and weird tubes coming out of him . . .

"Space Junk." Nicky said, grinning. "It's really a rad flick. See, that's the bad guy, and he's evil and he's got the good guys as prisoners. They're garbage men. *Space* garbage men. But they get away and the bad guy loses it and dies."

"Space Junk," Jane said wonderingly.

"It's funny. And there are girls in it."

"Girls."

"You know." Nicky held his hands out in front of his chest.

She laughed. Her fourteen-year-old nephew leering at girls in a movie.

"Ugh, gross," Kyle said, making a face.

"How's Grandma and Grandpa?" Nicky asked, turning his attention back to the movie.

"Fine," she replied.

"Cool. Grandpa's teaching us tai kwan do. It's so righteous. I can kick anybody's butt."

The two boys leaped up, feinting and kicking at each other, then subsided down onto the couch, where Nicky grabbed the bag of cookies.

"Give me some," Kyle cried.

"Oh, look, here's the part where the bad guy gets it," Nicky said, and they both fell quiet.

She watched them and eventually sat down, too, her heart again burdened, but now with regret that she'd missed so much of their youth. Nicky offered her a cookie, and she took it and determined to do better in the future. Life was just too short.

NINE

On the flight from Aspen to Denver the next day, Ray tried to pin down what he was feeling. Was he grateful to Jane for providing a convenient excuse for this trip to L.A.? Or was he a shitheel for using her? Because he *was* using her. Whoever asked—Stan, or Parker back in Denver, or one of the paper pushers in accounting—whoever, he could say he was still on the Lemke case.

In truth, all he cared about was revenge. He'd waited for an eternity, put up with being taken off the militia case, put up with the transfer to Denver. Spent eighteen months biding his time, frustrated beyond belief, unable to pursue the men who'd killed Kathleen and scarred him for life.

He'd considered quitting the FBI and going after the murderers on his own. He'd sat in the burn unit of the hospital and weighed his options. But he'd decided, cold-bloodedly, to stay with the bureau, because he figured he'd be more in touch with what was going on. So he'd accepted the desk job in Seattle that awaited him when he got off disability, and then he'd taken the chance to transfer to Denver, despite its plethora of humdrum cases. At least he'd be in the field again.

And that choice had panned out. The two militia men who'd set the car bomb, members of a sect called the Benton County Army, were on their way to Los Angeles. He didn't know what he'd do when he was face-to-face with them, but he knew he had to look each of them in the eye, see them for himself.

"Do we have time to eat something in Denver?" Jane asked.

"Uh . . . Denver. I guess so."

"When does our flight leave for L.A.?"

Irritated, wanting to go back into his cocoon of righteous anger, wanting to think about how he'd act, what he'd say. "Around five."

"Oh, ok, then there's time. I think there's a Pour La France on the concourse."

Pour La . . . "I'm not hungry."

"I am," she said quietly.

The small jet, half-empty, droned on over the mountains, the broad brown high prairie appearing below them sooner than could be imagined from the remote Shangri-la valley of Aspen.

He looked out the moisture-clouded window, unconsciously fingering his scars, and thinking of murder. No, not murder—execution, a simple, necessary killing. He was capable of killing the bombers. Maybe he'd just pull his gun out and shoot them and face the consequences. So what? There was no wife to cry for him. No kids. Not even a dog.

So what if he didn't solve the Lemke case? Someone else would take over. SAC Parker would send another case agent to Aspen. And Jane Russo was not going to help ID the UNSUB anyway.

They deplaned at Denver International Airport. He hefted his carry-on bag and followed her out into the busy concourse.

"I'm going to grab a snack," she said. "Do you want anything?" Coolly polite. He didn't blame her.

"I'll get some coffee. Meet you at the gate," he said.

During the wait for the flight to Los Angeles, he decided to put the bombers out of his mind. He'd been an ass to Jane. He'd probably never see her again after tomorrow, but she didn't deserve his rudeness. He'd try to be sociable. It would be a stretch.

Their flight was forty minutes late. He paced, checked his voice messages, called Bruce back in Aspen. Impatience clawed at him. Jane immersed herself in a magazine.

Finally, finally, they boarded. His blood pressure decreased, and he lay his head back against the seat and closed his eyes as the aircraft taxied out to the runway.

"Tired?" he heard her ask. Such a nice voice, smooth. When she wasn't pissed off at him.

He kept his eyes shut. "Not really."

"Can you sleep on planes?"

"Sometimes. On long flights."

"But not today."

"Probably not."

"Where are we staying? Are we renting a car? I'd really like to know what our plans are."

"We're staying at the Marriott near the airport. I've got a car reserved."

"And . . . your personal business?"

"I'll take care of it in the morning."

"When do we drive to Mammoth? I mean, we should get there as soon as possible. We don't know how much time Kirstin has left."

"We'll leave after I'm done."

"Okay." A pause. "Her name is Allison Sanchez. Allie."

"The girl in Mammoth?"

"Yes. The victim. Allie was thirteen when it happened. Five years ago."

"I've read the report."

"She's eighteen now. She's working at a gift shop in Mammoth Lakes over Christmas break. She's planning to go to U.C. Santa Cruz when she graduates."

He opened his eyes and looked at her. "How do you know all this?"

"I called her this morning."

"You called her."

"I've kept in touch." She gestured with a hand. "I keep in touch with all the girls. Not much, just a note or an E-mail once in a while."

"All the girls?"

"All the ones I interview. They're hurt. It helps them to know someone cares."

Her solicitude for the young women she interviewed made him ashamed of his attitude, his cynicism.

"I hope I can get something new from her. She tried so hard, when I first talked to her, but she hadn't seen much. The same thing Crystal and Melanie said, he was covered up."

"You going to tell her about his broken nose?"

"Not at first. I'd rather she came up with it. If I tell her, I'm giving her a suggestion, and then you never know whether her memory is tainted or not." She paused. "You know, I keep thinking it's cruel to make Allie go through this all over again."

"Think so?"

"I know so. It isn't pleasant to relive a horror like being kidnapped and raped."

"I guess not."

"But I have to try. Or he'll keep taking girls. You know that."

"He'll keep taking them till he makes a mistake and gets caught."

"But how many will be damaged or . . . killed before he gets caught? That's why I have to talk to Allie again. She understands."

"She understands, but can she help?"

She looked down at her hands and shook her head slowly. "I hope so. I hope so."

There was magnificence to her dedication. He could hear the caring in her voice, see it in the way she held herself. She wasn't jaded; she wasn't just going through the motions. All his words of doubt, of the futility of revisiting a girl who'd last seen her kidnapper five years before, evaporated. Suddenly he wished he were a better person, someone worthy of Jane Russo's respect. And he wondered if Alan Gallagher—whose dead child had inspired the man to become a child rights advocate—was worthy of Jane's admiration. Or her affections.

After the plane arrived at LAX, Ray checked them into the Marriott near the airport. He could tell she was restless, not really wanting to sit in a hotel room and watch television. He didn't blame her, but he figured he'd be lousy company tonight.

"You must be hungry by now," she said as they took the elevator to the tenth floor.

Mentally, he checked his stomach. Yeah, he could eat.

"The restaurant off the lobby looked okay." She held her artist's case in front of her with both hands. A barrier? Security?

"Give me half an hour," he said.

She cocked her head questioningly.

"We'll eat in the restaurant."

Her smile lit up the elevator. She looked awfully pretty when she smiled, and he wondered at the warmth that spread inside him at pleasing her. What else might he do to elicit that smile?

She ordered mahimahi, and he settled on seafood pasta. The restaurant was pleasant enough, the lighting dim. They'd been seated next to the large window that had a view of the airport runways, planes taking off and landing in the night.

"It always feels weird to me," she observed, "when it gets dark so early, but it's not cold out. I don't think I could live here. I need seasons."

"Is that because you were raised in Aspen?"

"Maybe."

Their salads arrived. She ate with a good appetite. He liked that she didn't try to impress him as a tiny eater.

"So, tomorrow we'll drive up to Mammoth?" she asked, buttering a roll.

"That's right."

"But you have some business to take care of in the morning?"

"I'll try not to be too long." *Right.*

"I guess I'll just wait here for you."

She might be waiting a long time. He felt bad about that, but he had to do what he had to do. It was just her luck that she'd come along on this trip.

"Is your business related to work?" she asked.

"Partly."

"You seem preoccupied," she said softly, leaning her elbows on the table.

Preoccupied. "Sorry."

"No, I mean, you don't have to be sorry. I just thought you might want to talk about it."

"Talk about what?"

"Whatever's bothering you."

"Nothing's bothering me."

"Okay." She sat back, and he felt her distance like a cold draft.

"Look," he said, "it's nothing you need to worry about."

"I said okay."

"Christ."

"You're an angry man," she said, and she reached across the table to touch his fingers. Lightly, just for a heartbeat. "It's eating away at you."

He drew his hand back, embarrassed. At a loss. His skin burning where she'd touched him. He had no answer for her, no smart remark.

The waitress set their plates in front of them. Jane ate in silence for a time, as if she hadn't made an intimate observation about him. He watched her surreptitiously, but her expression was neutral, the skin over her jaw bunching as she chewed.

Maybe he'd heard her wrong, misunderstood her remark. He was obsessing over what would happen tomorrow, not listening for nuances in a female's conversation.

It was rare that he dined with an attractive woman these days. Not since Kathleen. Too bad the whole situation was so touchy. Too bad tomorrow had to come. Maybe this would be his last meal as a free man, he thought dryly. The last supper.

"Sorry, if I'm nosy. I guess I get it from my mother," she finally said.

"No problem. I liked your mother."

"She's *direct,* isn't she?"

"I'll take that over the lying jerks I have to interrogate any day."

"What did you think of Roland?"

He hitched his shoulders. "Typical law-enforcement type."

"You're not going to go on record as criticizing a fellow lawman, are you?"

He let a corner of his lip lift. "Probably not."

She finished her fish and the last few vegetables on her plate. "That was good," she said. "I do miss seafood living in Denver."

"There're seafood restaurants in Denver."

She wrinkled her nose. "Not like on the coast."

"So," he said, suddenly curious, "how did you get into your work?"

"Oh," she put two fingers to her forehead, "it's a long story."

"We have time."

She told him about Lottie suggesting Kent use her to draw a witness's recollection of a man reported near a crime scene, about the sketch being an exact likeness of a local Aspen developer. "That was on spring break of my senior year at art school. When I graduated, I just sort of, well, word got around, and I worked in Grand Junction for a while, for the police there, and then I got an offer from the Denver PD, and, I guess the rest is history."

"But you freelance now."

"Um, yes. Well, it was a case I was on about, let's see, eight years ago? A bank robber in Denver. He killed a bank guard. The FBI worked on that, and I got to know some of the guys." She was pushing her crumbs around on the tablecloth, looking down. "They asked to borrow me from the police department, and things started getting too complicated, so I went out on my own."

"That case eight years ago. Calvin Lancaster, right?"

"Yes."

"He's serving life, isn't he?"

"Yes."

"You were on that case?"

She looked up and smiled mischievously. "Yes."

"You drew that picture of Lancaster? I remember, we got it in Seattle. One of the ten most wanted that year."

"He was caught in Phoenix."

"Yeah, I remember."

So *she*'d drawn that much-touted sketch. Maybe she did have a talent he'd been reluctant to acknowledge. He studied her with new eyes.

"What are you looking at?" she asked. "Do I have food on my chin?"

"No, no food."

She leaned forward, and, for a moment, he was afraid she was going to touch him again. But she didn't. "I can get something from Allie," she said. "I know I can. A detail. A little something. But it'll help."

"Maybe."

"I just need some time with her."

"You'll get your time." But perhaps without him.

After dinner they took the elevator and walked back to their rooms. The hallway was lit unevenly, unflatteringly. The walls were cream colored, scratched at suitcase level. Down the hall the elevator swished and hummed. Trays with dirty dishes sat outside a couple of the rooms.

"I'm leaving really early in the morning," he said at her door.

"Just grab me when you get back. I'll be packed and ready to go."

"I'm not sure exactly when that'll be."

"Whenever," she said. "I think we should get up to Mammoth as soon as possible."

"My business . . . ah, might take some time."

"You *could* tell me what it's all about."

"I don't think so."

She did touch him this time; she reached out and put the tips of her long fingers on the side of his face, on his scar, for God's sake. "I'm a good listener."

"I'm not a good talker." He fought the urge to draw away.

She cocked her head and smiled sadly, then she leaned forward and kissed him lightly on his cheek.

Sensation exploded in him. The whiff of her perfume, the scent of her honey-colored hair, the warmth of her lips—it was too much for him after eighteen months without a woman. His body flushed with desire, a kind of fever, that snatched his breath away, and sent a lightning bolt through him. He felt a stirring in his groin. This time he did step back. "What about you and Gallagher?" came out of his mouth. *Stupid.*

"What?"

"Nothing," he muttered, then he turned away and went to his own door, fumbling with the key before he got the damn thing open.

Friday dawned cool, with a yellowish haze over the sprawling megalopolis of Los Angeles. By seven a light drizzle seeped from the thick air.

The commercial flight from Seattle landed half an hour late. But it landed. And Ray and Stan Shoemaker were there to meet the U.S. marshals who'd brought the two bombers to L.A. A federal judge stood ready to arraign the two on charges ranging from illegal weapons possession to armed robbery to aggravated assault to one count of first degree murder.

Stan boarded the plane, Ray on his heels, and the papers

were signed and custody of the suspects turned over to the FBI case officer.

Stan did all the talking, paper signing, and exchange of keys to the hand- and anklecuffs. The airline crew, as always anxious and alert these days, seemed to breathe a collective sigh of relief when the men deplaned.

Stan and a federal marshal escorted the suspects, Joseph "Joe Bob" Perry and his younger brother Theodore "Teddy" Perry to a waiting car. The marshal ducked their heads one by one behind the iron grill in the backseat of the sedan. Even from where Ray stood, the two suspects looked shabby and unshaven, mouse-colored long hair, oily and stringy, blue eyes red-rimmed, necks grimy, flannel shirts and jeans soiled, hiking boots mud-caked. But when they were assigned lawyers—or someone actually paid for legal representation—and the FBI finished with its initial interrogation, the Perry boys would get haircuts and clean clothes, white shirts, suits, and conservative ties for their court appearances.

You bet, he thought. They'd look like fine upstanding citizens within forty-eight hours.

If they lived that long.

The U.S. marshal had driven onto the tarmac, and Stan took off with them while Ray was escorted by airport security back through the terminal to short-term parking, where he'd left the rental car. He was in a hurry. He figured he'd only get a few minutes alone with Joe Bob and Teddy before some pompous lawyer arrived to make sure they were afforded their due rights under the law.

A few minutes was all Ray needed.

Headquarters was located in the federal building in downtown L.A., and Ray took the 110 Freeway and got off at the Civic Center, only ten minutes behind Stan. Showing his badge, he parked in an official slot and made his way through the building. Stan had already told him where the Perry boys would be held.

Ray felt as if he were on autopilot, going through the motions until the moment of truth. But with each step, as he neared the holding room where Stan awaited him with the suspects, he felt his blood seething. It had occurred to him that Stan might read his real intent—not that Ray had an exact course of action mapped out—but Stan might ask him to leave his gun outside the interrogation room. Ray rounded the last corner, saw Stan shuffling papers at a counter, and he wiped his features clean of emotion. Hell, he was getting good at that.

"You got here quick," Stan said, handing the uniformed guard some paperwork.

"The traffic wasn't bad," Ray said, shrugging. "And the haze lifted, sun's out." Truth was, he'd exceeded the speed limit by twenty miles an hour in the outside lane the whole way.

"Well, the Perrys are in there." Stan nodded toward a heavy gunmetal gray door with a barred window in its center.

"They lawyered up yet?"

"Oh yeah, court appointed for now, but that won't last. I heard a PD is on his way."

"Um," Ray said, working at his neutral expression. "Mind if I poke my head in?"

Stan gauged him for a moment. "You sure? We don't want them claiming they were interrogated without their legal counsel present."

"I just want a face-to-face. They can't complain if I call them fucking asshole murderers, now can they?" Ray summoned up a grin.

"Ah, I guess not. Besides, you came all the way out here to get a firsthand look. Why not?"

"Thanks, Stan," he said.

When he opened the door and closed it behind him, it felt as if all the air had been sucked out of the room. He couldn't breathe. Blood surged to his face, and his pulse began to leap under his skin. For the first few seconds he stood, back to the door, staring at them, meeting their eyes, shifting his gaze from the older Joe Bob to his younger brother Teddy. Up close they looked smaller in person than he'd imagined. Pathetic. Dirty, stupid, *caught*. That these two had taken the life of Kathleen seemed impossible. Militants. Cowards. Men who feared everyone and everything that wasn't *them*. They feared blacks and Jews and Italians and Russians and anyone with a different-colored skin or tilted eyes. They hid themselves and located in remote areas where they'd avoid coming into contact with anyone they hated. Hated because they were too moronic to understand and accept the differences in races and peoples. Because they were so goddamn afraid.

And they armed themselves. To the eyeballs. They armed themselves and hid and only moved in the shadows. Like when they attached C-4 explosives to the underside of an FBI car in the black of night.

Ray studied them and choked on his own disgust. His hate was building to a crescendo. Those two. Sitting here breathing the air while Kathleen was six feet under.

Teddy sniffed and his stare fell to his lap, where his hands were cuffed to metal rings in the metal table. But Joe Bob's eyes didn't flinch. They were small and filled with the unholy light of hate.

It was Joe Bob who broke the silence. "You're Vanover," he said, the slightest smile appearing on his mouth. "I'd've recognized the burned face anywhere."

If Ray had a shred of control left it fled. His gun abruptly felt like a heavy stone against his side. He began to reach into his jacket. His hand knew the way.

* * *

He was unaware of the intrusion as he was aware of the feel of the cold steel in his fingers. The door behind him had opened and shut, but he knew only the stab of a red-hot poker of rage twisting in his gut. Somewhere behind him there was a noise. That didn't matter. He met Joe Bob's glare and thought, *See you in hell.*

"Hey." A voice. And again. "Hey, come on there. Ray? What the . . . ?"

Still he couldn't drag his eyes from Joe Bob. His fingers tightened on the grip of his revolver.

"Hey, *hey,* buddy." Stan? "Not like this, man, not like this. Cool off. Come on."

Ray felt an iron grasp on his arm, and he was cognizant now that his friend had entered the room and was talking to him, holding on to him. Sweat oozed from every pore, adrenaline fueled the fire inside him.

"Outside, Ray. No shit, man, you're outta here."

"Fuck that," Ray panted, ready to throw off Stan's hold, to squeeze off two rounds.

"Don't make me call for help. It's not worth it, Ray, come on, *come on.*"

How Stan got him out of that room and out of the building Ray never knew. It seemed as if one instant he was glaring through a crimson haze at the bombers, the next he was gasping in a lungful of air, his hands on the hood of his car, sweat dripping from his bowed head onto the cold metal.

"Jesus, Vanover," came Stan's voice at his ear. "Would you really have done those two?"

Ray sucked in another breath.

"They're small-fry, man."

"Fucking murderers is what they are."

"Okay, whatever. We've got their asses now, and wc'll ask for no bail and the judge'll give it to us. The point is we may get a shot at the mastermind of this militia. We squeeze those two assholes enough and they'll start to squeal. They're cowards. But we won't get shit out of them if they're dead, buddy. Right? You hearing me?"

"I hear you," Ray hissed, still not able to douse the flames of his fury.

"We have them dead to rights purchasing explosives," Stan said. "No jury is going to let them go."

Ray wasn't listening.

"And another thing," Stan said. "There's the head guy, the Northwest Bomber. Even if a jury gives these murdering bastards life without parole, we still don't have shit on the one who ordered the bombings in the first place."

They'd nearly had him, though. Three years ago, Ray and Stan had worked a case in eastern Washington State, a sporting goods store robbery and shooting. The two men under arrest upstairs had been in on that robbery; they left their fingerprints all over the place, even though they'd been smart enough to wear masks. There had been a third man there, too. Believed to have been the Northwest Bomber himself. He had stayed out of the line of sight of the shop's video surveillance camera, and it was believed he'd gone without a mask. He was also the one who'd put a bullet into the store owner's head—the surveillance tape proved the other two hadn't done the shooting—and he'd left the owner for dead.

But the gunshot victim had survived. The trouble was he'd never been able to ID the shooter. Ray wholeheartedly believed he'd suffered permanent amnesia or brain damage. Other FBI agents, Stan included, believed the man had blocked the shooter's face out of sheer terror. Either way, the Northwest Bomber had screwed up when he'd botched the murder, but they still had nothing on him. No name or face or prints. They only knew he existed.

"Hell," Ray said, "the one thing we have is the Perry brothers. We may never get their leader. And they have to pay. *Now,* before some sleazebag lawyer gets them off."

Stan was quiet, then he put a hand on Ray's shoulder. "Look, I know how you felt about Kathleen. We all felt the same. She was one of us. But someday you'll thank me for stopping you up there. It was the wrong way to handle it. Kathleen . . . she wouldn't have wanted it that way."

Ray reached in his jacket pocket and took out his car keys. "Wrong for Kathleen, but not for me," he said.

TEN

When he finally showed up at the hotel, Jane was white with anger. She'd spent half the morning pacing the room, pausing at the window and pulling aside the drape. She could see the parking lot ten floors below. *No rental car. No Ray.* She'd watched TV, but hadn't heard a bit of the CNN news, instead rehearsing the words she'd say to him: *"Did you forget Kirstin? Did you forget she's being raped, and we need to find her before he kills her?"*

But when he knocked on her door, and she saw his face, she shut up. Wherever he'd been, whatever had delayed him, it must have been bad.

"Sorry," was all he said, distracted, and he picked up her bag and strode toward the elevators.

They were out of L.A., heading northeast on Highway 395, before she dared to break the taut silence. "I don't know what kept you," she said. "I assume it was important, but there's an innocent young girl back in Aspen who's praying for someone to rescue her."

"Yeah," he said, attention locked on the road. He hadn't even heard her.

"It's not as if we have all the time in the world, Ray."

He remained tight-lipped, and she let it drop. For ten miles. "So what *did* happen his morning?"

"Nothing."

She laughed without humor. "For God's sake, I study faces for a living. Something happened."

"Don't worry about it."

"Okay, I won't worry about it, but maybe it would help if you get whatever's eating you off your chest. Bad cliché, I know, but it works. Talk to me."

The muscles in his face grew more rigid.

Men, she thought, but corrected herself. Not all men were repressed. Alan wasn't. Not in the least. Alan . . .

She shook off the notion and gazed out the window. They'd left behind the remnants of the dismal fog shrouding the flat basin that was Los Angeles, and the warmer temperatures, too, as the highway ascended into the Sierra Nevada foothills. The route followed the Los Angeles aqueduct past the El Paso mountains and up into the Inyo National Forest. Beautiful, unspoiled country. She remembered the last trip through these mountains. Christmas, five years ago. She'd been driven by another FBI agent, a woman. And she'd felt so confident she could get the face of Allison Sanchez's tormenter onto paper. She'd never failed before. Never known complete failure. Until the first time Allie had described the man who had raped her, the black room, the sheer horror of what had been done to her, the ensuing numbness of both body and mind.

And Jane had relived her own ordeal in vivid detail, as if it had been happening all over again. She'd tried to steer Allie in the right direction, tried to unlock the hidden memories from her wounded mind, but she'd failed miserably, been unable to get the poor girl to relax, to trust her, because Jane hadn't been able to release her own tension.

Then he'd struck again, same MO, three years ago in Snowbird, Utah, and again the FBI had flown her in to conduct the interviews when their portrait artist had failed to get a composite.

She had also failed.

Over and over, she'd fallen down on the job. Yet after working this case, she'd taken on many other jobs and succeeded. None were quite like this, though. None had brought home so intimately her own nightmares. And Caroline Deutch had still wanted her. Alan even trusted her to overcome her resistance and come up with a drawing. Alan, who knew what she'd been through.

She sighed and glanced over at Ray. *He* didn't trust her. Which wasn't helping at all. And his own tension was still palpable.

They'd been on the road for four hours and had barely spoken. Twice he had used his cell phone, first calling Aspen and then Parker in Denver. There was nothing new. *Poor, poor Kirstin,* Jane thought, knowing the girl was clinging to the thread of hope that she'd be rescued at any moment, a thread that was growing more frayed by the hour.

I have to succeed this time, she told herself. But, dear God, Allie's memories had been repressed and buried for years. Were they retrievable now?

She had to stop stressing and start focusing. She could do it. She could.

They were an hour out of Mammoth Lakes when she decided to practice on Ray. What did she have to lose?

"Um," she said, and she realized her throat was closed from so many hours of silence. She cleared it. "So, you said you're from New England?"

"I don't recall telling . . . Oh, right, at your mother's."

"Did you go to one of those preppy boy's schools?"

"Nope."

His reticence wasn't going to deter her. She spent the next few minutes prying his background from him until he was actually talking in sentences.

"You graduated from Boston University and were going into law school." She repeated his words. "So how did you end up with the FBI?"

"My father."

"Oh? You mean he wanted you to . . ."

"He was FBI."

"Oh, *oh*, I see. So you followed his footsteps. Dropped out of law school?"

"Never really started."

"Um. And is your father still . . . But no, I guess he'd be retired by now."

"That's right."

"Do he and your mother . . ."

"My mother passed away."

"Oh, gosh, I'm sorry."

"So am I."

"So your father lives alone?"

"On a boat."

"Really?"

"Yeah. Keeps it in Jacksonville, Florida."

"What a life. Do you see him often?"

"No."

She waited, instantly deciphering his tone of voice. Family difficulties were only too familiar to her.

"He's always been a prick."

Yet Ray had followed his lead, gone into the FBI. She supposed it was a father-son thing, competitive and not so pretty. And Ray's mother was not there to act as a buffer.

"Do you ever talk, I mean on the phone?" she ventured.

He appeared to think for a moment, and then he laughed wryly. "We talked, oh, I think it was last spring. He called to tell me he'd sold the house in Lexington and paid off the boat."

Better get off that subject. "Any brothers or sisters?"

He shook his head. "My mother died of breast cancer when I was seven."

She let out a whistling breath and nodded. His wounds really did run deep. She sought safer ground. "So, what do you think of Special Agent in Charge Parker?"

"He's all right."

"Kind of a stuffed shirt, isn't he?"

"I don't know him well enough to make that call."

"But I do. How about Caroline Deutch? A lot of the guys find her, well, let's say, intimidating?"

"Are you asking me if I'm intimidated by her?"

"Are you?"

"No."

"Do you think she's a good agent?"

"Barely know her."

"But you checked her record, didn't you? When Parker sent you over to my place with Caroline, I'll bet you went into her file."

Silence.

"I take it that's a yes."

They were passing through Bishop, a tiny dot on the map half an hour before Mammoth Lakes. *Almost there,* she was thinking, when he said, "You've been fishing all day." Belligerently.

"Fishing?"

"Yeah, that's what I said." He hesitated, seemed to decide something, then tapped his fingers on the steering wheel. He gave her a quick sidelong glance and then tapped some more. Finally he said, "Okay, so you want to know what happened this morning?"

"Only if you want to tell me." *Liar.*

"Well, here it is." He passed a car on the highway, pushing the rental car to its limit. "The two suspects in the Seattle car bombing were flown into L.A. this morning."

"Oh."

"They were apprehended in Washington State and escorted to L.A. for questioning, and I wanted to see them. Satisfied now?"

"Oh, Ray . . ." She drew in a breath. "Well, *did* you see them?"

"I saw them."

"And?"

"And what? I saw them, and they're just as stupid and guilty as I expected."

"What did you hope to accomplish? A confession?"

He laughed. "Right."

"Did you talk to them?"

"I doubt that you'd call it talking. I didn't give them any goddamn Play-Doh, if that's what you mean."

No wonder, she thought. His moodiness, his sudden acceptance of her plan to go to California, all explained. *Personal business,* he'd said. It couldn't have been more personal.

"You're sure they're the right ones?"

"Oh yeah."

"How were they caught?"

"A tip."

Of course. Most criminals were caught through tips. No honor among thieves. "Did it make you feel better?"

"No." A hard staccato.

"Will they be found guilty? Is there enough evidence?"

"Who the hell knows?"

"Um. Well, I guess you'll have to testify against them."

"If the case ever gets that far. Those slippery bastards, they could deal and be right back at their tricks again."

"Oh, I'm sure . . ."

"You're *sure*? Let me tell you how many times criminals have slid out from under charges. The legal system is enough to make you puke. I should have done those jerks this morning."

"No, Ray, that's not the way to go. You know that."

"Do I? You want to hear what I did this morning? I pulled my gun on them, I goddamn pulled my gun. I would have done them if Stan hadn't stopped me."

"I don't believe that. I just don't. Maybe you wanted to. Of course you did, but I simply don't . . ."

"Jane," he cut in sharply. "Believe it."

They checked into a log-cabin-style motel on the outskirts of Toms Place, a tiny mountain hamlet southwest of Mammoth Lakes. They were lucky to have gotten two rooms. It was almost Christmas, after all.

Jane sat on the sagging double bed in her room, her breath showing in the air while the heating unit groaned and rattled to life. She used her cell phone to call the Christmas Shoppe in Mammoth Lakes. She knew Allie wouldn't be off work till seven, when the store closed.

"Can we give you a ride then?" Jane asked. "Or did you drive to work?"

"If you don't mind, a ride would save me a walk. About ten after seven?"

"We'll be there," Jane said.

"I hope I can help. It's been so long."

"I know, honey," Jane said. "We'll just give it a try. See you after work."

Hugging herself, she got up, opened her door, and rapped on Ray's. "I talked to Allie. We can pick her up a little after seven."

"This is going to take all night."

But Jane knew it wouldn't. She didn't need to soothe Allie into relaxation. Allie already knew what was at stake, knew the drill. And Jane didn't expect to get too much. But even the smallest detail, anything, might be the key to breaking the case wide open.

"You want to eat before we pick her up?" he said.

She thought a minute. Shook her head. "How about after? Right now I'm going to huddle under the blankets and watch the news. Does your heat work?" She peered inside his room as if looking would answer her questions.

He didn't answer, just walked past her into her room and did something to the knobs on the heating unit beneath the front window. All he said was, "Helps if you close the vent," then he left, telling her to knock on his door when she was ready to go get Allie.

"Okay," she mumbled when he was gone and heat blew from the unit, "so I'm not mechanical. Big deal."

She switched the television set on and learned there had been a yellow alert at the 30th Street Station in Philadelphia. A Metroliner had been evacuated during the morning rush hour. False alarm. There was renewed Mideast tension. A suicide bomber in Jerusalem. Gold was up, the DOW down sixty points, Nasdaq up ten. An Arctic cold front was pushing down into the central U.S. And it was a balmy eighty degrees in Orlando. The Avalanche had beaten the Redwings in last night's game in Detroit.

She clicked off the TV and checked the digital clock. An hour before they were to meet Allie. What was Ray doing, making calls to Aspen, catching a nap, oiling his revolver?

He was full of it, she decided. He wasn't going to shoot anybody in cold blood. *Two* people. No matter what he'd told her. "Believe it," he'd said. Well, she didn't. Maybe she wasn't a perfect judge of character, but in his case she was positive he wouldn't have gone through with his threat. It was understandable he wanted revenge, for himself and for his dead partner, Kathleen. The partner that was so much more than simply a coworker. Anyone would want revenge. But he wouldn't have pulled the trigger. He was too . . . She searched for the word. Principled.

She found herself taking her sketch pad from its case and sitting cross-legged on the bed, pencil in hand. She often sketched to wile away the time. Drawing calmed her. Except recently. She hadn't been drawing as much as she usually did. But it was not a rapist's face she was after tonight.

She sketched in the lines of Ray's head, a nicely shaped head—perfect ears. She then went to work on the features, the long thin nose and narrow lips with the little dip in the center, and serious, almond-shaped eyes below dark brows. The hollows under the cheekbones and strong jawline, even shading the mottled skin, wondering how far below his neck the scars ran.

His hair, thick and slightly curling, a few gray tips around his sideburns. Every so often she cocked her head and bit her lip and held the sketch pad at arms' length, studying the emerging face. Not bad. Not too bad at all. It was pleasurable drawing Ray, a sort of release. She must have had the lines and contours and shadows in her head for days. The only trouble with the likeness was the lack of color. He had that rare golden skin coupled with pale blue eyes that was so terribly striking. Even his hair, a deep shade of brown, complemented his skin tones, making him all the more stunningly attractive. And the hint of silver at his hairline ... But, alas, she rarely sketched in color; black and white was her medium.

He was truly handsome. Even with the brows drawn together in a frown, he was good-looking, a little dangerous-looking, a man you wouldn't want to cross.

Studying her artwork once more, glancing briefly at the digital clock—still time before they had to leave—she turned the sketch pad on end and drew a stylized man's body with the lines and shaded hollows she imagined would be a good likeness to Ray. Long well-shaped limbs and hands, narrow hips and flat belly, broad shoulders and hard chest muscles. She shaded in the chest hair, knowing this was pure conjecture, then a thin line of hair running down his stomach and tapering, disappearing ... She wasn't about to sketch the rest of him, though in art school she'd certainly drawn her fair share of nudes, men and women alike.

She critiqued her work. It was Ray, all right, and she'd even captured the scowl perfectly.

She tore off the page, put the pad aside, stood and stretched, then opened her suitcase and took her makeup case into the bathroom. She washed her face, brushed her teeth, and reapplied her makeup. Her hair had been in a silver clasp all day and she brushed it out. That was better, less severe.

She checked the clock. Twenty minutes to wait. God, she hoped she could have even a miniscule success tonight. Time was rushing by, time that Kirstin didn't have. They needed to get a lead quickly, and the days were passing. Days that Kirstin suffered through, waiting, waiting. She felt the burden weighing her down, time rolling on like a steamroller, flattening everything in its path, and she was trying to find the key that turned the machine off, but she couldn't find it. She took a deep breath and bent her head, putting her fingers on her forehead. *They'd find Kirstin. They would.*

She glanced again at the sketch of Ray that lay on the bed. Why on earth had she drawn him? She'd never attempted a likeness to Alan. She stared at Ray's face and thought that despite the frown, she'd come up with a rather sympathetic rendition, captured the tormented soul in his eyes. Ray, who considered her life's work bullshit.

She was a sucker for strong, wounded men. First Alan, whose child was murdered and, on the heels of that unimaginable tragedy, his wife Maureen had walked out on him. Now Ray Vanover had obviously touched her deeply. She admitted she cared too much for what he'd suffered and, if he'd let her, she'd open her heart to him and do her utmost to help him.

God, who was she kidding? He was probably still in love with the woman who'd been killed in Seattle. Kathleen Bachman. His lover, the woman he wanted to marry. What in hell made Jane think *she* could help him?

She'd tried last night after dinner. It embarrassed her now to remember. Touched his face, kissed him. For a moment then she'd thought he thawed, his expression softening, his body leaning toward her. A single inexpressible moment, gone in a flash. Why did she do things like that? What on earth did she hope to gain?

Nice mess, she thought, and she gazed at the sketch and felt a pang of guilt. Why hadn't she spent the night trying to commit Alan's face to paper?

She picked up her cell phone, pressing Alan's number. He answered on the third ring. His voice, Alan's beloved voice. Her spirits took wing.

"Jane," he said, "it's great to hear from you."

Her heart was singing now.

"So where are you?"

"Oh, boy, well, not in Aspen. I flew out to L.A. yesterday with the FBI agent on Kirstin's case. I'm up in Mammoth Lakes. Actually, a town called Toms Place. Just a few miles outside the resort. No way could we get rooms over the holidays."

"I've been trying to follow the case through Caroline, but her information is sketchy. Have there been any breaks? Have you had any luck with the witnesses?"

"Some. Not enough, though." She told him about the broken nose and earring and Ford Ranger pickup. "But it's so little, Alan. I just thought if I could see Allie Sanchez out here again . . ."

"It's been, what? Five, six years? I don't know, Jane, you're asking a lot of yourself, not to mention the Sanchez girl."

She was ready to defend her decision to fly to California, when he said, "Just a sec," and she heard a muffled sound, as if he'd put his hand over the receiver. She could make out a few words. ". . . about a case. Okay, honey." *Honey?* "Be there in a minute. . . . Sorry Jane," he said, his hand obviously removed from the mouthpiece, "what were you saying?"

"Was that . . . Maureen?" she asked, her pride crumbling.

"Ah . . . yes. Look," he lowered his voice now. *Goddamn him.* "We're trying to work things out. You knew that."

Damn, damn, damn. "Yes," she managed, "but, Alan, I . . . I guess I just miss you sometimes, miss what we had. It's been . . . difficult." She couldn't believe how pathetic she sounded, how hurt and confused. She was practically begging for any tiny shred of encouragement from him.

He was clearly uncomfortable, and there was no way he was going to do any soul-searching with Maureen in the house. Was she living there now, or just stopping by?

"Listen," he said, "keep me posted on the case, okay?

And when you get back to Denver, we'll talk. I'm sorry I can't right now, but you understand."

"Oh, sure. Well, I . . . ah, I better go now. Ray's waiting."

"Ray . . . Vanover?"

"Um, yes, we flew out here together."

"I see. Well, good luck and call me."

"Bye, Alan." She severed the connection. *Shit,* she thought, squeezing her eyes shut, her heart hammering. *Shit.*

She sagged onto the bed, burying her face. She heard it then, the shower running next door in Ray's room. An instant, shockingly vivid picture of him materialized in her head. Her stomach clenched. She was so disgusted with herself she felt like vomiting.

It had been a super day on the slopes. The sun had been out and the temperature moderate for this time of year, but not too warm, which would have ruined the snow. A perfect powder skiing day. Though some of the runs had been a little too crowded for his liking. The best days were when he had the entire mountain to himself. But the holidays would be over soon enough and then, right after New Year's, the tourists would all go home to put their cute kiddies back in school and the mountains would be his again.

Good fucking riddance to the tourists. They did nothing to line his pockets.

He shouldered his way through the local drinking crowd at Zo's Bar and bumped open the door to the men's room with his elbow. There was a guy in the single stall on the shitter and one using the urinal. He waited. Then it was his turn. Christ, he had to take a leak. Four beers'll do that. He unbuttoned his 501s, held himself with his right hand, let the stream come arcing out while he hitched his shoulders and dropped them, rolled his neck from side to side until it cracked. Sweet Jesus, that felt good.

He shook himself off, rebuttoned his jeans, and noticed the sign: WASH YOUR HANDS. *Yeah, right.*

He shoved his way back through the door, and he ran directly into her. She was standing in the line for the ladies' room. So underage it was a joke.

She looked very shy and ill at ease, and her blunt-cut brown hair swung onto a pink cheek when she ducked her head and said, "Excuse me."

"Well, excuse *me*," he said back, pausing, grinning, noting the cute round glasses she wore. His penis sat up and noticed, too.

He made his way back to the crowded bar and drained his beer, sliding a dollar toward the bartender.

Time to split. No point risking a DUI. For more reasons than one. He was looking forward to getting home anyway. Though, he admitted, shrugging on his old navy-blue parka, she was starting to bore him. He still wanted her. But not with the overpowering urgency as before. Thing was, he was beginning to fantasize the end to their domestic arrangement. A few more days.

It was real cold out. Brittle. He climbed in his truck, warmed the engine while his breath plumed in the cold interior, forming little fog rings on the driver's side window.

Yeah, it would be good to get on home. Shove some food and water into her. Wouldn't want her to get weak. Not yet.

The needle of the temperature gauge crept upwards, and he put the truck in gear. Homeward bound. The little lady was waiting.

ELEVEN

Deputy Joe Delaney flashed the driver of the pickup truck over at the Buttermilk Mountain traffic light. It was going on 8 PM Mountain Time. The guy had been speeding as he'd left Aspen, then he'd pushed the yellow light at Cemetery Lane and gone over the centerline crossing the Maroon Creek Bridge.

The driver performed the roadside sobriety test poorly and blew a 1.2 on the Breathalyzer. He stank of beer and cigars, admitted he'd been at a ski patrol keg party. For Joe this pullover was routine on a Friday night. What got his attention was the make of the pickup—a Ford Ranger. Its color—deep red. And the man wore glasses and his hair was a dirty blond color.

Joe hauled him in, where Sheriff Kent Schilling met them, and sat the man down in the interrogation room in the basement of the Pitkin County Courthouse.

"You want a lawyer?" Kent asked dutifully.

The man said he had nothing to hide.

* * *

At seven-thirty Pacific Time, Jane heard Ray's cell phone ring. They'd arrived at the Christmas Shoppe at seven sharp, but were still waiting for Allie to run out the register for the night.

"You did?" Ray said into the handset, his tone on the verge of excitement. "Ski patrol on Aspen Mountain, huh? How about glasses? . . . All right. Earring? How about a broken nose?"

She listened, and her heart began a heavy cadence.

"Dark red truck, a Ranger? Jesus," Ray said. Then he listened, nodded, his eyes meeting Jane's over a rack of iridescent ribbons. "Uh huh," he went on. "A what? . . . An ACL? When?" He listened again. "Opening day of the season? When's that, Thanksgiving? Well, if he tore his ACL three weeks ago, couldn't he be back on skis?" Ray was saying, but Jane's hopes crashed to earth. No way could someone be back on skis—not until next year. And a ski patrolman wouldn't dream of risking a reinjury even if he were healing miraculously.

"Have you spoken to the surgeon?" Ray said. "Have you even *seen* the guy's knee? He might be lying." He listened, and then said, "Call me as soon as you talk to this doctor. Goddamn, I was hoping there for a moment. . . . Okay. I'll be waiting." He clicked off.

He turned to Jane. "You heard?"

"Yes. And unfortunately, assuming he's telling the truth about his knee, there's no way he could have been skiing last weekend. No way."

"He could be lying. He could have panicked when he got DUIed and come up with that story."

"He *could* be telling the truth," she said.

She felt a sudden weariness. Her emotions over the last

few days had been running the gamut. A moment ago she'd been awash with hope and now she was drained. Up and down, her pulse rising under her skin one second, sinking the next. But her problems were nothing compared to what Kirstin Lemke was going through. She clung to that thought and breathed in the spice-scented air in the shop, the Christmas lights twinkling merrily around her, candle flames dancing, toys shining on shelves, bows and ribbons glittering, ornaments dangling prettily from decorated trees.

Allie called from the rear of the store that she'd be just another minute, and again Jane felt a surge of emotion, but this time it was futility.

Ray was waiting an aisle over, cell phone still in hand, frowning, obviously disappointed. Jane joined him and together they watched a miniature toy train make its circuits, round and round, past the depot, past the forest, under a bridge, through the blinking railroad crossing lights, back to town.

"Had almost the same train when I was a kid," he said. "Wonder what happened to it."

And she recalled without a bridging thought a train her dad used to set up every Christmas. Funny, she'd never recalled that before. But then Roland had come on the scene, and her dad had left, a brokenhearted man. She wondered what had become of his train. Had her mother thrown it out, given it to a thrift shop?

Ray broke their shared reverie. "Goddamn it, for a minute there, I thought they might have him in custody."

"Me, too," she whispered.

They left the store shortly, Allie locking up behind them. She'd grown into a very responsible young lady. They even stopped by a night depository at the bank, where she dropped the deposit bag into the slot for the store owner to retrieve on Monday morning.

The Christmas Shoppe and the bank were both located in the core of Mammoth Lakes, the resort village that rested at the base of Mammoth Mountain ski area. The town was bustling with holiday revelers. Along Old Mammoth Road and Main Street couples and families walked past restaurants and saloons and rows of new condo complexes, chimneys spewing wood smoke into the black, star-studded sky.

Allie lived outside town in an apartment building that backed up to Mammoth Creek. She hadn't always lived here. When Jane had first interviewed her, she and her parents and one sister had lived farther down Route 203, which eventually ran into Toms Place, where Jane and Ray were staying. Now, it was just Allie and her mother. There'd been a divorce.

Allie showed Ray were to park, then led them into the apartment, explaining her sister had married and moved to Fresno, and her mom was at work running the front desk at a ski lodge till eleven.

So young still, and so grown up, Jane thought, taking off her coat, watching Allie as she let the cat out and switched on lights, checked for phone messages. Yet she'd stayed back a year in school and was not going to graduate until a year from the coming spring. With her dark hair pinned up—she'd long since grown out her bangs—her glasses, her shy maturity, she seemed so much older than eighteen. Then again, her ordeal had forced maturity on her far too early. Jane knew only too well about *that.*

Ray seemed particularly impatient as they settled in the small living room. Again Jane wished he'd waited in the car or stayed back at the motel. If only he'd just go for a drink. His tension was a living entity to her, hovering close, ready to pounce. She wondered if he was preoccupied with the Lemke case and the call from the sheriff or with his own personal troubles.

Allie was as forthcoming as Jane recalled from their first

meeting. She had not repressed her memories at all. And she was eager to learn about Kirstin's situation, asking Jane if the man had used a knife to subdue her—which Jane could not answer. Allie wanted to know if he still drove a truck, if he'd followed the Aspen victim on the ski slopes, if the two friends had been of any help in identifying him.

It turned out that the girl had been in counseling on and off since her kidnapping and rape. She'd apparently worked very hard to confront her feelings and not hide from them. Through her contact with Jane over the years, she knew that the same man had abducted at least two more girls—one of whom had died.

Allie had already spent a good deal of time with her therapist probing her hidden memories. "But even after trying for years, all I can see is just this vague face behind the goggles and neck gaiter," she told Jane. "I used to think maybe I blocked out his face or something, but now I'm not so sure. I never saw him, not really. And that room he had me in, it was so dark. Even in the day, only a little light showed from the sides of these curtains."

"He never came to you during the day, did he, Allie?" Jane asked.

The girl shook her head. "Never. I guess he was smart."

"More like calculating," Jane said. She hated to think of the UNSUB as smart.

"How about the vehicle he drove?" Jane said, switching directions.

"A pickup truck. I've always remembered the truck. He didn't make me wear that pull-down wool hat till after I was in the cab. So I knew it was a pickup. See, he asked me for directions when he was standing in the parking lot, and when he made me get in the truck, he sort of, well, stood there in the way, so I couldn't see much. And he had that knife, and I was so scared."

"I know, Allie. It must've been awful."

The girl's eyes shone with tears. She nodded.

"Okay, he asked for directions, then he pulled out a knife? I'm trying to get the sequence of events here."

"Yes."

"And then he sort of . . . herded you into the truck?"

Another nod.

"On the driver's side?"

"Yes. He pushed me so I'd slide over and then he got in."

Something itched in Jane's head then, as she saw the kidnapping unfold in her mind's eye. What was it? Had Lisa, the Snowbird victim, said something similar? About being herded into the truck?

She had assumed, as had the FBI, that the man forced the girls into the truck with only one goal—to keep them under control with his knife. But what if he . . . what if there was some other significance to his actions? What if he was trying to shield his truck from them? The license plates? But none of the victims or witnesses had ever seen a plate. They were probably too encrusted with road sludge to read. Almost all plates in the winter were. There was no way to tell if the UNSUB had deliberately obscured his plates or not.

What if he were trying to hide something else about his vehicle? An off-color door, a distinctive dent, a logo on the side? Something by which the victim could identify his truck.

Allie's gaze was fixed on Jane, and she had to shake off her musings. "Can you see the truck, Allie?" she asked. "Maybe the tailgate?"

Allie closed her eyes. "Um. It was . . . dirty. But I've always been sure it was red. A dark red."

"Any writing you can see?"

Jane had given her the Play-Doh at the start of the interview, but Allie hadn't done anything with it. Now she unconsciously rolled it in her hands, her eyes unfocused. "Um," she said again.

Usually Jane would never put an idea in a victim's head, but she felt Allie needed a nudge. "On the tailgate," she said softly, "was there any lettering?"

And after a long minute Allie's eyes flew open. "Oh, my God, it said . . . Ford. Not in like a different paint, but . . . the same paint."

"In raised lettering?" Another nudge.

"Yes," Allie breathed. "That was it. It was all dirty, but I'm sure now, yes, it was a Ford. Oh, my God."

"Good girl," Jane said, and she caught Ray's glance for a moment. He was only mildly impressed. This was mere corroboration to already known evidence.

Allie was eager to tell Jane small details she'd remembered while working with her therapist. She had recalled a few of the words the man had said to her before he'd forced her into the truck. "He told me if I didn't come with him he'd find my family and kill them. And he was poking me with the knife. I *believed* it was a knife, anyhow. It felt like one. And once he said if I looked at him he'd hurt me. But he was whispering, you know? So no one could hear?"

"Allie, did he ever speak to you when he came to you at night? I know this is difficult, but . . ."

She shook her head. "He said stuff in one word, like eat, or drink, and he'd untie my hands and leave for a while. Then he'd come back and tie me up again."

"Did he ever come in the room during the day?"

"A couple times. But it was so dark, and I think he was wearing that hat and neck gaiter. I *think*."

"Okay," Jane said.

She tried a few more tactics to prompt a new memory from Allie, but either too much time had passed, or the girl simply had no more information to be brought to light.

Allie never mentioned an earring or the misshapen nose, so Jane left those details alone.

"Are you going to talk to Gary again?" Allie asked. She was referring to the witness to her kidnapping, Gary Francis.

"Yes, tomorrow. We're lucky he's home on Christmas break," Jane said.

"He goes to Berkeley," Allie said in a regretful voice.

"I know," Jane said. At nine-thirty she gave Allie a hug at the door, promised to let her know as soon as Kirstin was found, and she and Ray left. She got into the rental car and bit her lip in frustration and disappointment.

Ray was infuriatingly quiet.

They were on Route 203 driving toward Toms Place when she couldn't stand his silent treatment another second. "Okay," she said, turning to him, "I know what you're thinking."

"You do?"

"Oh, yes. You're *thinking* this was a waste of time."

"You said it, I didn't."

She turned her attention to the road, the oncoming headlights blinding. "It *was* a waste of time. I just couldn't find a way to reach inside her. Damn. There has to be a way, something one of these girls . . . There's got to be a way to free their memories."

"Did it ever occur to you that there isn't anything to free? Maybe you already got it all. Years ago."

"Oh, bullshit."

"Whoa."

"One of them or all of them, it doesn't matter, but *one* of them holds the key, and I can't get it out of them. I can't reach them. It makes me want to scream."

"I really wish you wouldn't."

"Figuratively."

"Um. Good. I was worried for a minute."

"You're trying to placate me right now."

"No, I'm not. I just think you're being too hard on your-self. I'll allow that you've had some success with other cases. But this one has you stumped. You're making too much of it. There isn't anything more to get from these girls. Let it go, Jane."

She shook her head and squeezed her eyes tightly shut. He was wrong.

They parked at the motel and walked across the icy road to a diner. By the time they ordered sandwiches, it was nearly ten.

Ray had coffee while they awaited their dinners. At one point he stared at the cup, and he said, "Jesus, you see that? The coffee is shimmering, rippling or something."

"Earthquake," she said dully. "They have small tremors here all the time. Some big ones, too."

"Goddamn."

"Um," she said, distracted.

The food came, and she looked down at her plate, real-izing she had no appetite.

Ray dumped ketchup on his fries and dug in. "Aren't you hungry?" he asked after a minute, his mouth full.

She shook her head. "I shouldn't have come here," she reflected. "I shouldn't have even taken this case on again. I was on sabbatical. I . . . I needed time away from all this tension. Last year, after Jennifer Weissman died, I . . . I just couldn't take the pressure anymore."

He'd stopped eating, his attention focused solely on her. She felt her skin crawl. Why was she admitting this?

"So, what is it about this case, Jane?"

Her heart kicked against her rib cage.

"What is it?" he pressed, his voice gravelly and smooth at the same time. But with an edge.

She raised her glance from the untouched food and felt her neck muscles tighten. Would it hurt to confess the truth? She'd told Alan and lived through it. Even felt relieved.

"Jane?"

She let out a ragged sigh. "This case is too close to home. I've never pulled the right details from any of the girls' memories. I just can't make a breakthrough."

"*Too close to home*, you said."

She wrapped her fingers around her water glass and studied her fingernails, the blood rising to her cheeks. She just couldn't tell him the story. She couldn't.

"Jane?"

With effort she looked up, and she knew. She didn't have to confess, he'd already figured it out. She could read that look in his eyes, the pity, the disgust. He was a cop, after all. He *knew*.

She suddenly felt dirty and used and so ashamed, as if she'd been responsible for the violation of her body. Women always asked for it, right? Even innocent sixteen-year-olds.

Goddamn it.

She snatched her purse and coat and stood so fast her knee knocked the table, water sloshing from her glass.

"What are you . . . ?" he began, but she lifted a hand, shook her head, and walked out into the frigid night, coat trailing, clutching her purse to her stomach. She almost got run over by an SUV speeding through the town. She didn't give a damn.

Inside her room, panting, she put on the chain lock and flipped the dead bolt, then she tore off her clothes and dropped them on the bathroom floor, got into the shower, sagging against the back wall and crying her heart out.

She cried for Allie and Lisa and Jennifer. She cried for herself and the injustice of the world. Mostly she cried for

Kirstin. Needing Jane so badly, and she couldn't do a thing to help. *Nothing*.

Eventually, she managed to stop her tears and put aside the useless self-pity. So what if Ray knew? Screw him. *Screw them all.*

Ten minutes later she was in her pajamas, her wet hair combed back, teeth brushed. She'd fall asleep watching the news, and in the morning she'd feel much better and could face him again. Let him think what he wanted. She couldn't care less.

But she didn't watch TV. She sat on the side of the bed and stared at her artist's case and the sketch pad showing through the half open zipper. If she could just remember . . . Somewhere in a forgotten corner of her mind, where she stuffed all unpleasant memories, was his face. All these years she'd felt guilty and ashamed and dirty. She knew that. She also logically knew she was not responsible for the rape. She even accepted the misplaced guilt as normal. So if she knew all that, why couldn't she remember?

It had been an autumn weekend, Indian summer in the Rockies, and her mother and Lottie Schilling had cooked up the idea for one last camping hoorah before the early snows blanketed the high country. Everyone was up for the trip. Everyone but her, because she would have rather spent the weekend with girlfriends in town, ride their mountain bikes to Snowmass, catch a movie, see what was happening downtown. She hated camping and fishing. Boring.

But Hannah insisted. Even her sister was keen on the idea; Gwen's new boyfriend George had bought a brand-new CJ5 Jeep, and Gwen wanted to show off George and the Jeep to the family.

Roland and Kent, of course, were the first to say great idea. Kent would tow the speedboat up to Reudi Reservoir, twenty miles above the town of Basalt.

Lottie and Kent's twin girls were only five years old then, and they were excited. "Wow, camping! Can we bring marshmallows?"

And Scott, Jane's to-die-for stepbrother. A senior at Aspen High, he was game for the trip, too, organizing the fishing gear, showing Jane a bottle of brandy he planned on bringing.

"Big deal," she said loftily when he brandished it at her in the garage, then hid the bottle in his backpack.

"So don't have any." He shrugged. "All the more for me."

They left on Friday after school let out. Three vehicles to carry so much gear, Kent and Lottie and the twins towing the boat in their big Blazer. Even their two golden retrievers rode along. Roland drove Hannah, of course, and Scott rode with them. Jane went with Gwen and George in his new fire-engine red Jeep. She remembered the hard shell top was off, and the afternoon was glorious as they passed the bloodred mountains called Seven Castles on the climb to Reudi, the aspens and cottonwoods brilliant in their golden mantles, the sky utterly pellucid, the Frying Pan River they followed crystal clear, white rushing water splashing over smooth burnt umber rocks.

With little daylight left, the men only fished for an hour while the women and kids set up camp. Jane pitched her little orange tent away from the others. Oh so independent. There were steaks and baked potatoes wrapped in foil and cooked in the bed of embers from the campfire. The sun died over the shores of the reservoir, an evening breeze ruffled the surface of the water and stirred the leaves on shore. The earth smelled fecund.

Jane and the twins secretly ate Hershey bars before dinner. And after the steaks and potatoes, the dogs got the bones, Scott trimmed cottonwood twigs for everyone and they all had fire-blackened marshmallows—except for Gwen, who had become a dainty eater in front of her new love.

George did the dishes in grit from a stream with the help of Roland and Kent. Male bonding. Scott rebuilt the fire. Red embers burst from the fresh sap in the logs and shot into the night sky. The men had their share of stream-chilled beers, the women, too. Scott secretly nipped his brandy. Jane and the twins drank hot chocolate. The stars were brilliant diamonds in the black velvet bowl overhead. One of the twins spotted a satellite orbiting the earth.

"Or a UFO," Lottie Schilling suggested, teasing the girls.

They all slept well, snug in their sleeping bags, Kent's golden retrievers keeping the bears and raccoons away. Jane remembered hearing a coyote song from the ridge above, but she wasn't afraid. Foxes and coyotes roamed freely all over the valley. Only house cats needed to fear them.

The next day, Saturday, was deliciously warm. They fished and boated; Scott water-skied in a wetsuit. Jane hung out with the twins in the morning, wild mushroom hunting. In the afternoon she hiked above the ridge with Gwen and George. That night she was raped. On Sunday, no one seemed to notice how silent and withdrawn she was. She went for a walk, alone, and cried the morning away. She rode home with Hannah and Roland and Scott, huddling in the back, pretending to be asleep. Her heart pounded in shame and fear. It still did.

She picked up the sketch pad and her pencil and sat with the pillows behind her back in the backwoods town of Toms Place and began to draw, stream of consciousness lines coming out of her hand. A round face, but no features, square shoulders, sharp boned, a long body. But it was no good. The drawing was nobody or could have been anybody.

She put the pad aside, reached for the light switch, turned the lights off, and heard the knock.

"Jane? You asleep?" Ray.

"I'm trying to sleep," she called out.

"Sorry, but I thought you'd want to know Kent Schilling called to say the pickup truck driver was a flash in the pan. They let him go."

"Fine," she called, the paper-thin door no barrier.

"Ah," she heard him mutter, "I'll see you in the morning. Okay?"

"Fine," she repeated, but she was out of bed now, hugging herself, standing in the dark, her pulse heavy again. *Go to bed, Ray.*

She heard his footfalls crunch in the snow, made out the sound of a key being shoved in a lock. But then nothing. For an eternity, nothing. Then the footfalls again.

His voice through the wood. "Are you all right?"

"Damnit, I'm fine." She was standing in front of the door now, the room warm, but she was shivering.

"Look," he said after a moment, "will you open the door a sec? There's something I'd like to say."

She stood stock-still.

"I really don't want the whole goddamn place to hear, Jane. Open up."

"Go away."

"Just open the door. Damnit, Jane."

She felt uncertain and reluctant as she finally reached up and slid the chain aside, then flipped the dead bolt. She eased the door open a crack. The bitter cold air struck her face like a knife blade.

"That's better," he said, the light behind him, his expression hidden in shadow. "I just need to tell you I was an idiot at dinner. The last thing I wanted to do was embarrass you. Okay?"

She thought a minute, tried to still the rapid thud in her chest. Ray . . . apologizing? His voice, that honey-rough voice, probing her feelings.

Without thinking, she pulled the door open and stood aside. "Come in a minute," she said, and she made her way to the light over the table by the window, switching it on.

She turned back to him. "I'm the one who should apologize," she began. "You hit a sensitive spot."

She couldn't meet his eyes as she spoke. "I was sixteen. A bunch of us were on a camping trip. One of the men with us came into my tent and . . ." She swallowed hard, tried to continue.

He was listening, hands in his jacket pockets, his face carefully set in neutral. A professional interrogator's face. "You don't have to tell me," he murmured.

But she did have to. The words rose in her throat like a sickness, and she had to vomit them out to relieve the unbearable nausea.

She sank down on the side of the bed, her forehead leaning on her hand, the light pooling on the table, leaving her in shadow. He stood as still as a rock.

"It was dark, and I couldn't see who it was. Or maybe . . . maybe I did see his face, then I forgot it. But I remember the way it *felt,* the awful loss. And the shame. And I guess . . . I guess I never really got over it. That's why I can't, I tried, but the girls . . . they're like me, and I can't . . . get anything."

She took a deep breath. "So, I was raped. And the awful thing, the . . . Oh, I don't know, the worst part, was that it was someone I *knew.* One of those men you just met in Aspen. Now you know why I avoid them, why I didn't want to make the trip there." She drew in a shuddering breath. "So you can figure out why I failed with this case. If I can't put a face to the man who abused me, how can I expect to put a face to this monster who rapes over and over and over?"

He nodded slowly.

Then, not comprehending exactly why, she said, "You

remember when you asked me about Alan . . . Alan Gallagher?"

"Yes," he said.

"Well, Alan is the only man I've trusted since that day seventeen years ago. He's the only one who knows the whole story . . . except you. And he's the only man I've ever . . . ever . . ."

Ray again nodded. He understood.

"I don't know why I just told you all that," she suddenly said, fumbling, realizing she'd poured her guts out to this man, a man who was practically a stranger, who . . .

"Come here," he said, so softly she thought she hadn't heard. And when she didn't move, couldn't even take a breath, he came to her. He didn't say another thing. He didn't have to. He reached up and took her face in his hands, his pale eyes searching hers for a heartbeat, and then his mouth covered hers, gently, lips barely touching. She still couldn't make her muscles respond to the message from her brain—*no, Jane, no.* She just stood there, her knees softening, her hands hanging by her sides, gooseflesh raised on her skin, and she let him kiss her, his hands on her face.

Then he dropped his hands, stepped back. "I shouldn't have done that," he said.

But the terrible truth was she wanted him, every facet of him. *Wrong, wrong, wrong,* her mind cried.

Later she would analyze the next moments. Many times over. She would envision them as exquisite pearls on a long strand. Each pearl individual, full and round and glistening with promise, each bringing her closer to a decision until she'd come full circle. *Wrong,* this was all wrong, crazy, foolhardy, reckless . . . And he was in love with another woman, a dead woman, someone Jane could never compete with.

But all her mental anguish vanished and she said, "Hold me, Ray, make me forget." She closed her eyes and he was there again, his arms around her back, his mouth on hers, pulling her to him tightly, his lips parting hers, his tongue circling hers.

She responded with an abandon she had never dreamed of, even with Alan, patient, patient and gentle Alan . . .

Ray crushed her to him, and she held on shamelessly, her arms snaking around his neck as they sagged onto the bed, Ray cupping her hips in his hands over the slippery satin pajamas and forcing her up toward the center of the mattress. He rose above her for a moment, began to undo the satin covered buttons, slowly pulling aside the material over her arms until her breasts were bare.

"The light?" she whispered. She and Alan . . . Alan . . .

But Ray said, "No," and he threw his jacket aside, pulled his sweater and turtleneck off and tossed them. She saw the extent of his burns then, the red puckered skin that ran in a swath from his jaw down his neck to his shoulder and down his arm. *Oh, God, the pain he'd suffered.*

He started to say something, she never knew what, but she stopped him with a finger to his lips then she touched the scars, caressed them, and asked if she was hurting him.

"No," he said, "God, no," and his head lowered to her neck, her collarbone, her breasts, which he took one by one into his mouth, his teeth on her, softly, until her breath snatched in her throat.

Hands on her hips again, he raised her and slid the bottoms off, his lips on her belly, her hip, tingling, sending darts of need so deep inside her she gasped.

He took his own clothes off and kicked them away, stretched his long length against hers, easing her to him, kissing her mouth, her breasts again, his hands on her thighs, opening them.

He moved inside quickly, and her breath came in catches. She drew her legs up, receiving him. Then, as she felt the wild rising, he withdrew and coaxed her to straddle him.

She was panting, her skin sweat slick on his. "I don't . . . I've never . . ." she breathed, but he showed her, positioning her, his hands on her breasts as she arched her spine, her head falling back, hands finding his sharp hipbones, fingers pressing against him. And she took him and he took her.

Sometime before dawn she awoke and felt the sweet soreness between her legs. She smiled. She reached for him. The bed was empty.

TWELVE

"Your guy is going to escalate," Jack said.

"Yeah, I know," Ray replied.

It was very early in the morning in California, but late enough in Quantico, Virginia, for Special Agent Jack Singer to be in his office.

"The last three are closer together, right? The ones in Snowbird and Park City and now Aspen?"

"Right."

"This present victim, how long has she been missing?"

"Five, uh, six days."

Jack whistled. "He's getting ready to do her."

"Kirstin."

"Huh?"

"The girl's name is Kirstin Lemke."

"Oh, okay."

"Any ideas?" Ray pressed.

"You tried VICAP?" Referring to the Violent Criminals Apprehension Program, a national database.

"No matches."

"And NCMEC?" The National Center for Missing and Exploited Children.

Love those acronyms, Ray thought. "Nothing."

"Well, we can assume he's the inadequate type of situational child molester. He's probably a social outsider, a loner, a mechanic or a truck driver, something like that. And you know he has a pickup, so he can move around easily. He uses trickery to get his victim. He's the most uncommon type of molester, but the most likely to abduct and murder his victims."

"Terrific."

"Hey, you asked."

"This one is smart, too. He leaves no traces."

"Hmm. A thought-driven offender. He exercises discipline in choosing his victim. The UNSUB is not a family member, but you already know that." A pause. "White male, probably in his twenties or thirties, maybe sloppy looking."

"A broken nose," Ray said. "Blondish, tallish, thin. Truck may be a Ford Ranger, dark red or burgundy. Oh, and he wears glasses."

"And he always appears in ski areas. Interesting."

"Come on, Jack. Anything else?"

"Probably from a middle-class home, above average intelligence but an underachiever."

Ray grew impatient. "We know all that."

"Look, I'm not magic. Nobody's seen his face. You can work on a couple angles, his pickup or his job, without a face."

"You know how many pickups there are around Aspen? It's the West, man."

"You need a face."

There was a knock on his door. He got up from the bed

where he was sitting, cell phone to his ear, and went to open it. He figured it was Jane—who else could it be?—and he felt a spurt of relief that he didn't have to talk to her one on one right now. Hell, they were both adults. It had just happened. Big deal.

She stood there, and he was momentarily transfixed by her beauty, her complexion slightly pale above the tweed coat, her hair pulled back in a clip, strands escaping around her face. Hair he'd run his fingers through a few hours ago.

"Ray?" came Jack's voice.

"Yeah, I'm here." He gestured to the phone and waved her into his room. Mouthed *sit*.

"I don't really have anything else for you right now."

"Well, work on it. Bruce will keep you up to speed. And you have my cell number."

"Where in hell are you?"

"Toms Place, California. Near Mammoth Ski Area."

"The boonies."

"Yeah. Talk to you soon, Jack." He clicked off.

"Who was that?" she asked.

"An FBI profiler."

"Oh."

"He can't find a link, he can't give us more than we already have."

"I see."

"We need that face."

"Did anything happen in Aspen? I mean . . ."

"Nothing new."

"Poor Kirstin."

Maybe she wasn't going to bring up last night. What would he say if she did? Jesus, where had his brain been? Had he already forgotten Kathleen?

"We have to find her," Jane was saying. "It's been almost a week."

"I'm aware of that."

"So we go to Utah."

"That could be a waste of time," he said carefully. "I think you better . . ."

"Not that again," she said.

"I think it'd be better . . ."

"Okay, stop right there." She held up a hand. "Is this about last night? I'd never forgive myself if you used last night as an excuse to ditch me."

"It's not about that," he said stiffly.

Her glance shifted to her folded hands then rose to meet his again. "Look," she said, "last night just happened. It was a mistake. I'm hoping you can put it aside. I have. It's forgotten, okay?"

He felt a sudden kick in his gut. Relief? Regret? But he had no time to analyze his physical response. Barely missing a beat, he said, "Good. It's forgotten."

She held his eyes a moment longer, then nodded. "Now that we have that behind us, I still want to talk to Gary before we leave."

Gary? Then he remembered, the one male witness to the abductions lived down the valley on the route back to L.A.

"Gary," Ray said. "Fine." He would've agreed to anything just to get out of that motel and on the road.

Last night. He must've been out of his mind, especially after Jane had told him Gallagher was the only man she'd been with since she was raped. It was damn near impossible for him to believe she just wanted to forget that romp in her room. *No way.* In his experience women did not forget things like that.

He tossed his clothes and shaving kit in his bag, his back to her. *Shit, shit, shit.*

They drove to Bishop, the small town thirty miles from Mammoth Lakes where Gary Francis lived. A Berkeley student, home on Christmas break. Ray pulled up at the address. Nice place. A real log cabin nestled in the pines, a wreath on the door, three wood-stick reindeer strung with lights in the front yard.

Jane took up her artist's case and purse, half opened her door. "I don't suppose it would do any good to ask you to go get coffee or something and come back in a couple hours?"

He surprised even himself when he jumped at the chance. "Okay," he said. "I'll use the time to talk to the crew in Aspen. Couple hours, you said?"

"That should be fine. Thanks," she said, casting him a quick, doubtful glance before she stepped out onto the snow-packed walk.

Three cups of coffee later at the locals' breakfast spot, he tipped the waitress handsomely and started back through Bishop to pick Jane up. He'd spoken to Bruce and Sid in Aspen, talked to the sheriff, then wiled the time away thinking about Kirstin and all the other girls— victims because of their inherited need for glasses, their height and something as simple as hair color and style. Victimized women. Either they fit a certain mold, or they were simply in the wrong place at the wrong time. Like Jane. On her camping trip.

How could she *not* know which man had raped her? And how could she have sat at her mother's table a few nights ago knowing one of them had done that to her? He couldn't help wonder which man. Or maybe the man hadn't been there, maybe it had been Jane's brother-in-law who'd crawled into her tent, though somehow Ray couldn't see that. Grinell had all he needed with Jane's sister—or at least that should have been the case. Truth was, you never knew what motivated some of these sick bastards.

And Jane couldn't remember the face. Blocked it out.

Just as she was blocked on this case. *Jesus Christ,* he thought, frowning as he watched her saying her good-byes to Gary Francis at the door, even accepting a hug. *Had* she gotten anything from him?

She was still talking to the Berkeley kid, nodding, when Ray halted his musing. What Jane had suffered as a girl was none of his business. She was a victim. Hell, everyone was dumped on in his or her life, right? He, himself, was no exception. But his job was never to get too involved with the victims. Empathy tended to confuse the issues. What he felt last night and just now for Jane had been misguided protectiveness. Which had nothing whatsoever to do with the Lemke abduction case. Jane's problems were her own. He'd gotten involved. He was now going to *un*involve himself.

"A chipped tooth," Jane said a little breathlessly when she was settled in the passenger seat. "Gary thinks the UNSUB had a broken front tooth. Maybe the men in Aspen could add that to . . ."

"Jane," he said, casting her a quick glance as he pulled away from the curb, "the guy might have gone to the dentist. It's been five years."

"Or maybe he hasn't," she said.

He thought a moment. "Okay, dial Bruce's number. Christ, I don't know."

She called the info in on her phone.

They arrived at FBI headquarters in downtown L.A. only minutes before the offices officially closed for the day. She hadn't asked why he was stopping there, and he didn't say. He figured she had already guessed why.

Stan was putting on his jacket when they walked down the hall into the temporary office he'd been assigned. Ray's former coworker from Seattle shook Jane's hand and introduced himself. She gave him a warm smile.

"Well," Stan said enthusiastically, "how did the trip go? Get anything useful?"

"Not much," Ray said.

"A little," Jane said at the same time.

Then, before Ray could find out if they'd gotten anything out of the Perry brothers, Stan had to wax eloquent about the bank robbery case Jane had helped to solve some years back. "I remember seeing your sketch of the subject," he said. "Damned if it didn't turn out to be an exact photographic likeness of the man. Wasn't his name Lancaster? The federal prosecutor nailed his ass in court with your drawing. What was his name, the prosecutor? Seems I once did a job in Seattle with . . ."

"Stan," Ray cut in, "I'm sure you'd like to reminisce all night with Jane, but we've got a plane to catch."

"Back to Aspen?"

"That's right. I need to . . ."

And that was when Jane launched her latest idea. "I'm going to try to catch a flight to Salt Lake City," she announced.

"You're *what?*" Ray felt the skin on his face tighten.

"I'm going to Snowbird and then Park City."

"Now, look," he began, dropping into the hard wooden chair in front of Stan's desk. "First, I'm not budgeted for that. But more importantly, I need to be in Aspen, not off on some wild-goose chase."

"Then go to Aspen," she said in a matter-of-fact voice. "You might even make the last flight in from Denver tonight. But *I* am going to Utah. As for your budget, I'll call Parker in Denver, see what I can arrange on my own with him. If not, I have credit cards." She shrugged. "If there's any hope, any hope at all of nailing this man before it's too late for Kirstin, I have to try. You can't change my mind. Now, Stan?"

"Uh-huh?" Stan cleared his throat.

"Can you tell me where the ladies room is? Ray never seems to have to stop."

"Ah, right," Stan said, "down the hall. Last door on the left."

"Thank you." She threw him a winning smile and disappeared.

"Shit," Ray muttered.

"You're, ah, not going to Salt Lake with her?" Stan raised both brows.

"Oh, man," Ray said, "she just won't quit."

Wisely, Stan let it go. "Well, okay," he said. "Okay. I take it you stopped here to check on the status of the Perry case. And I wish I had some good news."

Ray looked up sharply.

"I'm sorry, buddy," Stan said, "but they're not talking. Got themselves a top defender and mum's the word so far."

Ray leaned on the desk, his arms locked and quivering with tension. "They won't cut a deal?"

"Not yet."

"Wonderful."

"It could take a while, Ray. Hell, you knew that. Cool down."

"I've been cool for a year and a half. I'm pretty goddamn fed up with being *cool*."

"Look, I'm going to send our portrait artist back to Yakima to work with the sporting goods store owner again." Stan rubbed the bald spot on his head, causing his fringe of hair to stand up.

"That's terrific," Ray muttered. "Guy got shot in the head. He didn't remember shit then, and he won't remember shit now."

"It's worth a second try."

"Christ, Stan, maybe dusting the shop again for prints is

worth another try, too. I mean, it's only been, what? Three years?"

Stan frowned and started to say something.

Ray smacked a hand on the desktop. "I knew this was going to happen! I should have done the assholes when I had the chance!"

"Hey, take it easy. We'll . . ."

He turned to see what Stan was looking at. Jane. In the doorway, holding the knob and staring at him. She'd heard it all. Goddamnit.

For a moment the three of them were frozen in an embarrassing vacuum, then Jane said, "Sorry, I, ah, thought you were, well . . ."

Ray whistled out a ragged breath. "It's okay, Stan, I told her about the Perrys."

"Um, I see," Stan said. Then he cocked his head at Jane. "Did he also tell you about the mastermind of this militant sect?"

"Not really," she said, and the next thing Ray knew, Stan was bringing her up to speed on the entire case. ". . . so we believe the Northwest Bomber was not only behind that car bombing, but six other previous bombings and the shooting of the shop owner in Yakima three years ago. Left the poor sap for dead. Ben Forsberg is the name. Real nice fellow, but our police artist was never able to get a composite of the shooter. Now Ray here thinks . . ."

"*Stan,*" Ray warned, but it was already too late.

"I wonder if *I* could have a shot at getting a sketch," Jane said.

And Stan. "You know, you just took the words right out of my mouth."

"If I'm already in Utah, I could take a few hours to fly up to Spokane, and . . ."

Ray could almost see the lightbulb switching on in Stan's

head. "Hey," Stan said, interrupting Jane. "Better yet, if I can get an okay from the SAC in Seattle, I could have Forsberg flown to Salt Lake. Even accompany him myself. Can't be more than an hour's flight. If you think you'll have time, that is. I know you're very busy with the Lemke case."

"I'll have time. I'll *make* the time," she replied.

"Okay, enough." Ray shot to his feet. "You're asking too damn much of her. How the hell is she going to focus on the Lemke case and try to get a sketch of the Northwest Bomber at the same time?"

"Now wait a minute," Jane broke in. "Why should you care when you won't even be there? You're heading back to Aspen, remember?"

She had him there.

"And furthermore, I freelance, as you well know. I can pick and choose what cases I take on."

Jesus. "I never said you couldn't," he began. "I just don't know why you'd want to."

She shook her head.

"What?" he said.

"You are really thick, aren't you?"

"I still don't see . . ."

"Oh, for Pete's sakes, I'd like to help, that's all."

Ray started to say something, caught himself, shut up, and the room went dead silent.

THIRTEEN

He barely spoke on the early morning flight to Salt Lake City. She tried to ignore his preoccupation, giving him a rundown on her phone call to the Snowbird victim, Lisa Turchelli.

"Lisa's sixteen now. She's working in her family's grocery store in Snowbird Center, and she was pretty upset when I called."

"Is that so."

"She said her parents don't want her interviewed anymore. They think she's been *tortured* enough. That's the word she used."

"Uh-huh."

"I think I can convince them. They're decent people, but you can imagine—they're just being protective."

She wished he wasn't so distant. He was dressed in his official clothes—dark suit and the same overcoat he'd worn the first night she'd met him. The formality of his attire would have made him unapproachable, even if his manner didn't. The whole situation was making her uncomfortable, and along with the discomfort, she simply couldn't dam the flood of emotions that sucked her along every time she glanced at him. She felt sympathy, certainly, for what he'd suffered in the bombing and what he still suffered, that all encompassing need to avenge the death of the woman he'd loved. He was so emotionally wounded, so very alone in his pain, and he was too proud to accept comfort from another human being. She badly wanted to help him. She needed to, if not for his sake, then for hers. *Don't shut everyone out,* Ray, she thought. *Don't shut me out.* And she had slept with him. Blood stung her face every time she remembered awakening yesterday to the empty bed. She had slept with him, touched every part of him, opened herself, body and mind to him, *trusted* him. Even with Alan she'd never let go like that, clinging and clawing and crying aloud her most intimate longings. She'd never known abandon. Why Ray? Why now? *Let's just forget it happened,* she'd said. Oh, sure. One of the biggest things that had happened in her adult life and she was going to forget it?

She glanced sideways at his profile: dark brows drawn together, deep vertical grooves in his cheeks. Had she ever seen him smile? Did he laugh?

She had taken the window seat, Ray on the aisle. The space between them was empty. She stared out the window at the harshly delineated land below. Once they'd flown northeast of the California-Nevada border, the landscape became rock and more rock, as far as the eye could see. The earth was so empty, a moonscape except for a dusting of snow on the northern exposures of the deep rifts.

She rested her chin on a hand and refocused, studying Ray's image in the thick glass. Okay, she'd slept with him, had herself a real one-night stand. So where did that leave her? Thirty-six hours ago, she would have sworn she was still in love with Alan. Maybe she was. She considered the idea that she might have slept with Ray as payback to Alan, but the notion didn't feel right. Vengeance was Ray's method of dealing with pain, not hers. Then why *had* she slept with him? Loneliness? Or as a few hours of release after so many days of unrelenting tension? Both scenarios felt closer to the truth.

She sighed, saw him give her a quick glance before he went back to the file he was studying. Maybe she'd opened herself to him, body and soul, for a much deeper reason. But she discounted the thought instantly. Love at first sight might exist for some, but not her.

She sighed again. This time he kept on reading. She might as well have not even been there.

They were met at the airport by a Salt Lake County deputy ready to deliver them to headquarters, where they would borrow one of the sheriff department's cars.

His name tag read Fairchild Smith, and he was very blond and very young. He drove so carefully she thought maybe this was his first assignment.

The day was bright and sunny and cold. Salt Lake City sprawled on a flat plain at the foot of the Wasatch National Forest, the Great Salt Lake glinting in the distance, the big white Mormon Tabernacle on the hill, the centerpiece to the city reminding her of the decoration on a wedding cake, beautiful and a bit unreal.

"Thank you, Officer Smith," she said when he pulled to a stop in front of headquarters.

"You're welcome, Miss Russo," the rookie deputy said, and he blushed.

The sheriff met them in his office. A gaunt older man, near retirement. Another Smith, Donald this time, and she recalled that a lot of Mormons had the surname of Smith. Joseph Smith had been the founder of the Church of Latter Day Saints.

Sheriff Donald Smith was polite but protective of Lisa Turchelli's rights. It took all of Jane skills to convince him to let her interview the girl, including a reference to the infamous Ted Bundy, who'd raped and murdered in both Utah and Colorado, and nearly gotten away with it except for the one girl who escaped him—a living witness. From Utah.

"I'm just so hopeful Lisa may be able to provide us with that break in the case," Jane said softly. Then she added, "If only Jennifer Weissman were still alive . . ." She didn't need to add, Jennifer Weissman, the rape and murder victim, also from Utah.

"Well," Sheriff Smith finally said, "you can give it a try again with Lisa. But when she pulls the plug, don't go overstepping yourself."

Jane nodded.

The sheriff loaned them an unmarked sedan, and Ray drove out of Salt Lake City with Jane reading the road map.

"Turn up there," she said, pointing.

He had that way of shutting her out, shutting everyone and everything out. He was doing it now. She tried again. "You didn't say two words at the sheriff's."

"Um, sometimes you can read a territorial thing the minute you walk into the local cop shop."

"I see. So you let me handle him?"

"Uh-huh. Woman's touch."

"That's sexist."

"Sure is."

She couldn't stop her glance from sliding surreptitiously to his hands on the wheel, the hands that had parted her legs, lifted her to meet him. Touched her hips and wound themselves in her hair, easing her head back as his lips had caressed her throat, her breasts, her belly. She still had pink whisker burn on her neck and breasts. Could he still feel her touch? On every inch of him, her touch and her breath on his scars, lovingly? How could he not remember? Or maybe she'd been a stand-in for Kathleen, nothing but a body.

She was bitterly ashamed of her weakness. Why was she such a sucker for men like Ray? What kind of masochist was she?

And sticking her nose into the Northwest Bomber case had made it worse. Why didn't she mind her own business?

They drove east out of town to Little Cottonwood Canyon and the two-lane highway that wound up between steep slopes to the eight-thousand-foot high resort of Snowbird. Snow lay thick on the pine-studded mountainsides, and they were in the shadows at the bottom of the Canyon. Along the road, signs were posted warning of avalanche danger.

"We're lucky it's not snowing out," she said. "Sometimes they close this road when the avalanche danger is too high."

"If they close the road, how do people get up there to ski?"

"They don't," she said. "The whole resort closes down."

They passed parking lots filled with cars of holiday skiers, and the valley widened, the first buildings appearing, the aerial tram cutting up the mountain ahead, skiers dotting the slopes like ants.

"What's the name of her condo?" he asked as they came upon a sign listing the buildings ahead.

"The Lupine," she answered. "I think it's further on."

"So, you're just going to show up, knock on her door? What if they're not home? What if the Turchellis are up skiing?"

"They know I'm coming."

"But they don't want you to talk to Lisa."

"It'll be all right, Ray. Trust me." *Trust me,* she'd said.

But he never would. And she'd trusted him with her soul.

She wanted Alan then. She desperately needed him, his calm wisdom and easy acceptance, his understanding when she failed to reach a climax or awakened from a nightmare or could not put the face of the man who'd raped her to paper. God, how she missed him. How could he have let Maureen back into his life after the woman had dumped on him, left him when he had most needed her? How could he not love her, Jane? She didn't care if their love was not passionate. He was her friend, her soul mate, damnit all. Alan kept her grounded.

How *could* she have fallen onto that bed with Ray and shamelessly responded to every touch?

Damn you, Alan, I need you.

"That the place?"

She started in her seat. "Oh, yes, yes, that's it. The Lupine," she said.

Lisa's mother was home. Lisa and her father were working at their grocery store.

"Please don't bother her," Mrs. Turchelli said. "She still has nightmares about that . . . that time."

"There's another girl missing, and we're sure she was taken by the same man. We're running out of time, and I think Lisa can help," Jane said gently.

"Oh God, I don't know what to do." The woman put her face in her hands.

"We'll go to the store, and I'll see what Lisa says. How about that?"

The woman looked up. "No, no."

"It won't take long."

"It happened three years ago! Three years. She won't remember anything more."

"She may. We think it's worth it try. She could save a girl's life."

Lisa's mother finally called her husband at the store, and he agreed to let Jane ask his daughter if she would consent to the interview.

"Good work," Ray said as they drove to Snowbird Center, where the store was located.

Her heart swelled with pleasure. *Sucker,* she told herself.

Mr. Turchelli was big and broad, with thick black hair and a walrus mustache. He was extremely angry. "I told you people, she doesn't know anything. Why won't you leave her alone?"

"Dad," Lisa said.

Jane went through her reasoning again for his benefit; Lisa had already heard it all on the phone.

"Lisa, honey, tell the truth," he finally said. "What do you want to do?"

Jane met the girl's eyes, holding them, smiling encouragingly. "You could really help us, Lisa. Maybe save Kirstin's life."

"Kirstin?"

"The girl who's missing. The way you were missing."

Lisa gave in then. In the office behind the store, the three of them squeezed in between a computer and boxes of groceries and piles of invoices and cash register receipts.

"Thank you so much, Lisa. You're a very brave girl," Jane said. "I know we've been over all this, but it's really important to go over it again now." She took out her sketch pad and a pencil and the lump of Play-Doh, handing it to Lisa.

"I can't do this clay stuff," Lisa said. She was a tall girl, with glossy straight dark hair and big brown eyes. She'd worn glasses three years before, but not now. She must have gotten contact lenses.

"That's okay. It gives you something to do with your hands."

Carefully Jane brought the conversation around to the kidnapper. Easy, she reminded herself. *Go easy.* Lisa was like a scared fawn, ready to run at the slightest provocation.

"Now, I just want you to close your eyes and try to recall anything you can. Any detail. Think of your five senses. Sight, hearing, touch, taste, smell."

"I'm not very good at this." Her hands kneaded the Play-Doh but not into anything recognizable.

"Okay, Lisa, we know he asked you directions to a gas station. You were at the bottom of the mountain after a day of skiing, waiting for the shuttle bus to take you home."

"Yes." She was nervous.

"You couldn't see his face."

She shook her head.

"He had a knife and made you get into his truck, right?" Jane thought of something then. "How exactly did you get into the truck?"

"What do you mean?"

"Which side did you get in on? Where was he in relation to you?"

"He was standing near the back, maybe putting skis over the tailgate thing. Anyway, he asked me directions, and I guess I kind of walked over toward him, and then he had the knife. . . . He . . . he made me get in on his side, the driver's side. I remember because the seat was all cracked and split when I slid across it."

"So it was an older truck?"

"I think so. All dirty and muddy."

"Do you remember the color?"

She shook her head again.

"And his face?"

She looked as if she wanted to cry. "He had a hat and a

thing over his mouth and nose. I told you that before. And he tied me up and pulled a hat over my eyes, and I couldn't see. I couldn't *see*."

Jane placed her hand on Lisa's knee. "I know this is hard, but you're doing very well. You really remember a lot."

"I do?"

"Oh yes." She smiled at Lisa, wanting to hug her and comfort her. But now was not the time.

Ray sat very still. She hoped he wouldn't say anything, ask any questions, and disturb Lisa's concentration. She glanced at him—he sat like a stone, his face without expression.

"Now, Lisa, let's think about the other senses, besides what you saw. Did you hear anything? Music, a radio, voices?"

"I can't remember."

"Any special tastes, food?"

"Mostly he brought cereal or hamburgers, you know, like McDonald's."

"Smells. Aftershave lotion, dirty clothes, air freshener, anything like that?"

Jane worked for an hour trying to coax the girl's memories from the shadows. It was rough going. Lisa was desperately unwilling to relive a moment of the horror perpetrated upon her. And Jane truly, deeply sympathized. Still, she kept trying. Behind the pretty eyes and contact lenses might be the means to break this case wide open. *Come on, Lisa, you can do it.*

Lisa's sight memory was useless. She'd been kept in the dark the entire time. Sounds were no help. She'd heard cars periodically. Which told them only that she was near a road. Tastes got them nowhere. So Jane went back to smells, trying a new tack.

"What did his truck smell like?"

"I don't know."

"Well, you think he owned a dog? You'd notice that in the car."

"No. No dog. But . . ."

"Yes?"

"Nothing." She shook her head vehemently.

"Lisa? What is it you don't want to recall?"

"Nothing."

"You're safe with us. You can remember. It won't hurt you, honey."

"No." She was fiercely kneading the Play-Doh. "No, no, no!" she suddenly cried.

"What is it, Lisa? Let us help."

"His . . . his hands."

"What about his hands?"

"They . . . they smelled awful."

"Like what? What awful smell?"

"He wore . . . he wore gloves. I could feel them when he untied me and let me eat. Oh God, those gloves. I saw them, too. Leather gloves, dirty. They smelled," she drew in a deep breath, "like oil, like that awful diesel smell, motor oil."

"Oily gloves," Jane said softly. "Very good, Lisa. See, you remembered something really important."

Lisa shuddered. "I hate that smell. I can't ever smell it without being scared. I never knew why."

"I know. But now that you've faced it, you'll get better with time. Trust me, you will. You'll never forget, but after a while it won't hurt so much." *Not true,* Jane thought. She should take her own advice, the platitudes she handed out so easily to other victims.

They left the grocery store, thanking Mr. Turchelli, who glowered at them even as he waited on a customer. The sun was gilding the tops of the mountains. All around them were skiers, dressed in brightly colored suits, carrying skis over their shoulders, clumping along in ski boots, sitting at outdoor cafes having a snack or an early lunch. And on the ski hill, the tram slid endlessly upward into the dazzling sunlight.

"Phew," she said, "I was afraid Mr. Turchelli wouldn't let me talk to her there for a while."

"You convinced them, I'll give that to you."

"Gee, thanks."

"And the gloves. That was good."

She looked at him, surprised. Her spirits lifted, and then she was angry with herself. Why was his acceptance and praise so damn important? She'd had more than her share of pats on the back from men just like him, initially cynics. Or was Ray unique? They neared the car and she felt heat rise to her face, pricking her skin. Of course he was unique. For God's sake, she'd made love to him.

She drove away from Snowbird Center while Ray called the new information in to Bruce. It occurred to her that Stan Shoemaker might already have landed in Salt Lake with the victim she was to interview. Then tonight she had yet one more interview, Jennifer Weissman's sister, a witness to Jennifer's abduction.

Talk about a full day, she thought, wondering if she were crazy, as she half listened to Ray's cell phone conversation with Bruce. "A new piece of info, okay? The UNSUB in Snowbird wore gloves that smelled like oil, diesel oil or maybe motor oil. Got that?" A pause while he listened. "Yeah, check every gas station, car repair in the valley. And the ski area mechanics. Don't they have people who work on snow cats and snowmobiles? And the lifts? Check for any employee driving a red pickup, chipped front tooth, blond, glasses, you know the rest."

She steered along the curves of Little Cottonwood Canyon Road and listened to his conversation, feeling good about herself. She'd made a breakthrough on this case—she'd finally made a breakthrough.

"How are the Lemke's doing?" Ray was asking. "Hmm. And is Josh Lemke still carrying on? Okay, that's good. Poor bastard." A pause. "Yeah, I know. A week. We may have a few more days. We may not. These creeps escalate, you know that. Okay, Bruce, keep me informed."

They were just pulling into Park City when Ray's phone rang. Every time she heard its distinctive ring her pulse leaped: *this is it; they've apprehended him, and Kirstin is fine.*

But it was Stan Shoemaker.

". . . still a bad idea," Ray was saying. "Yeah, yeah, I know she thinks she can handle it, but . . . All right, all right. We'll be at the . . ." He shot Jane a glance. "What's the name of the place the sheriff put us in?"

"April Inn."

"That's it, the April Inn." He paused on the line. "Hell, I don't know, maybe thirty miles from the airport. . . . Okay, say around five? But no matter what, Jane's got to do an interview tonight. . . . All right, see you." He clicked off.

"Um," she said, her eyes on the road. "Stan and the witness have landed in Salt Lake?"

"That's about the sum of it."

She started to say something, to tell him she could handle two more interviews, but she decided it was best to drop the entire subject. Instead, she smiled and said, "I'm famished. Mind if we stop before we get to the hotel?"

Park City was practically a suburb of Salt Lake City. Housing developments lined the highway, and amenities abounded. Still, the city itself was a small old mining town not unlike Aspen, with false front Western buildings and brick structures adorned with painted Victorian gingerbread. There was one noticeable difference: Aspen rested on the valley floor and was more or less laid out in flat grids, where Park City's blocks climbed a steep mountainside.

Jane found a parking spot in front of a family-style restaurant. "This look okay?" she said.

"You're the one who's hungry."

"True. Looks fine to me." She got out, locked the doors, and tossed him the keys.

Over burgers and cole slaw, she decided, What the hell? and said, "You know, I can do this."

"Do what?"

"Handle Jim Forsberg and . . ."

"Ben. *Ben* Forsberg."

"Right. I knew that. Anyway, I feel good about the interview."

"You don't even know him. I barely know the man, talked to him a couple times when he was still laid up in the hospital in Yakima."

She cocked her head. "So, what was your impression of Forsberg?"

"Does this matter?"

"Uh-huh. The more I know before I meet him the better. You *do* want this to work, don't you? I mean, you'd like to see this Northwest Bomber character behind bars?"

"Of course."

"Good. So tell me about Ben Forsberg."

"He's one lucky guy. Shot in the head and nothing to show for it but a little scar. The bullet hit his skull at an angle and ricocheted off."

"Besides lucky, what's he like?"

"Oh, he's nice enough. A little bit of a redneck."

"Is he married? Does he have kids?"

"I believe so."

"He was able to describe the men who held him up? I mean, really well?"

"The two men, the Perry brothers, that is, wore ski masks."

"So how . . . ?"

"The idiots left their prints all over the place."

"Um. Pretty dumb."

"Yeah. But smart enough to work with explosives. Learned their skills in Desert Storm, compliments of the U.S. Army."

"So, what about the shooter? Why didn't he cover his face?"

"Because he never intended to leave a witness behind."

"Wow. And you're sure he's this Northwest Bomber, the leader of the militant group?"

"Pretty damn sure."

"There were no surveillance cameras in the shop?"

"One. The shooter stayed out of its range."

"He knew the store then."

"Oh, yeah. Had to."

"Well," she said, sipping her Coke, "if his face is in Ben Forsberg's mind, I'll just have to get it for you."

Ray put his fork down, leaned forward. "Forsberg may have suffered brain damage."

"Or not."

"Whatever. I just don't think there's a chance in a thousand of retrieving the face after three years."

"Well, maybe you don't know what I'm capable of doing."

"I've seen you work."

"Only on the Lemke case. And I've admitted the problems I've had with it."

"Um," he said.

"You aren't being fair. I am good at what I do."

"I really didn't mean to get into a pissing contest."

"Well, for your information, the director of the FBI called me last summer and asked if I'd run a class on my technique at Quantico." She knew she was tooting her own horn shamelessly, trying to force him to acknowledge her usefulness. Trying to make him need her. The way he'd needed his partner Kathleen, the woman he hadn't forgotten for a second in all this time.

He stared at her, expressionless, his pale eyes under straight dark brows pinioning her. "That's nice, Jane," he said in his throaty purr.

They ate the rest of the meal in silence.

FOURTEEN

With Christmas only a few days away, the ski slopes of all four Aspen ski area mountains were jammed. Lift lines were long. Even to get a cup of coffee in a mountain restaurant meant waiting in a maze of ropes with a horde of boisterous tourists.

No, thanks, the man thought, leaving the restaurant at the top of the Exhibition lift at the Highlands Ski Area. It wasn't even noon, and he was ready to quit for the day. Too damn many people.

He hadn't worked in three days now. No new snow. No driveways to plow. He was growing bored. *She* was beginning to bore him.

He skied down to the day parking lot at the base of Highlands. Tossed his skis, poles, and boots in the back of the truck and put on his Sorrel boots.

And saw the cop. Walking the aisles of the parking lot, checking vehicles, notably pickup trucks.

Shit.

But the man expected this. He'd always figured the cops would find out that their man drove a pickup truck. The kid from Mammoth and the brat from Snowbird knew that much. And he'd always assumed the police might one day tie the kidnappings together. That, or one of the kids who was snowboarding with the Lemke girl here might have spotted the pickup.

Not that anyone could have gotten the numbers off his plates—he'd made sure they were way too filthy to read. He'd also made sure no one saw the front of the truck. If anyone had been able to give the cops a vague description of him, he'd carefully altered his looks for the day of the abduction: the shitty old nondescript ski clothes, crappy fifteen-year-old goggles, and neck gaiter. Today, as on most days he skied, he wore a navy-blue parka with a teal yoke and a matching blue hat, the latest goggles, and his contact lenses. Even his driver's license was from a different state—New Mexico.

Careful planning. He figured you could never be too cautious.

He got in his truck. No rush. Started the engine, backed out. The cop was still an aisle over, jotting plate numbers down, and there were plenty of cars moving in and out, hunting for parking spaces.

He drove out of the lot at the far exit from where the local cop had parked his distinctive blue-gray official Saab. Still, for all the precautions the man took, he was sweating. He hadn't seen anything in the papers about the kid's abduction since the first morning, when the *Aspen Times* had reported a local girl was missing after a day of skiing. Since then not a word. The feds probably hushed the papers up. In a large city that wouldn't have stopped the media, but here, in this close-knit community, the editors cooperated with the authorities. For the kid's sake, sure.

But also because reporting an abduction in a resort at
Christmas would've been tantamount to a shark attack alert
at a beach on the Fourth of July.

By the time he'd driven the few miles up the quiet valley where his rental cabin sat, he'd stopped sweating. They
weren't going to find him. And they weren't going to find
her, either, not till the spring thaw. By then he'd be well on
his way east. Been thinking about New England. Never
skied there.

He'd also been thinking a lot about the kid. In Park City,
he'd just sort of left the girl in that shithole motel. But this
time he wanted to be there when she took her last breath.
He'd contemplated many endings to her life. Some he
liked better than others. He was coming up with a short list
now. Each scenario equally delicious as the next. How was
he going to choose?

The cabin was cold when he walked in, so he rebuilt the
fire in the potbelly stove. Made himself a cup of instant
coffee and ate a bowl of Froot Loops. He guessed he'd take
her in some food, too. He dumped some cereal into the
same bowl he'd used and poured in a little milk. Didn't
want to waste any milk. She hadn't eaten hardly at all in
the last couple days, and he didn't want her getting too
weak too soon. Not till he fixed the day in his head. Maybe
Christmas. His present to himself.

He opened the bedroom door, light spilling in behind
him, and kicked it shut. Took a moment for his eyes to adjust
to the darkness. Not that he gave a damn if she saw him. She
was never going to get the opportunity to rat him out.

She was huddled in the corner of the bed, blanket
bunched under her, hands securely tied to the ring he'd
fixed in the wall.

The room stank. She'd soiled the bed several times.
That in itself was reason to get rid of her soon. He'd have

to dump the goddam mattress along with her. Replace it. Maybe he could find a used one at the thrift shop. Yeah. Good idea.

He put the bowl on the bed. "Eat, kid," he said. "You don't eat, you get punished. You hear me?"

"Ye . . . yes," she murmured.

Whining again.

He left the room, stretched out on the couch in the small living area, the stove giving off plenty of warmth now.

Closed his eyes. Might as well catch a nap. Then maybe a few beers in town, check the weather on TV there—he had no TV. Then home. And the girl.

His last thought before dozing was how in hell was he going to narrow his short list down to a single choice? *Problems, problems.*

Later, Ray would wonder how he'd failed to recognize the ripple effect of Jane's meeting with Ben Forsberg. Maybe he'd subconsciously seen the whole picture, and that was why he was so dead set against the interview. In any case, Stan blew it by bringing Forsberg to Utah, and Jane blew it when she so readily agreed to talk to Forsberg. And Ray? He just blew it when he allowed the situation to get out of his control.

He got them checked into the hotel in the Main Street historic district and handed Jane her room key. "Try to get some rest," he suggested. "Stan can bloody well wait."

"I'm fine," she insisted, "really. But it's nice of you to care." She gave him one of her heart-melting smiles.

Was she goading him? Sometimes he had no idea how to read her. "Are you being sarcastic?" he asked.

"Not in the least," she said. "I know you care. You just have an odd way of showing it."

Puzzled, he watched her cross the lobby and stride down the hall, her long blue-jean-clad legs catching every male eye in the place. Her legs seeming even longer because of the high-heeled boots she wore. She *was* disconcertingly tall.

Stan and Ben Forsberg arrived at the inn fifteen minutes later in an airport rental, a four-wheel-drive Jeep Cherokee. Stan was obviously sparing no expense.

"Hey," he said, walking up to Ray in the lobby, dangling the car keys. "The SAC said go for it. He's delighted Jane's going to do this interview." Behind Stan was Forsberg. He looked great, considering. Plus this had to be a nice vacation, all expenses paid.

"Look, Stan," Ray said, after shaking Forsberg's proffered hand, "are you aware that Jane's already had one interview this morning and now this?" He nodded at Forsberg, who was studying a wall-mounted elk head over the lobby fireplace. "*And* she's got another one this evening."

"Um," Stan said, rubbing his bald spot, "Forsberg could wait till morning, I suppose."

But Ray shook his head. "God only knows where we'll be in the morning. I've got to get back to Aspen. Time's running out."

"Well, then, maybe Jane could stay and . . ."

"Stan. Not a chance. I brought her on this insane jaunt, and I'll take her back to Denver."

Stan smiled mischievously. "Feeling responsible for the lady, are we? Or maybe there's more to it?"

"For chrissakes, Stan, give it a rest," he said hotly, then wished he'd let it alone.

Jane reappeared in the lobby as Stan was checking in. She'd changed clothes and now wore black denims and her boots, a purple sweater, her makeup freshened, her hair loose and swinging to her shoulders. She looked terrific, he couldn't help thinking, and the night they'd spent together came crashing back into his brain, muddling his thoughts so badly that Stan cleared his throat and made the introductions.

"Jane Russo, this is Ben . . . Ben Forsberg."

Forsberg was a good two inches shorter than Jane, maybe a little less, because she was wearing those amazing boots. Her height and ready handshake, coupled with the genuine smile and warmth she exuded had Forsberg mesmerized.

"Sure hope I can be a good subject for you, ma'am," Forsberg said, and he removed his baseball cap.

He was an all-right looking man, Ray supposed, if you went for the woodsy types. He wore brown leather cowboy boots, blue jeans, looked like Levi 501s, a blue wool, two-pocket shirt under a sage green down parka. Ben was slim and nearly fifty, with salt-and-pepper hair worn military short, soft green eyes, ordinary features. A bit of a down-home George Clooney look to him. Ray recalled telling Jane that Forsberg was married, but maybe Ray's facts were wrong. Forsberg wasn't wearing a ring, anyway.

Jane immediately chatted him up. And it seemed she'd once driven through Yakima, Washington, after a windsurfing trip on the Columbia River.

Ray listened to the banter and then raised his brows when she asked Forsberg where he'd be most comfortable for the interview. "Your room or mine?" she said.

Forsberg *um*ed and *ah*ed, then ducked his head. "Ah, yours, I guess, ma'am."

Lovely, Ray mused.

"Shall we get started?" she said.

"Fine by me."

Ray and Stan killed the time walking around downtown Park City, Ray phoning Aspen as they turned onto Main

Street. Nothing new. But it seemed every cop from Glenwood Springs to Basalt, Carbondale, and Snowmass, was on the prowl at gas stations, fender-bender shops, auto mechanic garages, and even car dealerships. The police and special agents were checking the ski company garages at all four ski areas and even Sunlight Ski Area outside Glenwood Springs.

"Keep them motivated," Ray told Bruce, "we're close, I can smell it." But were they? Or had Kirstin already suffered the fate of the Weissman girl here in Park City?

The small town was hopping by mid-afternoon. The restaurants, bars, and T-shirt shops in the quaint historic district were packed. He and Stan stopped for coffee, Stan chowing down on a cream-cheese-topped sweet roll, and then Stan wanted to head back to the inn.

"See what's cooking, huh?" Stan said.

"A warning to the wise," Ray said, paying the tab at the coffeehouse. "Don't go knocking on her door. When she's done, she'll let you know."

"It's been"—Stan checked his watch— "an hour and a half. How long does this take?"

Ray shrugged. "As long as it takes."

"Well, I'll ring your cell when she gets a sketch."

"You mean, *if* she does. Don't forget," Ray pointed out, "this Northwest Bomber has eluded us for years. I wouldn't get my hopes too high."

"Ah, don't be such a cynical old fart, Ray." Stan put on his wool-lined car coat. "I'm betting we get a face."

"Um," Ray said.

Jane had rarely worked with adults. At first she'd been hesitant to hand Ben the wad of Play-Doh, fearing he'd think she was treating him like a child. But he took to it instantly, even saying, "Hey, this is great. Who would've thought?"

She began the interview with small talk, learning he had a wife of thirty years and two grown children, one living in Spokane, the other in San Francisco. "A goldarn hippie." While he talked he shaped the Play-Doh into an amazing likeness of a deer.

She leaned forward to study the shape more closely. "That's very good."

"Oh, well, I do some carvings, you know, for a local art shop. Wooden carvings. I do deer, elk, Canada geese. It takes up the hours when my shop's slow. That'd be just about all winter." He laughed, but he was engrossed in his handiwork.

She took advantage of his focus. "The day your shop was robbed . . ." she began, and when she saw no hint of alarm or stress in his features, she eased into the crux of the interview, taking him back three years.

It had been a snowy late November day, hunting season in eastern Washington State still in high gear. Ben's shop was well stocked, his cash register bulging.

"Shoot," Ben said, "I knew the minute I seen those two with the stocking hats pulled down that I was in trouble. Big trouble, you know?" He collapsed the deer with his strong hands and kneaded the plastic into the shape of a head. She watched quietly. "Yeah, and they was toting, taller one in the cap pulls a .45 out of his waistband. Thought my bowels were gonna let loose."

He described the robbery, which he clearly remembered, and she was positive he had to have seen the third man, the leader who had stood to the side, unmasked and out of view of the surveillance camera. The face was imprinted somewhere in Ben's mind.

When he strayed from the moment, she carefully circled

him back to the store on the cold November day. "Was the third man standing near the counter or the door?" she prompted, guessing at the layout of the shop.

"Oh, not the door. Camera woulda gotten him. But then, FBI figured he knew that. No. He was standing to my left, 'bout maybe twenty feet, up against the rack where the fishing rods are. The one spot the camera couldn't get him."

"I see," she said. "And could you make out his clothes? The parka or boots or anything?"

Ben was molding away, as if she were not even present. "No parka. He was wearing a padded camouflaged jacket, the collar up."

"Oh. Okay."

"And army boots. Yeah, muddy ones." Ben kept molding and she began to sketch.

"Funny, but I can almost . . ." He paused, squinted his eyes, and looked bewildered for a moment, then said, "Gray hair. Well, not gray, more like a faded mouse color, as if he used that stuff . . . ah, what's it called? Grecian Formula? Yeah, that's the stuff. Oh, and he parted his hair way over on the . . . right side. Like if he pulled more hair over his bald spot no one would notice." Ben half laughed. "But them eyes. Real close set, you know? Like a ferret or a weasel."

Her hand could barely keep up. As for Ben, his deft fingers were going a mile a minute, shaping, gouging, Play-Doh caking beneath his fingernails.

Wow, she kept thinking, and Ben talked, shaped, sometimes cocked his head, trying to recall, and then his hands went to work again.

At six minutes past five, she followed him into the hallway, closing her door behind them. He still held the lump of plastic—that was okay, she had more in her case.

"You know," Ben said, "I never in a million years

woulda realized I had that bastard's face in my head all this time. How'd you do that, anyway?"

"*You* did it, Ben," she assured him, "you did it practically on your own."

They found Ray and Stan sitting near the big stone floor-to-ceiling fireplace in the lobby. Ben was grinning sheepishly, holding the Play-Doh face, shrugging, and Jane couldn't help herself, either, grinning broadly, elated as she flipped open her sketch pad and presented the drawing.

Stan rose, his jaw dropping. "Jesus Christ," he breathed.

Ray was slower to come to his feet. And he was deathly silent as his gaze fixed on the sketch.

"Well?" she finally said, unable to bear the glorious tension another moment. "Ray? Say something."

He drew in a breath. Held it. Then said, "My God, I've seen that face."

FIFTEEN

A million thoughts clashed in his head. How in *hell* had she gotten this face out of Forsberg? She must've copied it; she must've seen it somewhere in FBI files and subconsciously drawn it from memory. She must have . . . But none of those possibilities made sense.

Was it conceivable Forsberg had actually seen the man who shot him? *Son of a bitch.*

He held the sheet torn from her sketch pad and studied it some more. That face. Yeah, he knew it, all right. What was the guy's name? He'd scrolled by a mug shot of the man dozens of times in FBI computer files. A small time crook, spent a few years in a federal prison in northern California on illegal weapons charges. A while ago. Years. What in hell was his name?

"Stan," he said, "you remember this guy? From years back. Illegal weapons. Spent some time in a federal penitentiary. Maybe a tie to a militant group. You remember him?"

"Vaguely. A nobody. What was his name?"

"Can't remember. Damn, it's on the tip of my tongue."

"You really know who this man is?" Jane asked, amazed.

"Yes, yeah, I do."

"Did I help you?" Forsberg asked.

"Yes, you helped," Stan said. "You and Jane."

"So I can go home now?" He looked hopeful. "My wife was really mad I had to leave like that so near Christmas and all."

"Ben, don't worry," Stan said, "we'll get you on the first flight to Spokane. You've been great."

Ray wasn't listening. He was still fixed on the sketch. Trying to imagine the face years younger, with longer, thicker hair. There were computer programs that did this work for you, put age on people, took age off, thickened their faces, thinned their hair or, in this case, subtracted age and searched the National Database for a match. But Ray didn't have immediate access to the FBI's program. "Damn," he muttered. Then he looked up and found Jane's eyes on him.

She'd done it. She'd actually pulled from a man's memory this exact photographic likeness of the Northwest Bomber. The bomber was no longer an UNSUB. He had a face. And a name, if only Ray could recall it.

"It worked," Jane said, her eyes bright, her voice animated. "I knew it would. As soon as I met Ben. He was fantastic."

"*You* were fantastic," Ray said. "This drawing is . . ." He stopped short, frowning, thinking. "Something Polish or Russian. Damnit, Stan, what was it?"

"Got me."

"Yeah, I'm sure now, he was a white supremacist when he was young. A low-level risk, a small-fry. It's all coming back now. But the name, a *ski* on the end?" He put a hand to his forehead. "Like the ice skater, the one in the Olympics. Tara something or other. Tara, Tara."

He paced, his thoughts frenetic. This was the man who'd ordered the killing of Kathleen, who'd almost killed him. The name, the name.

No one spoke, waiting, watching him.

"Soon as I get a digital of Jane's sketch the computer will match them right up," Stan said.

"If I could just . . . Lapinski," Ray said abruptly. "Goddamn, Gerald *Lapinski*. Yes."

Stan left the hotel soon after, delivering Forsberg to the airport, then stopping by the Salt Lake County Sheriff's Department to have the sketch digitalized and sent out on a nationwide alert. Meanwhile Ray called Quantico and requested a search of a driver's license or address on Lapinski. He informed them the sketch would soon be in their hands; they were to send Jane's sketch out to every agency in the Pacific Northwest.

Things were moving. Soon Lapinski wouldn't be able to get gas for his car or cigarettes or a loaf of bread without a cop making him or his vehicle. They'd find him in short order.

Jane had done it. He clicked off his cell phone and stopped pacing. She was sitting on one of the sofas in the lobby, her hands locked around one knee, her expression expectant.

He walked over and stood in front of her, unable to find the words. He couldn't say what really needed to be said: he owed her an apology for being such a hardass idiot.

She looked up, her beautiful blue eyes full of light, but wary.

"Jane," he said.

"Uh-huh?"

He sank down beside her on the sofa, oblivious to the people milling around them: the holiday vacationers returning from the slopes in ski gear, the people checking in, the murmur and ebb and flow of strangers around them.

"Damnit, Jane." He reached out for her hand, and she let go of her knee and sat straight, staring at him, waiting. He held her fingers in his and he searched her face, and still no words came.

"Ray?" she said softly.

"You did good," was all that came to mind.

"Thank you," she whispered. Gracious, forgetting his past transgressions against her, smiling, squeezing his hand, and he felt a surge of emotion roar through his body.

Jane was still exhilarated when she and Ray started out for the Weissman's. Exhausted, too, she knew that, but there was so much adrenaline shooting through her veins she couldn't have rested in any case.

"You need to eat something," Ray said. "Take your pick, a sit-down restaurant, fast food, makes no difference to me."

"You won't believe this, but I'm not hungry." She glanced ahead at the highway. McDonald's, Taco Bell, Denny's, Burger King, Wendy's, an Arby's. None of them interested her. Had to be the high she was on. But, boy, when she fell back to earth she knew she'd crash hard. She'd keep going as long as she could, though, because she was on a roll and Jennifer Weissman's sister Caitlin might be the one to provide the big break.

Ray put on the signal director and pulled into Wendy's.

"I really don't think I can eat," she repeated.

She had a chef salad just to appease him, but she only picked at the food. And his burger and fries went nearly untouched, because his cell phone rang every other minute. It had only been a couple hours since Stan had faxed Lapinski's sketch and the all-out search had begun; the FBI was in high gear, already had an address on him, a credit card number, knew his driver's license number and the make and model of the vehicle registered to his name in Benton County, Washington.

When he ended one particular call, he shook his head, managed to take a bite of his burger. Mouth half full, he said, "That was Stan. Get this, Lapinski lives off some backwoods dirt road in an area known as Rattlesnake Hills. Figures."

"Has anyone gone there yet?"

"No." Ray took a drink of Coke, wiped his mouth with his napkin. "The FBI is coordinating a task force. State police, ATF, because of federal firearms violations and gun theft. The local county sheriff's department is in on it, you name it."

"Sounds complicated."

"Yeah, but there's a military reservation close by. They'll fly in and use it as a command post. Couple more hours, and I'm betting they're ready to go in after him."

"What if he's not there?"

"Then they'll wait. Rats eventually return to the nest."

She shivered at the image. Everything was developing with lightning quickness. Her head was spinning. And she still had the interview with Caitlin.

She checked her watch. "We'd better go," she said.

He nodded. Then his phone rang again. He talked on the way to the car, talked as he drove, hunting for the address in the sprawling subdivision.

A light snow had started to drift from a leaden sky. Ray slowed to make out a street sign in the fading light. He took another call while he steered. He was listening, then suddenly said, "No goddamn way! Are they nuts? We got them. You tell that high-priced lawyer no deal. He had his chance. He fucking blew it. The Perrys should have cut a deal when it was offered." He clicked off. "Can you believe that?" he said, as much to himself as her, "*Now* they want to deal."

"They don't have anything left to deal with, do they? Now that you've found Lapinski."

"*You* found him, Jane. And you're absolutely right, the Perrys don't have anything on their plates. They'll face federal murder charges. No way out."

"You're as high as I am."

"Yeah, I am. Damn, but I wish I could go join the task force right now."

The car was stopped under the street sign, the snow beginning to drift more heavily from the night sky, collecting on the windshield, muffling sounds. She felt as if they were being cocooned in a world of their own.

He glanced at the street sign, said, "Must have made a wrong turn." Then he shifted the car into reverse, put his arm over the back of her seat, turned his head. And stopped again.

"What?" she said.

He studied her face. After a moment, he moved his hand to her cheek, the back of it gently sweeping her hair away. Her breath caught in her lungs and halted. Her pulse began to thud in her ears.

Embarrassed, she smiled weakly and again said, "What?"

"I was just thinking."

"Thinking what?" God, if he didn't move his hand . . . But he didn't, and she couldn't help leaning a little into it.

"We're asking too much of you," he said in that voice that rippled along her limbs like molten gold. "You're exhausted. Maybe I should call the Weissmans. . . ."

"No, let me try." Her voice was a whisper. "Please, Ray, I have a hunch. I can feel it."

He kept his eyes on her, his fingers tucking the hair behind her ear. Her nerves leaped under her skin.

"Do you have to help every poor slob in the whole world?"

"Oh, don't be silly."

"Silly? I never thought of myself as silly."

"You know what I mean."

"I'm not sure."

"I just need to do my job."

"Oh yeah, your job. And I'm your newest case?"

"Ray, come on."

"You're very good at what you do, Jane."

She closed her eyes for just a moment and a wave of dizzy delight swept her. She opened them, tried to focus. What was he doing to her? Couldn't he read her thoughts, read the turmoil inside her? He'd transformed in front of her eyes, softened, showed the feelings that lay behind the hard facade. *What about Kathleen?* she wanted to ask him. *Do you still love her?* And she was abruptly afraid—he'd disappoint her, he'd hurt her. She couldn't bear it.

She drew back from his touch, pressed against the passenger door, put her hand up to smooth her hair where he'd swept it aside. She knew her face was set in a false smile, but she couldn't help it.

"My God," she said, trying to keep her tone light, "I forgot to call Alan."

His face was wiped clean of expression. "Alan."

"I'm dying to tell him about Lapinski."

"You want to call Alan." He wasn't looking at her; he was staring out the window into the storm. She could feel sudden tension crackling in the air, tearing at the delicate silk of the cocoon. Why had she done that? Brought up Alan in the middle of . . .

"What exactly is he to you?" she heard him say.

"Alan?"

"Yeah."

"Oh, well, he's . . . my friend."

He turned his head toward her, his expression guarded now. "I'm asking if you're still together."

"Oh." She had no idea how to reply. "I don't know if we're a couple anymore. His ex-wife came back onto the scene a couple months ago." She shrugged, glancing down, unable to meet his eyes.

"I guess three's a crowd," he said, and he finally backed the car into the deserted intersection, did a three-point turn, and headed the way they'd just come.

They located the house a block over. "This is it," she said. "I remember the garage." She grabbed up her purse and artist's case and pushed the door open, the snow riding on a frigid wind, the flakes tapping a cold tattoo on her face.

After Ray's phone rang for the fourth time, he excused himself and went outside to sit in the car while Jane finished interviewing Caitlin.

Unlike the Turchellis, the Weissmans were cooperative, but then their oldest daughter Jennifer had died.

"Closure," they'd kept saying. "Please catch this man so we can have closure."

What about justice? Ray wondered.

The first call was from Stan: the task force had advanced to Gerald Lapinski's property, advised him of his rights by bullhorn, and surrounded his farmhouse. He'd refused to surrender, and was taking potshots from one of his windows.

It was a standoff.

A second call from Stan relayed the fact that there might be other people in Lapinski's house, and the task force was holding fire, afraid of injuring someone. Nobody wanted a repeat of Ruby Ridge.

The next call: the media had gotten wind of the standoff and were arriving en masse.

"Shit," Ray said.

"I know. I'd like the balls of the guy who leaked this one," Stan said. "They'll have Lapinski looking like Jesus Christ and Mother Teresa, all rolled into one."

The fourth call was from SAC Parker in Denver: "Ray, listen, some stupid rookie at Quantico let it out that Jane Russo drew the sketch of the Northwest Bomber."

"Ah, Christ."

"I'll alert the sheriff in Aspen. And when you get back there, it's no comment, okay? And make sure Russo buttons her mouth, too."

"Got it."

That was when he left the Weissman house and retreated to his car. Snow had started to pile up on the windshield, and as he sat behind the wheel, the light was muted, claustrophobic. He put the key in the ignition and turned on the windshield wipers so that he could see.

His phone rang again. Parker's secretary this time. "Agent Vanover? SAC Parker wanted me to inform you that he had a call from Channel Nine here in Denver, and they know that Jane Russo is on assignment with the bureau on the Lemke matter."

Not good, he thought. If the media didn't trace Jane here to Park City, they'd certainly find her somewhere. The case would turn into a media feeding frenzy. Reporters would hound the sheriff's department, the Lemkes, and Jane. Make it impossible for her and the other agents to do their jobs.

Another thought struck him. What if the abductor heard about Jane being on the Lemke case? What might he do? Kill Kirstin on the spot and run? Go after Jane? Both?

This did not bode well.

He called Bruce in Aspen, and they compared notes.

There were already news vans parked outside the Lemke's house, but deputies were keeping them from intruding.

"For now," Bruce said.

"Damn vultures," Ray said.

"Nothing new at your end?" Bruce asked.

"Jane's talking to Caitlin Weissman right now."

"Nothing new here, either. We've got deputies of three counties working together with the state troopers, checking every red Ford pickup truck between Glenwood Springs and Aspen. No dice so far. Hell, every other pickup driver is blond and wears glasses. They're all workingmen, commuting to Aspen. Electricians, mechanics, carpenters, roofers. Any one of them could be our man. Or none of them."

"Great."

"Well, perseverance furthers," Bruce said. "That's from the *I Ching*. Good advice."

Perseverance furthers, he thought, shaking his head as he ended the call.

Jane surprised him by opening the passenger door a minute later.

"You're done?" he asked.

"Yes. I couldn't get anything new from Caitlin. She was so traumatized. It was her sister, after all. I thought, I really *felt* I might get something from her this time." She sounded dejected. Bone weary.

"I'm sorry."

"Me, too."

He wanted to pull her close, stroke her hair, comfort her. An odd kind of timidity held him back, as if Alan Gallagher stood between them. *Careful,* he told himself.

"We have to go back to Aspen," she said. "I can't do any more here. The answer is there. I guess I've always known that."

"Full circle."

"Yes," she said, her face so solemn, her hair tucked behind one ear, falling softly over the other cheek. "There isn't much time left for Kirstin."

The wipers swept back and forth, and in the warm car's interior snowflakes melted like tiny diamonds in her hair.

"We have to get back," she repeated.

"We can make the airport in forty-five minutes," he said.

She shook her head. "The planes may not be flying in this storm, and even if we could get to Denver, we might be stuck there."

The last thing he needed was to waste eight hours driving through the Rocky Mountains in a blizzard—at night. Alone with Jane for hours. Alone with this woman who'd forced him to face his own failings, who'd put him on edge, as if he were a callow youth again, unsure of how to act, what to do and say. Wanting, needing her approval but afraid to demand it. Liking her too damn much.

The windshield wipers swished in rhythm, like a heartbeat, clearing the glass, only to clear it of new snow again. And again. Silence ticked between them.

He'd been relieved when she'd told him she and Gallagher weren't really a couple anymore. Relieved that Gallagher's ex-wife was in the picture. He still didn't understand the relationship between Jane and the man, but he couldn't press her on it. And whatever that relationship was, it only made his situation murkier.

Then there was Kathleen. He'd thought her memory would hold him so tightly he'd never be free, never want to be free. He wasn't going to lie to himself anymore. Jane had altered his belief system. Hell, she'd shattered it. So where did that that leave them now?

"I'll check us out of the hotel," he said, breaking the silence. "I guess we drive to Aspen."

Goddamn, he thought.

SIXTEEN

The man started his pickup at 3:30 AM. The engine ground once, then caught, coughing like an old smoker. He let it warm up for a time, the wipers laboring to push snow off the windshield. He should have cleaned it by hand, but he was too lazy. He turned on the headlights, and the cones of light pierced the snow-filled darkness like beacons.

There was two feet of fresh snow. That meant work for him. And if he could get his jobs done by eight, nine at the latest, he'd be in the lift line before ten. Then if the snow kept up, he could go back and replow each driveway this afternoon. Double the day's earnings. What more could a man ask for?

He pumped the accelerator a few times, waiting until he was sure the truck wouldn't stall, then he got out and tramped back to the cabin while the engine warmed.

Checked on the kid. She was dozing. She'd been doing that a lot more lately. He hadn't touched her in days. She disgusted him now that she didn't look so pretty anymore. Or smell so pretty.

He'd dump her tonight. Lots of new snow to cover the body, four months till spring thaw. By then he'd be long gone.

He figured the truck had warmed up long enough. He went out into the storm, climbed in, and pulled the door shut. The wipers had finally cleared two spots on the windshield. Turning the radio onto his favorite country western music station, he heard the announcer giving the hourly news report. He switched the transmission into four-wheel drive, then backed out of his parking place onto the driveway. His tires left deep ruts in the smooth whiteness; oil dripped, hissing as it fell to the snow. He listened to the news with half his attention. The storm, which was big news, another Mideast peace proposal, a battle in Congress over campaign finance reform. Then to local news. "An update on the missing twelve-year-old, Kirstin Lemke, of Snowmass Village. There are no new leads, Sheriff Kent Schilling has informed us, but there is a promising development in this tragic case. A well-known portrait artist, Jane Russo of Denver, who has solved similar cases in an almost miraculous manner, has been interviewing past victims of the kidnapper. Ms. Russo is responsible for the apprehension of . . ."

He twisted the dial savagely so that the voice stopped. Felt as if he'd been punched in the solar plexus.

Jane Russo.

The sign announcing Rifle, Colorado, loomed out of the swirling snow. *Thank God,* Jane thought, her fingers white on the steering wheel. She knew exactly where she was and exactly how far it was to Aspen: sixty-five miles. An hour and half on dry roads with good visibility. Longer in this storm.

She glanced at the dashboard clock. It was just after five in the morning. They'd be in Aspen by breakfast time. Barring a commuter accident on Highway 82, which could tie up traffic for hours.

She was tired even though Ray had driven most of the distance through the night. He'd stopped at a rest area a couple hours before and said, "Either we both grab a quick nap or you drive. Your choice."

So she'd taken over at the wheel. The snowstorm had followed them from Utah, moving east just as they were. The trip had been miserable, wind and snow all the way, slippery roads.

But Kirstin was waiting to be rescued.

She peered through a sudden whirl of snow, mesmerized by the flakes battering the windshield and being swept away. She couldn't even see the town of Rifle, only the tall luminous lights set along the interstate at the two exits. Big yellow spheres with snowflakes dancing in them.

Ray was asleep in the passenger seat, his head resting against the window. She stole a glance at him—his neck was bound to be stiff when he woke—then fixed her attention back on the road. But a minute later she ventured another look; she never tired of staring at Ray, the handsome profile, his face relaxed in sleep, so that he appeared younger. In the dimness, she could even see the shiny skin of the scar on his neck, up along the line of his chin. To her the scars made him seem less perfect, a little vulnerable. And that imperfection gave her a perverse sense of comfort.

Years ago, she'd accepted the fact that strong wounded men attracted her. That's why she'd been interested in Alan. But he had taken a high road once he began to recover from the trauma of his daughter's death and the ensuing divorce. He'd become involved and healed himself through his dedication to the cause of children's advocacy. She understood that he needed to make some sense of a tragedy no parent should ever have to endure. How did the Chinese proverb go? The worst fate in life was to outlive one's children. Or something like that. She'd been there for Alan in his darkest hours, and now he no longer needed her.

She guessed she'd been losing him bit by bit. She'd been unwilling to face the truth: they had fallen in love because of a crisis, and the emotion faded when the crisis receded.

She drove along Interstate 70, past Rifle, on toward Silt, New Castle, and Glenwood Springs. The radio was tuned to a classical music station, the volume low so Ray could rest. She could just make out piano music, Rachmaninoff, she thought. Powerful music to accompany the storm.

So how did she really feel about Alan now? Sad, she supposed—they had been good for each other when both needed succor. Okay, she had identified the sadness, but there was relief, too, in an odd sort of way. But no matter what, she would always be grateful to him for teaching her to trust again.

The lights of a car swept upon her, passed, and were gone into the darkness. Damn fool, driving that fast in these conditions. She would probably find him upside down in the Colorado River in a few miles.

"Idiot," she said, then remembered Ray was asleep. He stirred, but did not awaken.

Ray. So different from Alan. Solitary. He'd been in love once, and then he'd faced tragedy and retreated into bitterness and the all-consuming need for revenge. It was his way of shielding himself from too much pain. And now he only seemed alive when he faced danger, craving the adrenaline high that came from his job. He was so afraid of his weaknesses he suppressed them with a kind of ferocity.

But underneath—she took her eyes off the road for a second to glance at him—she knew he was terribly lonely.

She had to admit how very hurt she was that he didn't return her feelings, but at least she had finally proven her worth to him. His acceptance and approval shouldn't have mattered so much, but it did. It had since the moment they'd met.

She steered along the curve of Six Mile Canyon that led to Glenwood Springs and the exit to Aspen. Right there, at that snow-encrusted sign reading SOUTH CANYON, was where that terrible forest fire had burned the mountainside years ago. Fourteen firefighters had been killed. There was a memorial at the site now. For a moment she was going to rouse him, point out Storm King Mountain, but she dismissed the idea. He didn't need to be reminded of fire.

Still, when she slowed to get off the interstate less than a mile farther on, he awakened. He was instantly alert, his face resetting into guarded planes and angles. "Where are we?"

"Glenwood Springs. Forty miles to go."

"Want me to drive?"

"No, I'm okay. And I know this road real well."

They stopped at a gas station to fill up, used the restrooms, and bought cups of steaming coffee. Then they were back on the highway, the sky beginning to lighten, a vague paleness in the blizzard.

"I want to talk to Crystal again," she said as they approached Aspen.

"The girl with the hippie mother?"

"Yes. She was the most observant. She gave us the Ford Ranger."

"Maybe that's all she remembered."

She shook her head. "I can get more from her, I know I can."

"Hey, you won't get an argument from me."

She flashed him a smile. Oh, yes, his approval mattered.

They drove straight to the Lemke's house in Brush Creek Village. As they climbed the hill, they looked for Bruce's car, but it was obscured by the snow, and by two satellite news trucks, their windows a cheery yellow in the dim morning.

"Shit," Ray said under his breath.

"Oh God, the poor Lemkes."

The moment she parked the car, the doors of the news vans opened, and people emerged to ask questions and stick microphones in their faces.

"Hey, it's Jane Russo," she heard, and the group converged on her. "Miss Russo, Miss Russo, how did you know it was the Northwest Bomber? What do you think of this standoff? Did you know Lapinski's wife is in the farmhouse with him? What's Ben Forsberg like, Miss Russo? Do you know who has the Lemke girl?" Questions, flung at her like pebbles. Sharp, hurtful. Of course she realized the Northwest Bomber was a big case—a huge case. But right now she had no time for that. She was focused on saving Kirstin. Couldn't the media see that?

Ray took her by the arm protectively and shouldered his way through the throng, repeating, "No comment, Miss Russo has no comment." Muttering under his breath as they knocked at the Lemke's door.

Bruce opened it a crack, then saw who it was. "Jesus, you got here fast," he said.

"It didn't seem fast," Ray replied, steering her inside, still shielding her from the most persistent reporters. "How long have all those vans been parked out front?" he asked Bruce.

"First ones got here last night. The others . . . I don't know, they've been arriving in a steady stream." Rumpled, bleary-eyed, shirttails dangling, feet sockless, Bruce led them into the kitchen where he was making coffee.

"You call the sheriff to hustle them out of here?"

Bruce sighed. "Schilling can't do too much. Long as they don't trespass. You know."

"Yeah, sure, I know the law," Ray said angrily.

Bruce handed them both mugs of coffee. She took hers, thanked him, and said, "Any news at all on the kidnapper?"

"Not much. A few possible suspects, one abandoned truck we're trying to trace."

"I'm going to talk to the Brenner girl again," she said.

Bruce cocked his head at her. "Why not? Give it a try. You sure as hell did a job on Lapinski. By the way, congratulations, that sketch you did . . ." But whatever he was going to say was left hanging when Josh Lemke entered the room.

He was in a bathrobe, unshaven, and hollow-eyed. "Oh, it's you," he said when he saw Jane. "Didn't think you'd grace us with your presence again."

She wasn't about to defend herself. "Hello, Josh," she said, her tone soft.

But he persisted. "Don't hello me. I can't believe you just took off like that to work on some goddamn old case that could have waited. How could you do that?"

"Look," she tried, "we've actually been working really hard trying to identify the man who took Kirstin."

"Oh, you have? Well, it seems to me,"—his voice rose—"you've been too busy making headlines to find the guy! If you're so fucking good, why can't you draw that . . . that bastard!"

"I'm trying, Josh. I'm trying so hard. I'm going to talk to Crystal again this morning."

"Go on, talk yourself blue. Why can't you find my little girl?"

Bruce was rolling his eyes, obviously accustomed by now to Josh's outbursts. But Ray took action. He grasped the man's arm and ushered him into a corner of the living room.

"Look, you can lash out like that, but it's not doing your daughter any good," Jane heard him say.

"What *are* you doing to find her?" Josh cried.

"We've just driven all night in a blizzard to get here, and we're trying our best. We're on your side. You understand that, Josh? We want Kirstin back as much as you do."

Josh stared at Ray for a moment, then burst into sobs, and sank onto a curved red sectional that looked out over the valley. Ray lowered his voice, and she couldn't hear what he said, but he put a hand on Josh's back and his tone seemed comforting, accepting. She looked across the dimly lit room at the two men, one collapsed on the couch, the other leaning over him, a hand resting on his shoulder. A shadowed tableau backlit by the pale dawn beyond the window. Outside, snow obscured the landscape, falling, covering every hollow and ridge and rooftop and tree branch. Blanking out the rest of the world. And it seemed to her that the men were isolated in that colorless universe, each alone in his pain.

"Remind me to take a long vacation when this is over," Bruce whispered at her ear.

She turned to him. "How is Suzanne doing?"

He shook his head. "Maybe you could give her some encouragement?"

"I can try," she said with more enthusiasm than she felt.

She found Kirstin's mother sitting up in bed watching television, her eyes unfocused, her expression slack, her hands lying white and lifeless on the coverlet. Her hair was unwashed and she wore a T-shirt that was torn, as if she'd clawed herself in grief.

Jane sat on the edge of the bed and put her hand on Suzanne's. "Hi, Suzanne."

"Oh, hello. You're . . . ? You look familiar, but . . ." Her voice trailed away. A man on TV talked cheerfully about food, what to serve for Christmas dinner, whether to have turkey or ham. Yams or mashed potatoes.

"Jane Russo, remember? I'm going to talk to Crystal again, and then I think I'll know more about the man who has Kirstin."

"Really?" Her voice was hopeless.

"Yes, really." Curiously, Jane felt a certainty that she'd lacked only moment ago. She squeezed Suzanne's hand tightly. "I think we'll find Kirstin soon."

The woman looked up into her face. "You really think so? Honestly? You aren't just saying that?"

"I honestly believe that. Just hold on, Suzanne, hold on." She wasn't lying, she *wasn't*. "We're going to find her."

But would they find her in time?

The man finished his last driveway at nine and had the rest of the day free. He could go skiing if he wanted to. Skiing in the fresh new snow, sharing the mountain with the other powder hounds, carving down the runs, searching for the perfect secret powder cache, the one that would provide face shots, where the snow was so deep it flew up off the tips of your skis and nearly choked you.

But he didn't want to ski. He'd lost interest. He was instead overcome by an urgent mission—to find out about this Jane Russo.

He parked in front of the Hickory House, one of the local workingmen's breakfast spots, and went inside. Picked a table in front of the television set and ordered his usual: scrambled eggs, toast, hash browns, and bacon. On the outside he appeared calm, unhurried; inside, he felt as if his blood was gushing through his heart, driving at the walls of the chambers.

Fox News was on, the usual blather about health and diet, political shenanigans, the volatile Mideast. He ate slowly and waited. The place was nearly empty; he was there, by design, between the breakfast and lunch crowds.

National news, finally. A blond woman reporting from a rural area outside Yakima, Washington: "Benton County militia leader Gerald Lapinski, aka the Northwest Bomber, is in a standoff with federal authorities, including the FBI, the ATF, and federal marshals. Lapinski has fired shots from inside his farmhouse, where he has barricaded himself, allegedly with his wife, but the federal agencies have withheld fire pending intelligence about who may be inside. We now return to Seattle, where Hodge Franklin will give a background report on Gerald Lapinski. Hodge?"

The man pushed his glasses up and forced himself to eat the potatoes, forced himself to savor each forkful on his tongue. He wasn't afraid of this Russo woman. No way. He convinced himself he was excited. Challenged. He carefully picked up a crisp strip of bacon and methodically bit off a piece. His eyes never strayed from the television screen.

Hodge Franklin, he thought derisively, then he listened to the man's report.

"And so Gerald Lapinski spiraled into ever more violence, all the while keeping his identity secret from the authorities," Hodge intoned. "Until one woman, a woman with an incredible talent, interviewed an ordinary man, but one whose visual recollection was extraordinary. Ben Forsberg, a sporting goods dealer, shot in the head by Lapinski, left for dead after a robbery. But surviving against all odds. And remembering. Remembering."

Okay, okay, the man thought, finishing his eggs, taking up another bacon strip. *What about Russo?*

Hodge might as well have heard him. "On your screen now is Jane Russo's rendition of Gerald Lapinski, drawn from Ben Forsberg's description. And next to it is a photo of Lapinski from his driver's license. Remarkable likeness." Hodge smiled his diamond bright smile. "Thirty-three-year-old Jane Russo, a freelance portrait artist hailing from Denver, Colorado, has worked for many law enforcement agencies, drawing criminals faces from their victims' descriptions. She has helped in the apprehension of many well-known criminals, including . . ." But the man shut out the list, because Fox News had put on the screen a photograph of Russo.

He stopped chewing, and he studied the face so that he'd know her anywhere. A pretty woman, with dark blond hair, wide-set eyes, high cheekbones, a determined chin. In the picture she looked very serious, staring off into the distance, and he wondered what exactly she'd been doing when the photo had been taken.

Jane Russo. Hodge was making her sound like a goddamn psychic saint. An avenging angel. And now she was on the case of missing twelve-year-old Kirstin Lemke, the reporter was telling his audience.

The tape switched from the studio to a live shot of Russo leaving the Lemke house, snow collecting on her pretty, honey-colored hair, a fixed smile on her lips, accompanied by a tall, grim-faced man who hustled her to a car.

The man couldn't believe it. A live picture of her. Here. In Aspen, only a few miles away from where he was sitting.

Hodge Franklin continued, his chocolate-mousse tones in voice-over: "Undisclosed sources tell Fox News that Jane Russo is on her way to interview a witness who will likely provide the break the FBI has been waiting for. Our next update on the hour. Hodge Franklin, live from Seattle."

It took a second for Franklin's words to sink in—Russo was on her way to interview a witness . . . provide the break they'd been waiting for . . .

That bitch, the man thought, and overwhelming hate enveloped him. On the heels of his loathing came fear and the knowledge of what he must do.

SEVENTEEN

They were everywhere, satellite vans, news anchors, cameramen. Outside of the Lemke's, on the road up to the house.

"My God," Jane said.

"Yeah, it's bad," Ray said, as they passed the airport, and he spotted another news van with a satellite dish parked in front of the arrival doors. The holidays, of course, and plenty of celebrities would be flying in. The reporters must figure they could fill dead air time by catching a star or two on video.

He'd never had any use for the media. With the exception of a couple of those *Most Wanted*-type shows, the press generally screwed things up. In this instance, they could do a helluva lot of damage if the UNSUB watched television. Kirstin was already in enough danger.

It was still too early to phone Crystal, so they stopped at the Grinell's house on their way into town. This time Jane invited him in, saying she was sure Gwen and George were at work by now, and they could get some coffee.

The Grinells were already on the mountain at their restaurant, but the boys were still home. When Ray walked in behind Jane, it looked to him as if a cyclone had blown through the living room. Breakfast dishes everywhere, pillows thrown on the floor, ski boots and hats littering the room. The TV was on, full blast, tuned to a robot monster cartoon. Lasers streaking from futuristic ray guns filled the screen.

"Hi, guys," Jane said, and the two boys sat up straight. "Can you turn that thing down?"

She introduced Ray to her nephews, Kyle and Nicky, and they stood and shook his hand.

"You're an FBI agent?" The one named Kyle was in awe.

"Yes, I am."

Then Nicky. "Do you have a gun?"

"I do."

"Wow, let's see it."

"No way," Ray said.

The boys plumped back down onto the couch and began asking Jane a dozen questions all at once. "We saw you on TV, Aunt Jane, out in Park City. That was so righteous. Why were you in Park City?"

Kyle began surfing channels, Nicky trying to snatch the remote controls from him. "Mom and Dad never told us what you do." Kyle shoved his brother in the chest. "They just said you were some kind of an artist."

"Well, I am." She stood over the couch and roughed Nicky's hair.

"But you draw bad guys' faces," Nicky said. "That's way cool."

"And you drew that bomber-dude. And now they're at his farmhouse, and they're going to arrest him."

"Or shoot him," Nicky said with devilish delight.

"They're going to try *not* to shoot him," Ray put in.

Kyle tossed the controls in the air, caught them; he was obviously restless. "I know Kirstin Lemke," he finally said.

"Me, too," Nicky added.

"I mean, I know who she is. From school."

"We're trying very hard to find her," Jane said.

"I know, but how come you haven't drawn the dude that took her, Aunt Jane?"

Ray saw the cloud cross her features. "I'm trying," was all she said. "We're going to see Crystal Brenner now to try to get more of a description."

"I know Crystal." Kyle made a face. "Her mother is, like, totally weird."

Nicky frowned at his brother. "Crystal's okay."

"Well, anyway," Jane said, "we're going to get some coffee before we go. Is that all right?"

"Nicky messed the kitchen up." Kyle gave his brother another shove.

"Fuck off," Nicky said, then he clamped his hand over his mouth. "Sorry," he said between his fingers.

"You know," Jane said, "using four-letter words is not cool. And you don't sound in the least bit sorry."

Nicky ducked his head for a moment and said, "I really am sorry, Aunt Jane. Honest."

She nodded. "Okay, then. I'll accept that as an apology."

"Will you be here for Christmas?" Kyle asked then.

"I'm not sure," she replied. "It depends on this case."

"We're going to help at the restaurant this afternoon, then get the Christmas tree. Will you be here to decorate?" Nicky asked. And Ray thought, *Christmas. Good God, tomorrow is Christmas Eve.* How had the holiday crept up on him? Not that he did anything about it. He bought no presents, sent no cards. What few relatives he had lived back East, and he'd never done much of a job staying in touch.

"Aside from too much cussing, they're cute kids," he said later as they drove to the mobile home park where the Brenner girl lived.

"Yes," Jane replied, "they are." Her tone was wistful.

She was biting her lip by the time they arrived at Crystal's trailer. "Oh God, I hope this works," she said.

He couldn't help putting a hand on hers. "You'll do fine. Just fine."

They had phoned from the Grinell's house, so Crystal was expecting them. Her mother wasn't home. *Thank God,* Ray thought. The place still reeked of pot, though.

Crystal was as willing as she'd been the first time. Ray sat quietly, the fat black lab Sherman again stretched across his feet as he watched Jane interact with the young girl. They talked about the weather and the upcoming holiday and snowboarding and a dozen other subjects.

"What did you ask Santa for?" Jane finally asked.

Crystal rolled her eyes. "Santa, right. I asked my *mother* for a new snowboard, one of those cool carving ones."

"Well, I hope you get it."

"She'll probably get me one from the thrift shop," Crystal said with resignation.

"I always had equipment from the ski swap," Jane told her, connecting, empathizing.

He marveled at her ability to establish rapport with the girl, the same way she had done with Ben Forsberg and countless others over the years. Where did her enormous reserve of understanding come from? How did she know with unerring precision what would reach these people?

Jane was handing a piece of Play-Doh to Crystal, explaining exactly why she needed to talk to her again. "You were such a good witness, the best, and I think there's more in your head. All we need is a tiny detail that might be enough to catch this terrible man."

"I tried, I really did. I told you everything I could remember. His face, the glasses, the truck. I can see that, but you know how you don't pay attention because you don't know something's going to be important?"

"I know. But the thing is, Crystal, you *did* see the whole thing, and it's in your brain somewhere. We just have to dig it up."

He was endlessly impressed with Jane now that he was able to see her work without his veil of skepticism. He could kick himself for wasting his energy in disbelief. He'd never met anyone like her, and he wished he had more time with her, to delve into her goodness and perhaps borrow some of her patience and caring. He wished he'd shown her his better side—if he even had one anymore.

That night . . . He should have stayed with her, woken with her in his arms. He should've been honest about his feelings instead of retreating into his shell like a turtle poked with a stick. He should have talked about Kathleen. Openly. Maturely.

He listened to her interact with Crystal; he stared at her, and he regretted what was never going to be.

The girl was molding the plastic, rolling it into a ball, flattening the ball, folding it over. He noticed her fingernails were bitten and had the remnants of blue nail polish on them.

"Okay," Jane was saying, "can you picture the truck again?"

"Uh-huh."

"Close your eyes and see it."

Crystal closed her eyes, her fingers busy.

"It was dark red, you said. Probably a metallic shade when it was new."

"Uh-huh."

"A Ford Ranger?"

"Yes. Dirty, all muddy."

"Now think, Crystal. Were there any dents in the truck? Broken lights? Rusted wheel wells, things like that?"

"Um . . ." Crystal thought, her eyes moving behind pale lids. "Um . . . The truck was pretty far away. And I wasn't even sure Kirstin was in it, not till way later. Melanie and I were, like, focused on the line for the shuttle bus."

"I know," Jane said softly. "But let's pretend you're not so far from the truck. You're looking right at it."

"Okay." She took a deep breath, let it out. Relaxing. "Um . . ." she said again. "The windshield . . . it might have been cracked. Like a spider web, you know?"

"Good. Now, pretend you're walking around the truck. The man's in it. He's got on a hat and neck gaiter, goggles pushed up on his hat. Glasses. You can't see him very well, but you can see the pickup. You walk along the side of the truck that faces you. What do you see?"

"Mud, dirt, a scrape, but it could just be a scrape in the mud, you know? Dark red. Faded metallic. It has . . . I think there's a stripe-thing along the side?"

"Molding," Jane supplied.

"Uh-huh."

"Now you're walking around the back. Can you see it?"

"I didn't really see the back." Her hands folded the Play-Doh nervously.

"When he drove away?"

"No, I wasn't paying attention. I'm sorry, I just can't remember."

"It's okay, Crystal, you're doing great. Now walk back along the side of the truck to the front. Did you see the front?"

"Sort of. I saw the crack in the windshield. The hood wasn't as dirty as the rest of it. It had big tires with those kind of deep treads. For snow."

"Good. Anything else? Writing on the door? Rust?"

"I don't remember rust, but there could have been some. I don't know." Her voice rose in distress.

"That's okay, you're doing great. You have a real eye for detail. Maybe you should become an artist," she said soothingly.

"Really?" Crystal opened her eyes. "You think so?"

"You should try taking some art classes in school. The high school still has Lottie Schilling as the art teacher, doesn't it?"

"I think so."

Ray watched in amazement as Jane brought the youth back from frustration.

"Sign up for a class from her. She's wonderful."

"I will. I really will. Do you think . . . I mean, I love to draw and all."

"Could you draw the red pickup?"

Crystal shook her head.

"But you remember quite a bit about it."

"A little."

"Where were we?" Jane asked. "Walking around . . ."

"We were at the front."

"That's right. And the hood was cleaner than the rest of the truck."

"Yes. Shinier. That's why I think it was metallic."

"Close your eyes again. See it in your head."

Obediently, Crystal did so. Her hands kneaded the Play-Doh.

"You're still walking around the front, big tires, mud and slush from the road, right?"

"Uh-huh."

"A license plate?"

Crystal frowned. "I can't see a license plate."

"The bumper? Was it chrome?"

"I can't see it."

"What do you see then?"

The girl hesitated, her brow furrowed in concentration. "The snowplow. I can see that."

"The . . . snowplow?"

Ray's heart clenched.

"Uh-huh. When he drove out of the parking lot, I thought he was going to take out a few skiers with it."

"You're sure about the snowplow?" Jane said, her voice rising.

"Uh-huh. I don't know why I didn't remember that before."

"That's okay," Jane said, "you remembered now."

Ray was already punching in numbers on his cell phone.

They left shortly after that, and Jane didn't know who was more satisfied, Ray or Crystal. She watched him with the young girl at the door, marveling when he held Crystal's hands and said, "You did a terrific job. Kirstin has a pretty wonderful friend in you, kiddo."

And Crystal's response was to smile at the same time her eyes glistened with tears. "Please find her," she said, choked up.

"We will, honey, we will," Ray said.

"That was nice," Jane began as they stepped out into the cold morning. The snow had stopped falling, and the sky was gray and heavy, the mountaintops wreathed in clouds. "She really . . ."

But a man was approaching them, microphone in hand, a cameraman behind him. "Agent Vanover, Ms. Russo, could you give us an update on the Lemke case?"

"No comment," Ray said in a hard voice. "Neither Ms. Russo nor I have a comment. Do you realize you're

endangering the life of an innocent twelve-year-old girl?"
And he pushed his way past them, strode straight to the car,
and gestured for Jane to get in.

"Goddamn vultures. Don't even have the sense to be
embarrassed," he said, wrenching the steering wheel around.

"I know. It's awful, but . . ."

Then he took a turn too sharply, throwing her against
the door. "I should have known this would happen after
you IDed Lapinski. I should've known. I never should've
let you talk to that Forsberg character. I knew it! Damnit
all. We should have gotten the Lemke case settled first."

She looked at his profile. "The reason I got the plow out
of Crystal was *because* of the breakthrough with Ben.
Don't you understand that, Ray?"

He muttered something under his breath.

"What?"

"I don't know what my understanding has to do with
this whole thing. But I do know that the coverage of this
case and of *you* is dangerous."

"It's worth the risk."

"Is it?" He flashed her an angry glance.

"Yes."

"Okay, so be it. Too late now."

"But the plow. Won't that help?"

He drove down the hill, crossed the river, turned toward
Main Street. "Yeah, it'll help. It'll nail the guy."

"Oh my God," she said, suddenly horrified, "do you
think . . . do you think he plows the Lemke's driveway?"

Ray smiled grimly. "I'd bet my life on it. The Lemkes,
the Sanchezes, the Weissmans, all of them. That's the
connection."

"Can it be that simple, a snowplow driver?"

"Oh, yeah," he said, "it usually is."

EIGHTEEN

The front door at the Lemke's wasn't even closed when Bruce pulled them both to the side. "Bad news, you two," he said, his voice low, and Jane just knew they'd found the snowplow driver, knew they'd found Kirstin's body . . . Her skin prickled in apprehension.

"What the hell now?" Ray said.

Bruce let out an exasperated breath. "The second you left that kid in the trailer park, CNN got to her. They just aired the info about the snowplow on the truck, and they're step in step with us on the assumption this guy is our UNSUB."

"Christ," Ray muttered, running a hand through his hair.

"You've got to realize," Jane said, "that if this snowplow driver has a TV and hears the report . . ." Of course they knew. She'd just stated the obvious. "All right, all right," she whispered, catching their looks. "But can you stop the media? I mean, if they know this information endangers Kirstin, won't they hold off?" But again, reading their exchange of glances, she knew there wasn't a chance of curtailing the press. The snowball was rolling nonstop down the mountainside now. *Oh God,* she thought.

She followed Ray into the kitchen where he sat down with Josh Lemke, who'd apparently not yet seen the news.

"Josh," Ray said, "tell me about the service that plows your driveway."

Josh was gripping a mug of coffee. "We, ah, don't use a service. Used to. But then we contracted with this guy . . ." Suddenly his knuckles turned white on the mug. "You think . . . Let me get this straight, you think this Kevin . . ."

"Kevin?" Ray broke in. "Kevin who? I need to know everything you know, Josh, right away."

Josh sucked in a breath. "Kevin Smith. Yeah, *Smith.* We've only written him one check, but it's Smith." He came half out of his chair. "Holy Christ! He drives an old red pickup truck! I just remembered! You mean, you think that *he* has Kirstin?"

Ray nodded, then reached out, took hold of Lemke's arm, and forced him back down into his seat. "Josh, you've got to focus. Do you have an address on this Kevin Smith? A phone number?"

"No, I mean, no address or phone. Jesus. He just shows up. It snows, he's here."

"How do you pay him? How you know *what* to pay him?"

"He . . . Look, he knocked on our door about a month ago, right before Thanksgiving, said he'd do our drive for twenty dollars a time. We were paying Mountain Maintenance twenty-five or something, so Suzanne said sure, he could have the job, but if he didn't show up, you know, missed plowing us sometimes, we wouldn't be able to use him."

"Did he leave a business card?"

"No, around here, guys that do odd jobs and cut you deals operate pretty much by the seat of their pants."

"Great," Ray said.

Jane and Bruce were both hovering close by, and she couldn't stop herself from interrupting. "Josh," she said, and he pivoted. "You paid him once so far this winter? Maybe at the end of November? Did he leave a bill?"

"Ah, yes, in the mailbox."

"Do you still have it?"

"I, ah, maybe Suzanne does. She pays the monthly bills."

Ray looked at Bruce, who took off down the hall toward Suzanne's bedroom. In the meantime, Sid Reynolds was in the living room flipping through the phone book. Agent Canning, who never seemed to leave his electronic equipment, was shrugging on his down parka and hurrying out to join the other sheriff's deputies in a house-to-house canvas of the neighborhood. Presumably, the Lemkes were not the only Brush Creek residents to have switched plowing services. *Someone* had to have a line on this Smith character.

Jane's attention was drawn to the television in the corner of the living room. The volume was turned down, so she could barely hear the report, but there was that still shot of her face on a split screen with video on the other side of her and Ray getting into the car in front of the Brenner's trailer less than a half hour ago. Then the shot of numerous federal and local authorities in the Washington State standoff at Lapinski's farmhouse. Finally they showed Lapinski's face from his driver's license and superimposed it over the sketch Jane had done yesterday.

Yesterday, she thought. It seemed weeks ago, and she felt a wave of exhaustion nearly overwhelm her.

Lapinski, Smith. And Kirstin. How could she have forgotten Kirstin for even a second?

Bruce came back into the kitchen brandishing a piece of paper, shaking his head. "This is all Smith gave them for a bill. His name, Smith, *sure,*" Bruce sneered, "and the number of the plow jobs times twenty dollars, then the total. Suzanne says she put the check in an envelope with his name and left it for him the next time it snowed. It was gone from the mailbox the following morning. She remembers looking in the mailbox, because she didn't want the mailman to take it by mistake."

Jane hovered over Ray's shoulder while he scanned the bill. She even put a hand on his jacket, then quietly removed it, afraid of what Bruce might think. And Ray . . . But he didn't seem to have noticed.

They were still studying the bill when Kent Schilling arrived with an entourage of deputies and a couple officers from the Aspen City Police, though this was county jurisdiction. He stationed the uniformed cops at the front door and the head of the driveway, as more and more media vans were chugging up the hill, reporters positioning themselves with the Lemke house as the backdrop, speaking into microphones while cameramen hoisted video equipment on their shoulders.

It was as if someone had dropped chum in the water, and now there was a feeding frenzy.

Ray finally stood and steered her aside. "I know you're beat," he said, his expression genuinely concerned, "but could you make a couple calls for me, and then I'll have someone drive you back to your sister's and you can get some rest?"

"Sure, but who . . . ?"

"The other victims. Lisa and Allie, and try the Weissmans, too. You have the numbers. Find out who plowed their drives."

"Oh, right," she said. "Of course."

"And see if there's anything they can remember. Anything. Maybe he used a different name. I don't know. Maybe he has a phone here and uses a name he's used before. It's a long shot, but worth a try."

"I'm on it," she said. "But my cell phone battery is dead."

He reached in his jacket pocket and gave her his phone, but when she started to take it, he held on to her hand, giving it a gentle squeeze. "You sure you're okay?"

"I'm fine. Really I am." She was surprised at the calm in her voice when her heart was hammering so loudly everyone had to hear. "I'll, ah, make those calls," she said, reluctantly pulling her hand from his. How could his touch alone, the mere brush of his fingers on hers, suck the breath from her lungs?

She sat in the family room and made the first call, reaching Allie at the Christmas Shoppe. But Allie had no recollection of the man or service who'd plowed their drive all those years ago before they had moved to the apartment complex. She gave Jane her mother's work number at the Mammoth Ski Lodge. "My mom, she remembers everything," Allie said. "Do you think this guy is the one?"

"Could be," she said.

"Will you call me right away when you know?"

"Right away, honey."

She spoke to Allie's mother. Afterwards, she talked to Lisa Turchelli's father at their convenience store in Snowbird Center and then to the Weissmans in Park City. Finally she returned to the kitchen where Ray was near the back door talking to Kent Schilling.

"Well," she announced, "you were right. That's the connection. The snowplow driver. A Kevin Smith plowed their drives. Always early in the morning and sometimes late in the afternoon. He left monthly statements, all handwritten, by the way, in their mailboxes or under their doors. He was always there after a fresh snow. No one ever remembers having to call him or even if he had a phone number. No one really remembers much about him at all."

"Real inconspicuous fella," Kent said.

Ray met her gaze and lifted his shoulders, then dropped them. "Didn't think you'd get much. But at least now we know. And it'll make solid courtroom evidence."

"*If* we find him," she pointed out.

"Oh, we'll find him," he said.

"Damn right," Kent agreed.

What no one said, what Jane knew they were afraid to voice aloud, was whether they'd find Kirstin in time. And out front the press just kept on running the story, making it sound as if the cops were closing in on their quarry. If Smith were watching the news, he'd have to react. He'd have to get rid of Kirstin.

But she shut the thought down hard. Last night it had snowed fourteen inches. Smith was out on the job. He would have been out since before dawn. He hadn't seen the news. He might not even own a TV. *God, don't let him have a TV.*

"You ready for a ride back to your sister's?" Ray was asking her.

"Oh, oh no, I couldn't rest. I *won't* rest until we find Kirstin."

"You can't keep up this pace." He took her arm, leading her toward Bruce. "I slept for hours in the car last night. You barely got a wink."

"But I . . ."

"For me, Jane, okay? Just try. Plug your phone in, and I'll call the minute we know something."

She thought a moment. He was right. She was completely done in and of no help to anyone. She'd take that ride and maybe she'd sleep. "Okay," she said. "But you promise to call?"

"I promise." He smiled, and she realized she'd give anything to have a lifetime of those smiles lavished on her. But on the heels of that notion her spirits dropped. *Fat chance, Russo*. She'd be lucky if she ever laid eyes on him again after this case was concluded. Another painful regret to add to the stack she'd amassed this week.

Ray instructed Bruce to do his best to lose the press then hang out at the Grinell's house until he was certain the media had not followed, and if they did, Ray said he'd have Schilling station a deputy there. He helped her on with her long tweed coat and walked her to the door, touching her cheek with a finger. "Thanks, Jane," he said, "you've been amazing."

"Call me," she said.

"I will."

Bruce evaded the two vans that followed them down the hill to the traffic light at the bottom of the Brush Creek subdivision. He sped up at the yellow signal and took the right turn toward Aspen practically on two wheels, and then he passed everything on the highway. At the roundabout, he darted up Maroon Creek Road and made the left up the hillside a good half-mile in front of the vans. They'd lost them.

Her nephews had gone to the restaurant, and Gwen and George wouldn't be home till after five. And hadn't Nicky or Kyle said something about getting the Christmas tree this evening? So maybe, she thought, she'd have some privacy. She plugged in her phone and stretched out on the guest bed, pulling the comforter up to her chin. She was sure she'd never sleep, but she could at least lie here. Unless something broke with the case. Which she prayed would happen. And Ray had promised to call.

She turned her head. Yes, she'd put her cell phone right

next to her on the bedside table. *Okay*. She could close her eyes now. Finally. If only her pulse would slow down. If only Kirstin . . .

She sat up with a jolt, her heart leaping. What? Where was she?

Her phone was ringing. She grabbed it, realizing she was at Gwen's and had dozed off.

It was Ray. "I woke you," he said.

"No, no, it's okay. I . . . Let me just catch my breath. God, I'm a wreck. What's happened? Have you found . . . ?"

"We've got a lead on Smith," he told her. "About an hour ago, we got a call from a guy who said he rents a cabin to Smith out on a road called Little Annie's."

"My God, that's not far from here. And it makes sense. It's totally isolated up there but still close to town. Ray, have you . . . ?"

"I'm there now."

"Oh, *oh*. Did you find Kirstin, is she . . . ?"

"The place is deserted. Looks as if Smith must've heard the news and taken off."

"Oh no! Oh God, Kirstin . . ."

"We knew this could happen."

"Is there . . . is there any . . . sign, you know, that Kirstin may still be all right?"

"I know what you're asking. There's absolutely no sign of that kind of violence. And we're damn sure this is where she was being held. There's a mountain of evidence in the bedroom. I won't go into detail."

"No, please don't," she said, images of ropes and badly stained mattresses assailing her.

"Look, I'm reasonably sure the girl's okay, or *was* okay a few hours ago. The potbelly stove is still warm, so we can assume he didn't take off with her too long ago. That's what Schilling thinks, anyway."

"He'd know." Kent had a potbelly stove in his home.

"That's what I figure. We've put out an APB on Smith and his vehicle. Odd thing is there's no truck, no Ford pickup, anyway, registered in Utah or California or Colorado to our Kevin Smith."

"He could be using an alias. Or he registers the truck in a different state. Kansas, Nebraska, Arizona, New Mexico? All he'd need is a P.O. box."

"I know. But it's going to be tough for him to get out of the valley. Too little time before we put out the APB."

She exhaled and kicked away the comforter. There'd be no more sleep this day. "You'll find him, Ray, I know you will."

"You bet," he said. "Look, I've got to go. I just wanted to update you."

"Thanks, I mean that. But is there anything I can do?"

"Not a thing. You've done enough. By the way, you still alone there?"

"Yes. I'm okay though."

"You're sure?"

"Positive."

"You have my cell number. Call me if you need anything."

"I will. And good luck, Ray. Let me know as soon as you find Kirstin."

The whole Grinell family arrived home just after six, dragging in a seven-foot tall Christmas tree, everyone talking at once, Gwen giving Jane a quick hug then hurrying to find the boxes of decorations in the garage. Jane watched the madcap scene and swore to herself that if she ever had a family of her own, she'd do things at a reasonable pace. Christmas was supposed to be a peaceful time of good cheer and warmth, friends and family, not a rat race.

George carried in the boxes of decorations and set them

on the living room couch, while Gwen put a casserole in the oven. She'd prepared the dish that morning at the restaurant. Oh so organized.

The boys punched and pushed at each other and fought over who was going to string the lights on the tree.

"I do with every year!" Kyle yelled. "Mom, make Nicky do it! *Mom!*"

"Asshole," Nicky fired back.

"That's enough of that," George barked.

In the background Jane had the TV tuned to a Denver news channel. Every ten minutes or so a live update from Aspen came on. There was a report Smith had been apprehended at a cabin on Little Annie's Road. Another report correcting the first report. Smith had *not* been found. The national news was still covering the standoff between the federal authorities and the Northwest Bomber in eastern Washington State, video shots through a telescopic lens wavering and grainy in the waning light of day. Speculation as to when the feds would storm the place abounded, as did mention of the Ruby Ridge and Waco fiascoes.

"The standoff between the federal authorities and Gerald Lapinski could go on for days or even weeks," the reporter intoned.

Wonderful, Jane thought, her head aching from the lack of sleep and constant tension.

"Look," George said from the living room, "you're on again, and right there with the Veep, who's here for the holidays. Kyle, you step on that string of lights one more time like that and you can spend Christmas in your room, boy."

"Sometimes I wonder how I cope," Gwen said, checking the casserole, then striding to the laundry room, where she sorted a load of wash.

Yes, a madhouse, Jane thought again, and Gwen wouldn't let her do a thing to help.

"Have they found Kirstin yet?" Nicky called, dashing into the kitchen and out again.

"Not yet," Jane said to his back.

"The boys think it's cool, you know," Gwen said, pausing for a moment, her expression grave. "At their age they just don't get it. They know their schoolmate is in danger, but they're more interested in phoning their friends to tell them *the* Jane Russo on television is their very own Aunt Jane."

Jane leaned against the kitchen counter and folded her arms. "I suppose that's par for the course at their age."

"They can be so dense at times . . . Well, sometimes I wonder. I should've had girls, I guess, maybe then I wouldn't worry. Except for that old adage, what is it? Oh, right, if you have a son you only have to worry about one little prick on the block, but with a girl, you worry about all the little pricks."

Suddenly Gwen grew still. Then she bit her lip, exactly the same way Jane habitually bit hers. "That was stupid of me," Gwen said. "I mean . . . Well, you've always thought you were . . . ah, you know . . . molested."

"*Thought* I was molested?" She unfolded herself and stood straight.

Gwen eyed her. Then she shrugged. "This has gone on long enough. I mean, my God, Mom told me what you said. About Roland. Or maybe it wasn't Roland, maybe it was Scott. Or let's see. It could have been Kent. Um. Will the real rapist please stand up?"

Jane felt as if Gwen had just slapped her face. Every nerve ending in her body sizzled. She and Gwen had never directly spoken about the camping trip, though Jane was aware their mother had told her sister. But to find out like this, to have Gwen stand there and insinuate, with that imperious tone of hers, that Jane was . . . making the story up . . .

"Can you believe it?" came George's voice at the door.

"Jane is on *again*. My little sister-in-law, a celebrity. Who'd of thought it?" Then he was next to her, oblivious to her inner turmoil, to his wife's frozen stance. "It really is great to have you here, Jane. I mean aside from what that poor Lemke girl is suffering, it *is* good to see you. And Gwen and I were talking on the way up the mountain this morning. We really want you to stay through the holidays. No matter what happens with this god-awful case, we want you here with us. Tomorrow we're all having dinner. It'll be the four of us and Hannah and Roland, the Schillings, oh, and Scott, can't forget the Wonder Boy, and a couple other friends. It's become an annual Christmas Eve gathering. Gwen? Tell Jane she isn't getting out of it this year."

"You're doing just fine," Gwen said coolly, and George, still oblivious, put a hand on Jane's arm.

She couldn't help her knee-jerk reaction. She recoiled from him. Then she muttered something and beat a retreat to the guest room, where she began to pace, one hand on her brow, the other on her hip.

Goddamn Gwen, she thought over and over. *Goddamn George.* But then she had to step back and take a look at it from her sister's point of view. Why *would* Gwen believe her? Jane couldn't even identify the man who'd raped her. Who would believe that? She could hardly fathom it herself. If it weren't for all the years she'd spent working with young, abused girls, she'd never believe to what depths the human brain would go to protect itself.

Don't blame Gwen and don't blame George, blame yourself.

Who in hell was it? *Which* man, which one had sneaked into her tent that long ago night and robbed her of her pride and innocence? She could almost see him, almost . . . Damnit, why wouldn't she let the face come into focus?

She clenched her jaw and squeezed her eyes shut and

thought she was going to scream. Then Gwen knocked on her door and begged her to come out, and said, "Jane, I'm so sorry. I'm as stupid as those stupid boys of mine. I'm just all stressed out over the holidays and the restaurant . . . Jane?"

"I'm here."

"Will you forgive me? Can we talk about it? We should've talked years ago."

Jane looked at the closed door, then picked up her coat and gloves. She pulled the door open.

"Jane? Where are you going? You aren't *leaving?*"

"Oh, Gwen," she sighed, "I'm not leaving. I'm going for a walk before dinner. Okay?"

"You're sure? I mean . . . Look, you're my little sister. I really do want to sit down with you and talk. Jane, I love you, and I've missed you." She gave Jane a hug. "You will stay through Christmas, won't you?"

She nodded. "I'll try to stay. I just need some fresh air right now."

"It's my fault."

"No, no, it isn't. I'm uptight about Kirstin. I've been uptight for a week. I just want to walk for a little bit."

Somehow she got out the front door, the raised voices of Nicky and Kyle fading as she reached the street, trying to make the ugly images of the scene in Gwen's kitchen recede. She stared up at the star-studded night and felt the cold, pure air fill her lungs.

Gwen wanted to talk. After all these years. Maybe, just maybe, there was hope for their family after all.

NINETEEN

Smith saw the woman come out of the house. *Well, well.*
He couldn't believe his luck. Where was she going with
her determined air and long stride? Was she on her way to
meet someone? He searched the darkness—no vehicles, no
headlights. Nobody on the dead-end road in this nice, private neighborhood.

He turned the key in the ignition, holding his breath.
Would she hear? Would she notice?

It was full dark now; he could hardly make her out. He
slipped the gearshift into first, engaged the clutch, and let
the truck roll slowly down the hill after her. No headlights.

In the passenger seat, the Lemke brat stirred. He
glanced over at her, and she cringed. She sickened him.

But the other one . . . Not his type. Too aggressive, too
confident. Dangerous.

A car approached, climbing the hill, its lights illuminat-
ing her and sweeping on. At a safe distance, he rolled along

behind her, wondering where she was going, why she'd left the warmth of the brightly lit house.

She never turned around, not till he was right next to her. He leaned across the girl and rolled down the window. "Get in," he said.

She stopped short and turned, started to say something, then he saw recognition burst in her.

"Get in," he repeated.

He took the knife out then, holding it to the throat of the girl huddled, tied up, next to him. Making sure that *she* saw the glint of a streetlight off the blade. "Get in or I'll kill her."

There was an anxious moment when he thought she might yell or run, but he twisted the knife—just a little—and the girl made a noise, like a wounded rabbit, and the woman named Jane Russo held up a hand as if to stop him and moved toward the truck. Females were so fucking dumb.

At 9:06 P.M. Ray was informed there was a call for him from a woman named Gwen Grinell. The call had been routed through the sheriff's office and patched through to Kent Schilling's cell phone. It took Ray a second, but then he placed her—Jane's sister, right.

"I'm so worried," she was saying. "Jane went out for a walk, oh, I guess around seven, and she's not back."

"Let me get this straight," he said. "Jane went out for a walk at seven this evening? In the dark?"

"Yes, I didn't think . . . I mean, she just said a short walk, but then she didn't come back and George said . . ."

"George?"

"My husband. He said with all the publicity maybe the media was bothering her, or . . ."

"Two hours ago? She left your house two hours ago?"

"Yes. Oh, I'm so upset. I shouldn't have . . ."

"Okay, Mrs. Grinell, *Gwen,* you stay right there. I'll be over in a few minutes."

There was no question in his mind. He knew with the kind of clarity that didn't need proof. He knew Kevin Smith had her. The son of a bitch had her.

How in hell had he found her?

Fear seized his belly with a cold hand. *Not Jane, not another death.* But he had some time. Smith was running scared, desperate, or he wouldn't have taken her. She didn't fit the mold. She wasn't like the helpless young girls he preyed on. The man was desperate, all right. Knew they were hunting him. Was he planning to use Jane as a shield? *Not Jane.*

He sped down the dark highway like a madman, the sheriff, another vehicle with two deputies and two agents following. His hands shook on the wheel.

The Grinell's house, lit up for the holidays, was so innocuous looking. Somehow, he thought fleetingly, it should be blazing, exploding, anything but squatting quietly on its snow-covered hillside.

Gwen opened the door before he could knock. The deputies and agents pressed close behind him, so many men crowded into the warm, pine-scented living room. A Christmas tree stood in the corner, half decorated.

"Kent?" Gwen cried. "Where is she? Have you found her?"

"Now calm down, Gwen. We don't even know for sure if she's . . ."

Gwen collapsed on the couch, face in her hands. "It was my fault. I never should have . . ."

"Now, dear," her husband George said.

The two boys sat in chairs, stock-still, white faced, scared.

"Mrs. Grinell, Gwen," Ray said. "Let's start at the beginning. Tell me exactly what happened."

She told the story. Tearfully. A quarrel. Jane suddenly needing to go for a walk.

"I waited and waited," Gwen said. "And then it got so late. And I looked in the guest room to see if she . . . she'd taken her cell phone, but it was on the night table, so I . . . I couldn't call. And then George went out and drove around, to see . . . to see if she was on the road. And then, I called. Oh my God, where is she?"

While Kent talked to the Grinells, Ray issued orders. Cool, collected on the outside, professional. Roadblocks, descriptions; they knew the drill. And all the while, random thoughts darted through his mind, bouncing off one another, uncontrollable, even as he discussed plans with Bruce and Sid. Feelings bounced off each other, too, electrical surges that drowned thought. White-hot fear.

There wasn't much time. A little. Yes, a little, because Smith had to find a safe place where he could hole up, do whatever he planned. To Jane. To Kirstin.

Time thundered in his ears, every precious second taken away, never to be retrieved. *Not Jane.*

He forced her to drive. He had to, she knew, because he couldn't control her the way he had Kirstin, who was tied up. So he held the knife at the girl's throat, sitting in the middle of the front seat, between Jane and Kirstin.

He smelled of sweat, a sharp acrid odor, and motor oil, dressed in stained overalls, a lined flannel shirt, heavy engineer boots.

"Turn here," he said, gesturing with the knife.

She registered the route, her mind skittering from one insane idea to another. Try to overpower him. Drive into another car, a tree, a ditch. Anything to stop this deadly journey.

He was avoiding the main highway; he must have figured there were roadblocks. But now that she hadn't returned to the Grinell's house, someone would know she'd been taken. Wouldn't they? Wouldn't Ray?

How long would Gwen wait before she got worried? Had George or Gwen called anyone yet? Was there an alert out? Did anyone know?

She tried to think and steered the balky truck on the snowy road. Down Cemetery Lane, crossing the river, up the other side, the two-lane winding road that paralleled Highway 82. Not many cars. A few, their lights brushing her eyes and speeding past.

He wasn't stupid. He knew the area.

"Take a right," he said.

The Lenado Road. Where were they going? And Kirstin? Jane couldn't even see her, the man's bulk was in the way. But she was alive.

Make the abductor identify with you, feel your humanity. Oh, she knew the rules, what she should do. Talk to the monster.

She steered the truck up the Lenado Road, into the dark and the unknown, passing a few old ranches, some new mega homes, built by the rich for genteel seclusion.

"Your name is Kevin Smith, isn't it?" she tried.

"Shut up."

"If you let us out here, you can drive away. We can't stop you."

"Just drive."

Kirstin whimpered, and she wished, oh God, she wished she could do something to alleviate the girl's terror. How much longer could Kirstin bear this?

God, she'd been foolhardy. Broke every rule. The last

thing you did was to go quietly with an abductor. You did anything to avoid that: kick, scream, run, even risk injury or death—because once you were in his power you were as good as dead. But there'd been Kirstin. All the rules were changed, and he'd had the upper hand, because he had nothing to lose now. He'd kill the child in a heartbeat.

How far had they come? Five miles? Ten? She couldn't tell, hadn't been up this road in years. And it was so dark, the truck's headlights skimming white fields, trees, an occasional house.

Think, think.

How could she overpower him? Save Kirstin and escape? She could jerk the steering wheel, drive off the snow-packed pavement, hope he hit his head. But then she remembered that there was a drop-off along this road. A cliff. Crashing the truck would kill them all. Oh God, what could she do?

Kirstin moaned. "Shut up," Smith repeated harshly. The truck tires thrummed along the lonely road. She struggled with the tight steering wheel; the cab bounced over rough spots. Like last night—driving endlessly through Utah and Colorado in the darkness—only nothing like last night.

"What are you going to do?" she asked. "Where are we going?"

"Not your problem."

"People will miss me," she said. "My sister . . ."

"Keep driving," he said.

Think, she told herself. *Think or die.*

It took all of Ray's willpower to ward off the panic. His clothes felt stiff with dried sweat. One of his eyelids wouldn't stop twitching. His hands shook from the count-less cups of coffee Gwen Grinell had supplied him, Kent, and Bruce.

The boys had been sent to bed. Poor kids, they were probably listening at their doors, scared to death. Gwen cried quietly on the couch, and her husband had an arm around her, trying to comfort her. George Grinell. He was one of the men who'd been on the camping trip with Jane all those years ago. Maybe he was the one who'd raped her. Maybe his face was the one she couldn't remember. Was that what Jane and her sister had been arguing about, what had driven Jane into the arms of danger?

On the surface George appeared to be a nice enough guy, tall, with sandy hair thinning at the top. He'd probably been good-looking back then. A charmer, a ladies' man. Maybe he was glad Jane was gone, so that his dirty secret need never be aired.

Jane. Every law enforcement officer in the valley was on the lookout for the truck with the snowplow. Deputies from three counties, the state patrol, local police, agents from Sid Reynolds' office in Glenwood Springs. Every major road was covered. Even the ski company personnel had been put on alert. Someone at the ski company's main office had found a record of Smith's season pass, with his photograph. Lousy picture, barely recognizable.

Not a soul doubted that it was Smith who had Jane, yet no one had seen him take her. Not a neighbor, not anyone. How had he found her? Had Smith been following them all day?

Bruce's cell phone rang, and he answered it, turning away for privacy. The call was quick; when he clicked off, he shook his head. "They've gone through Smith's cabin now with a fine-tooth comb, tagged and sealed everything he left behind. Boxes will be sent to forensics."

"Did they find anything new? *Anything?*"

"Nothing's that going to tell us where he is now."

Ray felt dead inside. Full of anger and fear, yet dead at

the same time. "There's got to be something, something we're overlooking."

"This guy's smart."

But I'm smarter, Ray told himself. *I have to be.*

It was no use grilling the Grinells anymore. They knew nothing. Only that Jane had put on her coat and gloves and boots and gone out for a walk.

He couldn't stay in the house another second. "I'll be outside," he told Kent. "Need some air."

The night had turned clear and cold. There was no moon. Blackness extended all around him, with barely enough light to reflect dimly off the snow. Overhead stars blinked and glowed, so many, more than you could ever see in rainy Seattle. He walked to his car, put both hands on the hood, so cold the metal burned, leaned there, head down. Breathing hard, gulping great lungfuls of frigid air.

Jane. Where are you? What has he done to you?

All right. Okay. Smith was a criminal, a sick man driven by uncontrollable urges. Criminals were never as smart as they thought they were. Funny thing was, they planned every last detail of the crime: the who, what, where, when, and why. Planned for months and sometimes years. But once the crime was committed, they always screwed up, always left some glaring evidence behind. Even Smith had never counted on one of the girls recalling the snowplow attached to his truck. He was probably still wondering how Jane had gotten onto him. Unless she'd told him by now, been forced to tell him.

Shit. What were they overlooking?

He braced himself against the car, and he tried to put himself in Smith's mind. A twisted brain but one that worked according to its own strict logic.

Where would he take his two captives? Someplace he felt safe. Someplace private, where he knew no one would come barging in. He couldn't leave the valley, because there was an APB out on his truck and all the roads were blocked.

There were a few private roads leading to multimillion dollar fortresses equipped with state-of-the-art security systems. Smith couldn't get into them even if they were empty, but it was Christmas, and all the second homes would be occupied for the holidays. So where could the man hide? And how long before the bastard killed Jane and Kirstin?

How long?

TWENTY

It was late, after midnight. Five hours since she'd left her sister's to get a "little fresh air" before dinner. By now Gwen must have reported her missing. *She must have.* Or did Gwen just think she was pissed off after their quarrel? Had the Grinell household gone to bed, ignoring Aunt Jane's childish behavior?

She didn't know exactly where they were, how far they'd driven up the Lenado Road. She'd checked the odometer in the truck, but it was broken, frozen on 116,328 miles. Then Smith directed her to turn into a long driveway that led, finally, to a log house nestled into a hillside, surrounded by stone walls and tall blue spruce trees.

Whose house? Somebody wealthy who wasn't here this Christmas? Perhaps the owners were in Bermuda or Paris or Bangkok. She surmised instantly that they must have hired Smith to plow their driveway. So he knew the place, knew they wouldn't be in residence. And in order to keep the driveway clear, he'd have to plow right up to the garage doors; so he'd know the security code to open them.

Would he park his truck inside? But no, he ordered her to drive around behind the garage to park—he had everything figured out. Even if someone checked inside the garage, they wouldn't spot his vehicle. No one would know they were there. Nobody. Not a soul.

He ordered them out of the truck, shoving both of them, making sure they saw the knife. Around the front of the house, he punched numbers into the security pad. Then, as soon as the garage doors began to crank open, he pushed them inside and finally into a pantry, through a kitchen to the living room, where there was a lamp turned on, presumably hooked into a timer. Her nerves scratched against her skin, and her chest was so tight she couldn't seem to get her breath. But Kirstin . . . the poor child was numb with prolonged shock, moving like a mannequin, following commands woodenly. *Damn you to hell, Smith.*

She sat on a leather couch, both arms around Kirstin. She might have appreciated the faux hunting lodge decor of the room, but all she had was an impression—Navajo rug, heavy leather furniture, log walls, an elk-antler chandelier.

She tried to take calming breaths while her eyes tracked Smith, who paced back and forth, back and forth, his knife catching the light of the single lamp as he pivoted. She should have been exhausted; instead adrenaline was gushing like liquid fire through her veins.

"We'll be okay," she kept whispering to Kirstin. "We'll be fine."

"Shut up," he rasped. "Shut up."

"Why don't you leave us here and drive away? We won't tell anyone. You can cut the phone lines. Just leave us here."

"Ha!" he said scornfully. "They're looking for me. You stupid bitch, you'd love that, wouldn't you?"

Kirstin cowered at the anger in his voice. She hadn't said a word. Not one word. Her thin body shook, and she smelled stale. Rage stabbed at Jane's chest.

But she couldn't lose herself in anger. She had to narrow her thoughts down, concentrate. Could she surprise him somehow? Knock him out? Her eyes darted around, searching for a weapon. A wrought-iron lamp, a fireplace tool, a candelabra on the counter dividing the living room from the kitchen. Anything.

She prayed that Gwen had reported her missing. She had, of course she had. And Ray would know what had happened. He'd know instantly; he'd warned her that she was in danger when she'd identified the bomber and the media went wild. And she'd gone for a walk. *Stupid, stupid.*

But how would Ray find them? Would he figure out they were at the house of one of Smith's clients? It was pretty far-fetched to imagine he'd check out Smith's clients, even if he could find out who they were.

It was up to her if they were to get out of this alive. She looked at Smith. "Please, just turn us loose. It'll take us forever to get to a phone."

Smith paced, not answering. He moved jerkily. His body language told her he was scared, trying to figure out what to do. He'd broken with his normal MO, and he was confused and anxious. *Good.* Or, she thought, maybe the anxiety made him more dangerous, more unpredictable.

She studied him, holding Kirstin, whispering to her, stroking her tangled hair. But in her head, she was sketching his face. Every detail. The hollow cheeks and straggly beard, the muddy-colored eyes, the nose—yes, a bump. An earring in his left ear. A crooked front tooth. Not chipped, crooked. Five ten, one hundred seventy pounds, she estimated. Pitted skin from teenage acne.

She watched him and she assigned his face to memory, in

case she ever had to identify him. In case she got the chance.

She was afraid, but not paralyzed. Not yet. Her heart pounded, and her senses were knife-sharp. She felt as if she could see everything in the room, hear everything. Her muscles were ready to leap, to fight, to escape.

"It's okay, Kirstin. We're going to be fine. They're already looking for us."

"Shut up," he snarled.

By four in the morning, Ray was in a suspended state of dread. He'd gone back to Smith's house himself, combing through every piece of garbage, every scrap of paper, even sifting through the ashes in the woodstove and the woodpile out back. Nothing. No idea where Smith had gone or what he planned to do.

He returned to the Lemke's house, and he spoke several times with Jane's mother, then Hannah's husband Roland, who was dying to join the manhunt. Ray finally turned him over to the sheriff to handle. Every ten minutes someone from the Grinell house called, Gwen or George, and Ray spoke with them three times before he asked Bruce to take their calls. What more could he tell them? He didn't even know what to tell himself.

He checked in with the sheriff's deputies and state patrol manning the roadblocks so many times that he knew they were sick of hearing from him. Wondering why he was behaving in such an unprofessional manner.

Josh Lemke poured mugs of coffee and brought them to Ray and Kent Schilling. How many cups did this make? Six? He'd lost count.

"Okay. He was a snowplow driver," Ray said for the tenth time that night. "There's got to be a way to . . ."

Kent pursed his lips and shook his head. "Hard to trace,

no real records. I mean, it's not like he ran a legitimate business or had a bookkeeper."

"He can't get out of the valley," Ray repeated. A mantra he clung to. The words were true, but that fact wouldn't keep Jane and Kirstin alive. Hell, no.

"He's got to be someplace close." Ray had said that many times before, too. "He knows we're onto him. He needs a hideout, a safe house."

"Jesus, who'd put him up? Everyone knows he's on the run. And this Smith's a loner, probably doesn't have many friends here. Not the kind that would aid and abet him, anyway."

Ray stood up. He couldn't sit still for long. His body craved action. "The people he knows are mostly his clients, right?"

"Pretty much, I'd say."

"So he could use one of their houses, but none of them will be empty. It's Christmas. Everyone is here. All the places are occupied. So where would he . . . ?"

Kent sat straighter. "Now, hold on. Plenty of people have second homes here, but the real rich ones have *third* homes. Hell, yes. They could be anywhere right now."

With surprising clarity, Josh Lemke agreed. "Empty houses? Sure. Some of these people spend Christmas in London or Paris. Or stay home and come here after New Year's when it's not so crowded. I personally know people who do just that."

Ray could barely fathom the concept—owning an Aspen home and not using it during the holidays? "You're saying . . . ?"

"Oh yeah." Kent nodded.

"And you think they'd hire someone to plow their drive-way even if they're not planning on being here?"

"Hey, winter or summer, they demand their services

whether they're here or not. Housecleaning, gardening, window washing, Jacuzzi maintenance, every goddamn thing you can think of. Snowplowing, absolutely."

Ray's pulse quickened. "So he'd know . . . an empty house."

"What're you thinking?" Kent's brow creased.

"Jesus Christ," Ray said. "He left his bank statements at the cabin!" He turned on Lemke. "You said you paid Smith by check, or your wife did, right?" But he didn't give Josh time to answer. "A check." Ray was thinking furiously. "And there'll be records of his deposits. The statements were from a local bank."

"I'm on it," Schilling said, flipping open his cell phone.

By five in the morning they'd awakened the bank manager. By six, Ray and Schilling were at the bank, studying a printout of the activity on Smith's account. They derived eighteen names from the deposited checks. Eighteen addresses.

They all went into high gear.

Jane came up with a plan. Ridiculous, risky, but it *was* a plan. The hardest part was that she needed Kirstin's help, and she wasn't sure the girl could understand what was required of her. Or if she understood, carry through her role. She stroked the child's hair, talking soothingly to her, telling her about Crystal and Melanie and her mom and dad, how everyone in Aspen had been looking for her for over a week now. How much they loved her.

Kirstin gave little sign that she heard. She clung to Jane, shivering, her eyes closed.

Smith finally stopped pacing. He slumped into a leather armchair, his hands nervously flipping the knife end over end, catching it. He gave up telling Jane to shut up. He just sat, watching her with hooded eyes. Figuring his next move while he adeptly caught the butt end of the knife without fail.

"Can we use the bathroom?" she finally asked.

He gestured with the blade. *Thank God,* she thought, *thank God,* a minute or two alone with Kirstin. But would that be enough time?

With the powder room door closed, in a semblance of privacy, Jane whispered her plan to Kirstin. But all the girl did was shake her head, over and over. How to reach her? *How?* And they were taking too long in the bathroom, too long . . .

"Kirstin, honey," Jane whispered, holding the girl's shoulders, trying so hard to reach her. "We're going to make it through this. We are. You have to believe me. Listen, the same thing happened to me when I was young. I was raped. Really, it happened to me. I *know* how you feel. I know how afraid you are. But you'll be okay. Your family will help and your friends will help. Kirstin, can you hear me? Are you listening? See? I'm okay. You'll be okay, too. But you have to help me now. You *have* to. Can you do that?"

Kirstin finally stopped shaking her head. She stood there, skinny, dirty, half out of her mind, and she drew her head back to meet Jane's eyes. "Promise?" she whispered.

"I promise," Jane said.

She flushed the toilet, and then led Kirstin back to the couch. Smith was standing at the window now, knife still in hand, watching the faint light of dawn. Time was running out for him. For them, too.

Ray and the deputy named Bernie were on their way to check out one of the eighteen addresses when he got the call.

"Okay," Schilling said, "we've found him. It's the address out in Lenado. Saw some fresh tire tracks and spotted his truck parked in the back."

Lenado. Ray was heading in the wrong direction. "I'm on my way. Tell Bernie exactly how to get there." He tossed his cell phone to the deputy and spun the car around, its wheels finding no purchase on the slippery road.

He drove too fast in the pale dawn, Bernie directing him. Down Cemetery Lane to the river, up the far side, along a narrow, winding road. Far too fast. Sliding out on one curve.

"Holy shit, man, take it easy." Bernie clutched the dashboard.

"Yeah, right," Ray said. He pressed the accelerator, feeling the wheels spin and catch on a dry spot in the road. The car surged ahead. *I'm coming, Jane. I'm coming.*

TWENTY-ONE

She had managed to position herself so that she was at the far end of the tobacco-brown leather couch. He must have noticed; did he wonder why she and Kirstin were huddled next to the fireplace now?

His face was pasty and drawn; he was exhausted. How long could he stay awake? Maybe she had to do nothing more than wait until he fell asleep. He'd have to sleep eventually, wouldn't he?

Kirstin had rested for awhile, head in Jane's lap, but now she was awake. Waiting. They were all three waiting. For what? For daylight, so he could drive back down Lenado Road and use them as hostages to escape the valley? And then what?

He paced, he played with the knife, flicking it so that it stuck into the log wall. She wondered if she could grab him while the knife hung, quivering, in the wood, but he was always too quick to retrieve it.

She kept talking to Kirstin, meaningless reassurances,

but she tried to send signals with her eyes. *Soon. We'll do it soon. Be ready.*

The sun was slow to rise in the narrow Lenado Valley. Finally it streamed in the window, lying in bright swathes across the golden pine floor and the brightly colored Navajo rug. It reached the big chair where he was sitting. In the warmth he almost dozed off, his head sagging, then jerking up.

Should she wait? Or would he kill them when he realized he was going to fall asleep despite everything?

Only the on-and-off hum of the refrigerator broke the silence of the house. And Jane's words to Kirstin, a low murmur. Smith remained eerily silent, chin on his chest, eyes on them. His lids lowered at times, his head nodded, then he got up, moving around, shifting the knife from hand to hand.

The next time he sat down in the chair, she squeezed Kirstin's arm. Surreptitiously. Afraid to look at her in case he noticed. Surprise was her single advantage.

She waited, on the verge of terror and desperation and reckless resolve. She couldn't do anything yet; it was up to Kirstin. But could the girl summon the strength to carry out the plan?

Finally, *finally,* Kirstin whimpered, her voice weak, quavering. Her moans grew in intensity, becoming rending sobs, then screams, and she doubled over. Terrible wails that pierced Jane's ears. All the pain and fear of the last days emerging in awful, choking cries.

"Oh my God!" Jane breathed, trying to hold Kirstin, but she wrenched herself out of Jane's grasp and fell on the floor, still screaming. Jane kneeled beside her writhing body and tried to still her.

"Shut her up," he yelled.

"I can't! Something's wrong with her. Help me!"

"Shut her the fuck up!" He rose and took a step toward them.

Kirstin screamed louder.

He broke. "I'll shut her up," he hollered, and he came, fast, in a fury, hands outstretched.

Now it was Jane's turn. She lunged from where she was crouched on the floor, snatched the fireplace poker—she'd rehearsed the moves in her mind a hundred times—and swung the tool at him as hard as she could. But his reactions were too quick. He put up a hand and half turned, and her blow glanced off his arm, knocking the knife out of his hand. He dropped to his knees, clutching at his arm.

"Run!" Jane cried out. "Kirstin, run!" Raising the poker again as he lurched up and grabbed it in midair, yanking.

Stumbling backwards, terror ripping through her, trying to pull the fire iron from him, the world turned into snatches of movement, too fast and too slow at the same time. She could hear his breath rasping and animal sounds coming out of her own throat. He was too strong; she was losing the struggle.

And then, behind him, a movement that didn't belong to this violent tableau. The front door burst inward, and Kirstin was there, pointing at them, and then Smith's fist slammed into Jane's cheek, her head exploded, and she fell back while the world tilted and rocked. Sprawled on the floor, she was aware of vast confusion, chaos beyond her comprehension, men shouldering into the doorway, loud voices. Was that a gunshot? But she couldn't get up, and the noises receded into the fog of unconsciousness.

Awareness returned in disparate pieces: the slight sway of a vehicle, pain, a man's voice, hot air blowing on her legs. She was in a car, yes, the heater was on. She pried her eyes open. "Uh," she groaned, "what . . . ?"

"You're awake. Thank God." Ray, driving, glancing over at her. "We're almost there."

"God, that hurts," she said, touching her cheek.

"That son of the bitch."

She sat up shakily. "Where . . . ?"

"He's under arrest. Kirstin's safe. Right behind us in Schilling's car. We'll be there in a few minutes."

"Be where?"

"Hospital."

"No," she said without thought. "Please, Ray, I'm okay."

"You probably have a concussion, Jane. Don't be stupid."

"No hospital."

"*Christ.*"

"Please?"

"You scared the hell out of me," he said.

"Me, too."

"Why'd you go for that walk? What's the matter with you?"

"Oh, Gwen . . . Oh, Ray, does she know I'm okay?"

"Yes. Everyone's been notified." She moved her jaw from side to side. Oh, wow, that hurt. Her cheek felt swollen. But she couldn't face the hospital—doctors, nurses, reporters, cops, questions.

"You want to go to your sister's place?"

The boys. Gwen and George and all the explaining. *No. Not yet.* "I'd rather not."

"Okay, you got me. Where *do* you want to go?"

"You're mad at me."

"Jesus, Jane. Mad? I haven't slept in thirty-six hours, I was scared shitless all night, and the son of the bitch punched you out."

"But you got him."

He glanced over at her. "*You* got him."

"Don't be mad."

"All right, I'm not mad. Where do you want to go?"

She tried to collect her thoughts. "Um, how about the place you're staying?"

"The Mountain House?"

"No one will be there."

"No, they're all kind of busy," he said dryly.

"Then let's go there. I just want to put ice on my cheek and have a good cry."

She felt better after a half hour on the couch, feet up, a bag of ice from the mini refrigerator on her cheek.

"I'm hungry," she said.

"You want me to get you something?" He'd been tiptoeing around her, obviously unsure of himself.

"No." She put a hand out. "Not yet. Come here."

He sat gingerly on the edge of the couch. He looked weary, dark stubble on his cheeks, his shirt wilted, his sweater creased, worn for too long.

"I was so scared," she mumbled against the ice pack.

He took her hand. "You were brave."

The tears came then. She cried for her fear and for Kirstin and the other girls and for what might have happened. She cried for Alan and her mother and her sister. Ray sat still for a minute, then he gently gathered her in his arms, and she leaned into him and let her tears flow.

"Better?" he finally asked.

"Yes." She sniffed. "And you're sure Kirstin is okay?"

"Well, not okay, but safe. When we saw her run out of the house, Kent grabbed her, and she told us what you were doing."

"Did she tell you how she helped?"

"Yeah. In hindsight, it was a good idea."

"And Smith?"

"He'll be charged with four, no five, counts of felony

kidnapping and four of rape and one count of capital murder. They're taking him to Denver later today, and he might be arraigned this afternoon if they can find a judge. It's the day before Christmas, after all."

"I forgot," she said. "Christmas."

"Uh-huh."

"And Smith won't get off on an insanity plea or anything?"

"No way. He'll never see daylight again. These are federal charges."

His cell phone rang then, and he reached into his pocket to get it. He listened for a few minutes, and she could see the lines tighten in his face.

He clicked off. "That was Bruce. He said to turn on the news." He rose and located the remote, switched on the television set, found one of the news channels.

"What?" she asked.

"Gerald Lapinski just shot himself inside his place."

"*Oh*. Oh, dear God. He did?"

But Ray was focused on the report from a helicopter hovering above Lapinski's farmhouse. She listened in a daze, more interested in how this was affecting Ray than the report. Lapinski dead. The man who'd ordered the killing of his Kathleen, dead. The man who'd scarred him and cost him so much emotional anguish, dead.

She touched his shoulder, but he didn't acknowledge her. She was afraid. What if he shut her out? "Ray?"

"Yeah," he said, his eyes still on the screen.

"What are you feeling?"

"Feeling?" He laughed harshly. "I'm feeling cheated. Lapinski took the coward's way out. I should have known."

"You wanted to see him arrested, tried, and found guilty and locked up."

"Goddamn right I did. Well, it's over. Water under the bridge."

"At least he can't hurt anyone ever again. And you still have the Perry brothers in custody. And *they* carried out the bombing."

"Yeah, they did."

"Ray . . . would you tell me about Kathleen now?"

His eyes finally switched to hers, and her pulse throbbed in her veins.

"Kathleen."

"Only if you want to."

"Yeah, I guess it's time to talk about Kathleen," he said.

She slept for a little while after that, using the bedroom while he manned the phone, tying up loose ends, talking to Stan Shoemaker back in Seattle. She felt good, even happy, despite the nightmare she'd been through. Kathleen no longer haunted her. She'd been laid to rest at last.

But when she woke up, lying there in the mussed bed, hearing Ray's voice in the other room, she remembered Kirstin and what she'd told the girl. "It will be all right. Your family will help you. See me? I'm all right."

Lies. Blatant lies, just to get the child through the crisis. To save her life.

What about the girl's future? Maybe Kirstin would suffer as she had, for years and years. Maybe Kirstin would be crippled emotionally, too. Maybe one day she'd remember the lies Jane had preached, and she'd hate Jane for holding out false hope.

She was crying again when Ray went in to check on her. He didn't say a word, just held her until her sobs died down.

"Sorry," she said, wiping at her eyes.

"Don't be."

"I must look like hell."

"You look pretty damn good, considering."

She smiled, and he loved her courage. "Your mother called. Around five times now."

"Oh God."

"I guess no one knows what to do. They were supposed to gather for an annual Christmas Eve dinner, but they were up all night and pretty worried, Jane."

"So what does Mom want me to do? Cook something and take it up to the house and pretend everything's wonderful?" Then she seemed to catch herself. She put a hand on her forehead, which must have hurt as much as her cheek now from all the crying. "That was bitchy of me," she admitted. "Of course they were worried, and I should at least call them."

"Jane."

"You think I should go up there?"

He nodded slowly.

"Damn. It will be like a wake, everyone tiptoeing around me."

"They need to see you, see that you're okay with their own eyes."

"Damn," she repeated, but he could tell she knew he was right. "I guess it won't kill me to stop in. But just for a few minutes." She sniffed again and looked at him. "Will you drive me? I just don't want to go there by myself."

"I'll drive you."

"I won't stay long."

"You can stay as long as you like," he said.

He waited patiently while she showered and fretted about putting the same clothes back on.

"We could stop by your sister's place first," he suggested.

"God, no, I don't have the energy."

"You're sure you don't want to go to the emergency room?" he asked, worried again, watching her keenly. The purple bruise on her cheek was a personal affront to him.

"No," she said firmly. "My mother's little get-together will be enough to wake the dead."

He loved her sense of humor, her courage, her unself-consciousness. When *had* he fallen in love with her? That first evening he'd met her with Caroline? Or had it been later, when he'd watched her work with the girls? Maybe he'd never know the exact moment, because he'd only realized the depth of his feelings last night when he had to face losing her.

In the car on the way to the Zucker's house, she fidgeted, wiping at the inside of her window with a gloved hand. He knew the signs; he knew her so well. "What's wrong?"

"I wish I didn't have to do this."

"We won't stay long. No matter what."

"Promise?"

"I promise."

She was abruptly quiet. Then, "That's what I told Kirstin. I promised she'd be okay. But will she?"

"You saved her life, Jane."

"But will she get over this?" She was looking down, biting her lip. "I never got over it."

He couldn't think of anything to say. Maybe she was right, and Kirstin Lemke would be emotionally scarred for life. But, he was coming to realize, you could live with scars.

Her family insisted on hearing every last detail of her ordeal. Hannah interrupted to ask dozens of questions. Gwen apologized over and over. Roland took Ray aside to pump him about the rescue. And all the while, Ray kept an eye on Jane, watching her for signs of exhaustion, of stress. Every time he looked at her and saw the bruise, rage ignited like tinder in him again.

Despite everyone having been up all night, Hannah had

obviously gone into high gear the minute she'd learned Jane was safe. Hannah truly was an amazing woman, energetic, organized, and tough as nails. The house was warm and scented with cider and pine and bayberry candles. A fire was blazing; there were presents under the tree. Platters of food covered the table—an impromptu potluck dinner.

Christmas Eve.

Lottie Schilling stopped by, weary and nervous, but Kent was absent, accompanying Kevin Smith to Denver. Her two girls and the Grinell boys were sent to the bedroom to watch DVD movies. Scott was there, without a date this time. It seemed to Ray that Jane's stepbrother felt upstaged, a bit sulky. Quiet.

Ray studied the men: Roland Zucker, George Grinell, Scott Zucker. Eliminating Kent Schilling from the list of suspects, one of these men here was a rapist. One of them had hurt Jane. Wasn't it ironic that she'd helped bring so many criminals to justice, but couldn't help herself? A surge of protectiveness swept him. And he wanted to draw her from the people who surrounded her, some of whom had wounded her so terribly, and hold her, comfort her, banish the bad memories. He wanted to get her out of there.

But he waited and he watched.

"I can't believe you had the guts to do that," Hannah kept saying. "He had a *knife*."

"Oh, Mom, come on. I had no choice."

"We're so proud of you."

"I was dumb."

"I shouldn't have let you leave the house," Gwen said. "I'll never get over it."

"You couldn't have stopped me," Jane said. "And, besides, they never would have found Kirstin if I hadn't."

They all ate, but everyone's appetite was subdued. Ray

hadn't had a bite since some doughnuts at the Lemke's house. When was that? Three or four in the morning? Still, he only picked at the food.

Jane was handling the situation well. Realizing, perhaps, that she had a family who cared about her. He guessed it was a beginning.

After an hour, their eyes met over the holly and pine arrangement on the coffee table. *Enough.*

She stood, tall and lovely, despite all she'd been through. "That's it, everybody," she said. "I've got to get some sleep. Ray and I both do. And in the morning I have to get home to Denver."

Her mother hugged her, teary-eyed. "Please come back and see us soon. Don't be a stranger, Janey."

Gwen squeezed her hand and Lottie embraced her, too.

Even Roland. He told her she was a brave, wonderful girl. And Scott kissed her on the cheek, saying, "Come back soon."

Ray watched all this, accepted their relief and gratitude, too, but mostly he watched. And weighed reactions.

He drove her to her sister's house and stopped in the driveway. "You going to be all right?"

"Yes."

"Lock the doors."

"Then how would Gwen and George get in?"

Ray just shook his head.

"I'd ask you in, but . . ."

"I'd fall asleep."

"Good night, then."

"Hey, sweet dreams. And Merry Christmas." He leaned close and gently kissed her lips, stroked her cheek where it was bruised. "Does it still hurt as much?"

"Not quite."

"See you tomorrow."

"Not too early."

"Hell, no." He hesitated. And then he put to words the idea that had been percolating in his head all night. "I have a present for you."

"A present? But . . . Oh, Ray . . ."

He shook his head. "I hope you'll accept it."

"You know I'll treasure anything you give me."

"We'll see." This was certainly not the kind of present she was expecting. Not at all. "Tomorrow," he repeated.

"Tomorrow," she said in a husky voice that was full of promise.

TWENTY-TWO

Kyle and Nicky woke her on Christmas morning. "Mom said we could," Kyle explained, "because they have to go to work soon."

Of course. The Christmas crowds would ski today, and they needed sustenance. No breaks for the Grinell family.

"Um." She stretched, and then winced. Her face hurt.

"You got a big bruise," Nicky informed her.

"Thanks," she said.

"That guy called."

"That guy?"

"You know, the FBI guy. Ray."

"He called already?"

"Mom talked to him. She told him you were still asleep." Kyle hopped on one leg. "Come on, we're opening presents."

The Christmas morning tradition was a hurried affair; George and Gwen had to go to work.

"You're okay?" Gwen asked.

"Sure. Not so pretty, though."

"You look just fine," George said, giving her a kiss.

She held her breath, recoiling mentally. Would she ever get over this knee-jerk reaction?

Ray arrived later that morning, presumably to drive her home to Denver. He looked like a new man. He wore a pale blue shirt that matched his eyes and a navy blue fleece pullover under his leather jacket.

"Hey," he said.

"Hey yourself." She was decidedly nervous, not knowing where she stood with him. And she was sad; the case was over. They had no reason to work together anymore. Would they ever see each other again?

But he stood in front of her, the boys sitting there watching TV, with torn wrapping paper, open boxes, ribbons on the floor at Ray's feet, and gave her a kiss. A long, sweet kiss on her lips.

"Merry Christmas," he whispered.

"I don't have a present for you," she said.

"What? You didn't have time to do your Christmas shopping?"

"Well, you said you had something for me, and . . ."

"In a little while. Okay, boys, you can quit the giggling. Can't your Aunt Jane have some privacy?"

They drove straight to the hospital from the Grinell's house. The sun was out, but downvalley, over the snow-covered pyramid of Mt. Sopris, clouds were gathering. Another storm was coming. And no Kevin Smith to plow his clients' driveways.

They visited Kirstin, who'd been kept in the hospital overnight. Josh Lemke and his wife Suzanne were there.

"How are you, honey?" Jane asked the young girl.

"Really happy to be back home," she said. "I didn't get a chance to thank you, you know, yesterday, and I wanted to."

"Oh, Kirstin, you don't owe me any thanks. You were so brave. You got us out of that . . . that awful fix."

"No." Kirstin shook her head. Her hair was clean now, and shiny, and there was some color in her cheeks. "*You* did."

"We both did, how's that? And I'll keep in touch with you, I promise. If you ever want to talk, I'll give your dad my phone number. Anytime."

Suzanne accompanied them out into the corridor when they left. She clutched Jane's hand, tears in her eyes. "Thank you, thank you. I can't ever . . ." She stopped, choked up.

"Please, Suzanne. Listen, Kirstin was great. I couldn't have done it without her. You've got a terrific daughter."

They hugged each other, Suzanne crying, holding on to her.

"I'll call," she said, crying herself. "In a few days."

She thought they'd head out of town on the highway toward Denver, but Ray turned in the opposite direction onto Main Street, and eventually he pulled up in front of the Mountain House. She looked at him questioningly.

"Come on. I promised you a Christmas present," he said, his face deadpan.

"What's going on?"

"Patience, my dear."

The suite was deserted, the agents dispersed to Denver and Glenwood Springs. All trace of the operation was cleared away: no file boxes, no dirty clothes hanging from chair backs, no cigarette butts from overtired, overworked men. The room smelled faintly of disinfectant. Why had he brought her here?

He had carried her art case in from the car. Without a word, he opened it, and removed her sketch pad and pencils, handed them to her.

She accepted them, frowning. "What is this?"

"Just cooperate. I want to try something."

"Ray."

"Humor me." He put a hand on her arm and led her to the pullout couch, pushed her gently into it. Sat across from her in a matching green plaid armchair, his hands on his knees, his eyes on her.

"What do you want me to draw?" she asked, mystified.

"Nothing yet. We're just going to talk."

"About what?"

"That night seventeen years ago."

"What is *wrong* with you?" She was bewildered. A Christmas present? What was he talking about?

"Nothing's wrong with me. But I want to fix what's wrong with you. That night . . ."

"I don't want to talk about that night." She dropped the pad on the floor.

"Then do it for me, Jane."

"Ray, please, can't we just go? This is ridiculous."

"That night. In your tent. Tell me." His voice was calm, without inflection. But insistent.

She put a hand to her forehead, hiding her eyes.

"Jane."

"God, this is cruel of you."

"That's just your defenses talking. Let's get to the crux. That night. You can do it."

She felt herself becoming agitated, her heart pounding. "I don't want to," she said in a low voice.

"You need to."

She drew in a quavering breath. "I already told you."

"Tell me again. In detail." His voice, the rough-smooth cat's tongue, soothed her. Compelling her.

This is crazy, she thought. He was emulating her techniques. It just wasn't going to work. "I honest to God don't want to do this, Ray."

He looked at her in earnest. "Close your eyes, and go back to that night. Was it dark?"

Reluctantly, she closed her eyes. "Yes, sure, it was dark. It was *night*."

"And where were you?"

"You mean when it happened? I was in my own tent. I *told* you all this. I was so proud of myself, having my own tent. It was a big deal. I hadn't really wanted to go on the camping trip, anyway. I wanted to stay in town and hang out with my friends, but Mom made me come."

"Go on."

She opened her eyes. "This is humiliating."

"Close your eyes again. Think. What did you have for dinner that night?"

He took her back in time. She protested; she twisted and turned mentally. She got up and paced the way Kevin Smith had. Once she swore at him, to no avail, and once she put her face in her hands and sobbed. He held her then, stroking her hair, handing her his handkerchief.

"Was it warm out that night?" he asked softly.

"Cool. It was cool. September. But I had a down sleeping bag."

"Were you asleep when he came into your tent?"

She blew her nose. This was so hard. No, impossible. What made him think he could wrest the face from her? Ha! But she said, "Yes. He woke me up."

"Did you recognize his voice?"

"No. He whispered. I couldn't tell. Maybe he didn't whisper at all, maybe he didn't say anything."

"How much light was there? A moon? The campfire?"

"No. Yes. I don't know. A moon, I think. Some light. And a big campfire. Earlier we roasted marshmallows."

"Was the fire still going?"

She stopped and thought. Her forehead creased. "I don't

know. I was asleep. But . . . I remember, there were voices. Somebody laughing. So there must have been people still up. Around the fire."

"Okay, good. We're getting there."

"Are we?" she asked, ready to burst into tears again.

"Let's take it a step further. In the tent."

Her heart clutched. "I didn't see his face. I *didn't*."

"Maybe not."

He led her on, backtracking at times, talking of other matters. "Smith was arraigned late yesterday afternoon. He asked for a public defender," he told her.

"I'll have to testify, won't I?"

"Yeah, you will."

She finally picked the sketch pad up from the floor, removed a pencil from the plastic case. It felt familiar, comforting in her hand. This is what she did.

He sat across from her, leaning forward. "Some light came into the tent. A little. You knew him. You had to. That's what's been blocking you."

"I always thought he was young," she said. "For some reason. But all the men were younger in those days. And Kent, I never believed it was Kent. But I wasn't sure. I'm still not sure." She drew a curved line, recalling a shadow, a certain shape to it, a reflection. Another line, bent over the pad, biting her lower lip, her hand steady.

"That's good. It's coming."

Her hand sketched, her brain seemingly unattached. She stopped once, panic making her heart flutter. Snatches of memory battered her: a mouth, an ear, hair, scratchy whiskers, a certain smell that flooded her senses. But Ray was there, his arm around her, murmuring encouragement. And her hand began to draw again.

A face slowly emerged from the blank page. Eyes, nose, mouth, jawline, forehead. Cheekbones. She couldn't look at it as a whole, only the parts that her hand created out of excavated memories.

Finally, drained, she stopped, put the pencil down, and let the pad drop onto her lap. Leaned back and closed her eyes.

He picked the pad up out of her lap. "Christ," she heard him say. Wonderingly.

She opened her eyes, saw him staring at the drawing. Then he held the pad out for her to see, and she *did* see now. There was the face, unmistakable. Scott Zucker.

"Oh my God," she breathed.

"You did it," he said.

She burst into tears then. How many tears had she shed in the past two days? A lifetime worth of them, all those tears she hadn't shed up to now. And he held her, once again, until she was spent.

"I'm sorry," she finally said. "I've never cried so much in my life. I'm a mess."

He smiled. "You're not a mess."

They were quiet for a long time while she tried to fit her thoughts around the meaning of this breakthrough. Would she be a different person now? Able to grow and flourish? Or would she be the same, merely wiser for the revelation? And what about *him,* her stepbrother? *My God. Scott.*

She blinked and focused on Ray. "What should I do? I mean, about Scott?"

"Yeah, I've been thinking the same thing. It's a problem. You can't file charges against him anymore. The statute of limitations ran out years ago."

"And no one would believe me."

"I'd be happy to beat the shit out of him for you."

"Ray."

"I'm serious."

She knew he was. "Well, that's not going to happen. But I can't just let it go, can I?"

"No."

"I'll have to . . ."

"Whatever it is, you don't have to do it right now. Wait. We'll figure it out."

"He can't . . . he can't get away with it."

"That's a girl."

"All these years. And every time he looked at me he *knew*." She stared past Ray's shoulder, remembering. "I never liked him. Is that why?"

"Could be."

She picked up the sketch pad and studied it. "He was so young."

"Not *that* young."

"I should hate him," she said, but she couldn't dredge up the emotion. Not right now. Not yet.

"It's okay to hate him."

"I have to think. I don't know *what* to do yet."

"Like I said, we'll figure it out."

"We . . . ?"

"Yeah, that's what I said."

"Ray?"

"I'll be right there with you, whatever you decide to do about Scott."

She stared at him, his face so familiar now. He'd seen her at her worst; he'd seen her at her best. He'd helped her, and she'd helped him. But she still wasn't exactly sure how to define their relationship.

She leaned into his shoulder, buried her face in his chest, breathing in his scent. His arm was strong, enfolding her.

"So," he said, his voice casual but with an edge, "what are your plans?"

"My plans?"

"You're going back to Denver, right?"

"Of course."

"What about that job in Quantico you were offered?"

"What?"

"You told me . . ."

"I know what I told you."

"Well?"

"Why are you asking?"

"No particular reason. Either place is fine with me, whatever you decide."

She twisted her neck to look up at his face. "What . . .?"

"You're not going without me."

"You mean . . . we should be together?" she asked carefully.

"Something wrong with that?"

"No, but . . ."

"I think we should live together. Then get married, maybe have some kids. Stay together for a long, long time. Like forever."

"Forever is an awfully long time," she said, her heart buoyant as a cloud.

"Not long enough," he replied.

Berkley Books proudly presents

Berkley Sensation

a brand-new romance line
featuring today's best-loved authors—
and tomorrow's hottest up-and-comers!

Every month…
Four sensational writers.

Every month…
Four sensational new romances
from historical to contemporary,
suspense to cozy.

To sign up for the romance newsletter,
visit www.penguin.com